TRUCKER'S DEADLY HAUL

No One Outruns Bad Decisions

While every precaution has been taken in the preparation of this book, the publisher assumes no responsibility for errors or omissions, or for damages resulting from the use of the information contained herein. In recounting the events for this book, some details have been compressed, altered, and omitted to better fit the narrative. Some of the dialogue has been changed and/or abbreviated.

TRUCKER'S DEADLY HAUL
NO ONE OUTRUNS BAD DECISIONS

First edition. November 2025.

Copyright © 2025 Craig Handel and Don Corbett.
All rights reserved.

Published by Big Kat Kreative LLC, 2025.
Printed in the United States of America.

Cover designed by Michael Mazewski.

ISBN: 978-1-962796-14-9

Written by Craig Handel and Don Corbett.

THE CAL RAVEN FILES

TRUCKER'S DEADLY HAUL

No One Outruns Bad Decisions

CRAIG HANDEL
DON CORBETT

Craig: To my wife Isabel for her support in me writing my first fiction book. Sometimes, being creative puts me in another world, which makes me distant. Thank goodness, she likes her quiet time as well.

Don: To my beautiful loving wife Marsha. She is a true angel, my rock, the matriarch of our family. And to all the suffering police officers who need our help!

Contents

Authors' Note

Loosely inspired by real events, *Trucker's Deadly Haul* contains graphic descriptions and language, particularly in reference to the human body. Great care was taken to tell this fictional tale as realistically and unfiltered as possible. However, the names, characters, locations, dates and incidents are products of the authors' imaginations or are used fictitiously and are not to be construed as real. Any resemblance to actual events, locations, organizations or persons, living or dead, is entirely coincidental.

This book is not meant for youths under the age of 18. You will learn about the birds and bees soon enough. And it's highly suggested you do not read *Trucker's Deadly Haul* while eating. It could turn your stomach.

Reader discretion is advised.

Weight Of The Badge

It only weighs between 2 to 4 ounces, but when that police badge is pinned on, there is an enormous weight that comes with the responsibility of being a law enforcement officer.

The true weight of the badge is not overcome by muscle, not found in the gym, not measured on a scale. The weight of the police badge is immense. It requires a mental strength and conditioning that can't be trained for, and an inner fortitude to handle the evils that officers face on the job. The heaviness of the badge makes the law enforcement officer different from other professionals.

The badge is not just pinned on a chest. It is pinned on a lifestyle.

Introduction

In 1956, President Dwight D. Eisenhower established the U.S. Interstate Highway System by signing the Federal-Aid Highway Act.

It has been called the greatest public works project in history.

Besides creating thousands of jobs, these roads have helped truck drivers transport goods from one coast to another. The food on your table, clothes on your back and fuel for your home were delivered by truckers.

The highway system has helped budget-conscious families take road trips all over the USA. High school and small-college teams take the interstate for competitions, connecting communities. And "snowbirds" travel from the North and East to Florida, Arizona and California in the winter.

This way of life has been part of American culture for more than 70 years.

However, within the rest stops and truck stops along this vast interstate system, there has been a subculture.

Prostitution.

Drugs.

Stolen property.

Murder.

Serial killings.

It is a problem now; and in the heart of the Midwest, it was a huge problem in the 1980s and 1990s.

I Know Death

**"I saw bodies contorted in ways
I didn't think possible. I saw
missing heads as well as only
heads or missing body parts.
I saw people with no faces."**

– Cal Raven

The question from Oldsmar Police Sergeant Frank Jamison during my job interview led me to pause, flash back and recall that snowy, icy Sunday afternoon several Decembers ago.

Car hitting telephone pole. A teenager, like me, in the road, severely hurt. Trying to get her to breathe in the ambulance.

The drive to the hospital seemed like hours, etched in my memory like a morbid scene from a horror film.

It doesn't mean I wanted to remember. But those moments aren't just something you can unsee, unfeel, unhear. At least I couldn't.

"Mr. Callaghan Raven, what experiences have prepared you to be a police officer?" Jamison asked.

———

I grew up in Oldsmar, Illinois, population 75,000, about a two-hour drive southwest of Chicago.

We're known for a Chrysler plant, iron ore production, a great small-college basketball team and being located in the middle of three major roadways – SR45, which ran north to south; I-62, which ran east to west; and a major toll road I-68, which ran from the northeast to the southwest. Truck drivers from around the country traveled these routes night and day.

It's a blue-collar area, a shot-and-a-beer community. If you grew up here, most people either knew you or recognized you.

I experienced death as a youth. Three uncles on my dad's side died before I was 12. That included Uncle Jack when I was 4. He had won an election of the steelworkers union; and he unseated a man who had been president for 12 years. The man, who also lost in the recount, had told others, "This wasn't over."

A few months later, my dad found Uncle Jack dead in his bed in the late afternoon with one shot to the head by his own Colt blue-steel hand gun with ivory grips. The coroner's report said he was shot from a short distance and that he was believed to be killed in the morning because he was nearly dressed. His gun had been returned to his drawer.

Almost all signs pointed to my Aunt Lauren, who had psychological issues because she couldn't have a child. She offered $10,000 to adopt a baby. Police detected gun-shot residue on my aunt, indicating she may have recently fired the gun that killed Uncle Jack. Since she knew where Uncle Jack's weapon was located and she had experience firing guns as a hunter, police incarcerated her in Richland County Jail, evaluated her and then transported her to the Illinois State Psychiatric Institution on suspicion of murder. During the trial, my aunt did not understand what she was being charged with and was subsequently found guilty by reason of insanity. This followed a lengthy psychiatric exam.

We often visited the institution, with its Victorian-style exterior. It gave me the creeps.

You know, when you hear other kids talking about their retired uncles, I realized I didn't have that. One day, I thought, "I hope nothing happens to my dad." You also realize the lily-white image of growing up in an idyllic childhood in a smaller city didn't have the happily-ever-after ending you read about in books or watch on TV.

I met Mr. Mack Thomas of Thomas Funeral Home at age 17. He saw me "pumping ethyl" at Universal Fuel Station and we chatted. Hearing a teen say, "The job has its perks but it's boring," Mr. Thomas replied, "Cal, we can use guys like you. Saturday morning, be at the funeral home in a suit and tie."

Mr. Thomas knew my parents.

He buried my grandparents, family members and friends. … Maybe there's a better way to say that.

I wanted to make a good impression so I wore a white shirt with a black tie, pressed black pants, buffed black wingtip shoes and a gray suit coat.

When my mom dropped me off early on a dark, chilly, dreary morning in October, I couldn't tell which door to enter. No one else had arrived. Community trust ran so high, citizens and businessmen didn't lock their doors.

In the first room, caskets and tombstones greeted me as I entered through the door closest to me. I got tangled in a cobweb, messing up my suit coat.

A strong, pungent smell – which I later learned was formaldehyde – engulfed me in the second room. I soon forgot about the smell when I saw a dead body on a porcelain table. I realized where I was –- the embalming room.

Finally, Door No. 3 took me from the garage to the visitation room after I took the steps. A man lay in a casket, arms folded. Mr. Enzo Calabrini. I could tell by a card on a nearby table.

Do I really want to do this? What in the hell am I doing here? Am I crazy?

If I came in my own car, I think I would've aborted this job offer and driven away. Reality smacked me in the face. As I waited in the room, it was so quiet, you could almost hear the dead people moving.

Thank God, living people arrived. Ed the embalmer and Al the ambulance driver. Thomas Funeral Home doubled as an ambulance service so the job included taking severely injured people to the emergency room, picking up the dead from homes, hospitals and the morgue, and transporting them to the funeral home, churches and cemeteries.

Think of it as an all-in-one service for the dying and dead. Stephen King would love this place.

"Are you the new guy?" Ed said.

Sucking it up and burying my nervousness, I confidently responded, "Yeah. What's up guys?"

"Not Mr. Calabrini," Al replied quickly.

The joke broke the tension hanging heavy in the air.

Now I know why I didn't have to go through an interview or even fill out an application. Mr. Thomas must've figured if I survived the "doors of horrors," then I had the guts to do the job.

I soon received the grand tour, which included the place I'd stay in for a 32-hour shift on weekends. No it wasn't another room within the funeral home. There was a small duplex, which had a bed, refrigerator, black-and-white TV with rabbit ears and a designated phone line for emergency calls. Two people needed to be on call at all hours of the day, hence the duplex. When that phone rang, away you went on assignment.

My fears literally took a back seat when Al had me go with him on an ambulance run. When he put on the flashing lights and siren, cars darted to the roadside like the parting of the Red Sea. I liked that power. After returning, I assisted during Mr. Calabrini's visitation.

When bodies came in, Ed went through the process of cleansing – extracting blood and body liquids – and replacing them with embalming fluid. I'd cleanse and comb the person's hair, and clean the fingernails. If a woman died, a beautician came in to style a beehive or any hairdo the family asked for.

Getting dead people dressed often meant cutting the back of their shirt, sportcoat or dress and then tucking it in the casket. Our ultimate goal, the litmus test, was to get visitors to come in and say, "Doesn't he look peaceful?" or "Doesn't she look beautiful?" even though they're stone-cold dead and pale as a ghost. We were like a halfway home for the departed.

I remember one embarrassing moment early in my career. One time, a stray cat sneaked into the embalming room. Scratched up a woman's face something fierce. Weird to see the marks but no blood. We had to put a lot of makeup on that one.

———————

I had a couple of fringe benefits with the job.

We constantly took friends to the embalming room. Unbeknownst to them, my partner Al laid down on the embalming table and covered himself up with a sheet.

We'd walk in, stand next to the embalming table and Al would sit up and scream "Hallelujah, I'm still alive!" I never saw so many people run for their lives with a look of pure terror on their faces.

Of course, Halloween was our time to shine. I'd invite high school classmates for costume parties. My go-to costume was a vampire. I considered using some real blood, but thought better of it.

We'd bring over the girls at night. We had one guy wrapped up like a mummy who would come out of a room. We had a guy inside a casket and when we'd open it, he'd pop up. The girls would scream and the guys would howl. Also, the trunk in my 1971 Chevrolet Chevelle contained a giant pillow, foot pillow and blanket that funeral homes use. Guys loved to lay in there and have their picture taken.

At night, we'd get everyone together and drive in the limo and other vehicles to Hope Cemetery, next to St. Michael's Church. Now, it was illegal to enter after dark but the cops didn't patrol that area. We'd have scavenger hunts where we'd put candy or money in the mausoleums.

No guts, no prizes.

Thank God, Mr. Thomas didn't find out what we did, otherwise he may have had a heart attack. We also never got any emergency calls or visits from Officer Not-So Friendly.

I used the limos for two of my proms. I took my girlfriend Jan. She thought it was the coolest thing. I think I was one of the pioneers of taking a fancy car to prom.

Hours of downtime had you wanting to get in that ambulance and start those sirens; but I realized I needed to be careful what I asked for.

One night, we received a hospital call to pick up an elderly woman who appeared to be dying but had labored breathing, which we called a death rattle. In those days, "do not resuscitate" wasn't put in writing, so if she was not still breathing, you had to give CPR – cardiopulmonary resuscitation.

CPR includes breathing into a person's mouth and doing chest compressions. When I started doing the chest compressions, I heard a crack. I broke one of her ribs. I thought I killed her! Thank God, she passed quickly.

When we arrived at a scene, sometimes our victims were dead. Sometimes they weren't. For those, we applied the "snatch and scoot" routine. Snatch the live body, scoot and get them to hospital as soon as possible. Time was critical.

And sometimes those calls hit close to home. One of my duties was to pick up Aunt Lauren from the mental institution and bring her to the funeral home to be embalmed. That opened up some old scabs.

On a snowy, icy Sunday in December, we received a call that changed my life.

While watching a Chicago Bears game, we responded to an accident two villages over. I had only been on the job for about two months.

Normally a 15-minute drive, it took us twice as long due to the slippery road conditions.

When we arrived, we saw a two-door Chevrolet Impala upside down after hitting a pole. It lost control while taking a turn on those slick roads.

The driver, Marie Roberts, had minor cuts and bruises. Her friend and passenger, Nancy Jones, was thrown from the car.

Only 16-years-old, Nancy had severe head and neck injuries. You could tell by the swelling in the eyes that she had massive head trauma.

Somehow, I got the job of trying to save her. Just one teenager helping another. I had Advanced Life Support and CPR training, but this was beyond that. All we had was a mobile radio, some oxygen, air conditioning and rudimentary medical supplies. I had no ability to communicate with the emergency room. I was on my own.

Just five or 10 minutes into our 30-minute drive to the Southside Emergency Room, Nancy stopped breathing.

I suctioned out the blood, tried to respirate her and gave her chest compressions. Nancy had a cut between her eyes on the bridge of her nose. The oxygen mask was lower than the bridge of her nose. Every time I blew oxygen into her, a mist of blood pushed out through the wound. Cold air hit the misting blood. I focused on trying to save her.

When we finally reached the hospital and the ambulance doors opened, the trauma unit came in and took over. Nancy's parents stood in shock.

When I went into the bathroom, I looked in the mirror. It looked as if I had been sprayed with maroon paint. The special smock I wore along with my pants also had been soaked in blood.

Traumatized, I avoided the investigators, doctors, nurses, grieving parents and TV cameras and returned home. When I told my dad what happened, he shook his head. My mom had tears in her eyes. I went upstairs and replayed the events in my mind over and over.

Nancy didn't survive. I had to relive the trauma when her parents hired Thomas Funeral Home for the visitation. I worked the event while many of my high school classmates looked on. Awful, just awful.

Shortly after that incident, while staying at the duplex during my shift, I fell asleep. When I awakened, I found myself standing outside in only my underwear and T-shirt, freezing.

I had been sleepwalking.

———

Snapped back to the present from Sgt. Jamison's question, I reflexively replied, "Obviously. I have seen death. I have seen homicides, I have seen suicides. I saw a mother and daughter in a VW after a bus crushed it into a utility pole. I also responded to a murder involving a classmate's father who was shot to death in the kitchen."

I saw bodies contorted in ways I didn't think possible. I saw missing heads as well as only heads or missing body parts. I saw people with no faces. I also saw floaters, people who had risen from lakes and retention ponds after the chains holding them to the bottom had loosened.

All these are images teenagers shouldn't see, indelible images with long-term effects. That's what happened to me. That's how I became acquainted with death.

———

But taking this job earned me a lot of respect. After rigid testing, I became one of the first nationally registered EMTs. The state of Illinois honored me. I received a patch, a pin on my smock and a certificate to recognize my achievement. I really felt like I became somebody.

My friend Mike, who later became a cop, liked to keep my ego in check. When I arrived late to school because the funeral home needed extra help, Mike said, "Raven found a dead rabbit and had to embalm it."

My parents showed a lot of pride in me and bragged about the community service I provided to family and friends.

Mom always told me, "What you've seen had to be terrible, but you did it for a reason. God put you in those places for a reason."

In my four years of working for Thomas Funeral Home, I saw death in just about every way that was unnatural as well as natural. Three semesters at Oldsmar State College and sixth months at the Illinois Police Academy felt like a walk in the park.

As a police officer in the Oldsmar Police Department, I would become acquainted with life.

That also had an ugly side.

And we're not even talking about the 44 Magnum Lounge.

CHAPTER 2

A Cop's Beat

"Go to it kid."

– Words of wisdom from
Sgt. Frank Jamison on my first day

My first day on the job.

Picture day. Jan took a Polaroid of me holding 3-month-old daughter Janet with me in dress uniform – blue shirt, epaulets on each shoulder, Oldsmar Police patch, navy blue tie, police badge over my heart, two pens in a breast pocket, navy blue pants with light blue stripes on the sides.

Underneath my uniform, I wore a two-pound Kevlar vest, which doubled in weight after I sweated for eight hours on a shift.

Because I lived less than a mile from the police station – I could see it from my kitchen window – I often walked to work. It allowed me to think before and decompress after. Also, we only had one car and Jan often needed it.

When I left home that winter day, it was cold but sunny and windy. In the 15 minutes it took me to get to work, snow pelted me in the back and side which got me all wet.

Great way to start my first day.

After I arrived at the station, I joined other officers for roll call. As I walked in, I heard chants of "virgin, virgin, virgin."

I smiled and sucked it up.

Tony Blackstone came up, reached out his hand and said, "Hey man, if you need any help, just ask me. These other assholes still believe in initiations."

I quickly learned ball busting became constant. Nobody was spared. If a guy messed up on his beat or filled out paperwork wrong, he'd hear about it for days. Guys also decided what watering hole they'd meet at after 10 p.m., who failed to fill up the cruiser with gas the day before, who left coffee cups under the seat, the typical roll-call bullshit.

In his roll-call notes, Sgt. Jamison reviewed things to look out for.

"Men, watch for a wanted fugitive who was seen in our district," he said. "Also, you didn't check that vacant house where neighbors had complained about people getting high or selling weed and cocaine. Also, you're not making enough traffic stops."

One of the cops replied, "Frankie, I also hear you're nailing the chief's daughter."

Shaking his head, Frank Jamison said, "Dismissed."

The police department handed me a badge, gun, handcuffs and a cruiser with lights and a siren.

Besides saying, "Go to it kid," Jamison quoted Teddy Roosevelt when he said, "Walk softly and carry a big stick."

I went through a mental checklist before starting the car and beginning my day.

- Hat? Check.

- Calibrate K55 Radar unit on dash? Check.

- Black jack with a strap? It had black padding surrounding a steel frame. Guaranteed to leave a mark with a drunkard or a dude on drugs. Check.

- Sap gloves with lead knuckles? Check.
- Overhead alley lights and siren? Check.
- Fuel gauge? Check.
- Shotgun? Loaded with one in the chamber. Check.
- Radio and scanners working and on TAC 1? Check.
- Briefcase? Check.
- Sweep car? This included dumping ashtrays and cups of coffee left in the car on the last shift. Pete Devita's shift. Nice guy but what a slob. Check.

———

But the euphoria overwhelmed those nuisances when I got behind the wheel and turned on the engine. This is where I wanted to be career-wise.

Called Second Watch, my 2 p.m. to 10 p.m. shift prepared me well for my future. It's the busiest shift a person could work. Most citizens get off work around 4, 5, 6 p.m. There's a lot of activity. College students, couples and "thirsty" individuals heading to the bars and restaurants.

I worked alone. Outside of Christmas, everyone did, unless training officers – basically an observer – paired a rookie with a veteran cop.

My training officer three months earlier offered a glimpse into some officers' habits. We began our day by going to D Squared – Dunkin Donuts. After buying me donuts and coffee, he drove to an apartment where he told me to take the wheel and make some rounds while he "got his finger wet." This guy had a wife and two kids but that didn't stop him from having sexual activity, even if on the job.

I actually did rescue cats from trees, help people unlock their cars and homes, oblige mothers who wanted us to give stern and firm chats with their mischievous children and took calls from little old ladies, who just wanted to talk.

One called me "pretty." So glad I didn't have a partner. I already heard enough from my 13-year-old niece Lisa who called my wife Jan and I "Ken and Barbie." My medium-cut blonde, wavy hair had a perfect part on the side. A bump of hairspray made me look, like, you know.

"I think you need a new look," Lisa said sarcastically.

I knew what she needed – a swift kick in the tailfeathers – but I resisted because of how much respect I had for her mom.

The only thing worse is being called "good buddy." More on that later.

Dorothy Douglas became one of my favorites. She always seemed to invite me in when it was 7 degrees or 87. Her apple pie was sooo sweet but the bitter, dark-roast coffee offset that. Cup after cup came my way even when I said no. She loved to regale me with stories of her deceased husband – a respected state accountant – who took her on trips all over the world.

"Jack knew everybody," she said. "We went on cruises with a lot of his clients."

Dorothy also asked me so many questions, I barely could answer before she asked another.

"What bad guys have you arrested?

"Did you tell the third-watch officer to keep an eye on my place?"

"Did you watch the latest Days of Our Lives?"

"Did you see Bo and Hope are trying to have a baby?"

"Did you know Bo wants to be a detective?"

"Would you like more apple pie with ice cream?"

By the time I left, I was so wired on sugar and caffeine, I could've climbed the tree and plucked the cat.

I really wondered how much Dorothy listened – or if she could listen.

As I did these minor but meaningful tasks in neighborhoods, a thought came to mind: cops are about the only people who still made house visits.

————————

I had to make sure I'd alter routines. Some were unavoidable. Certain restaurants like McDonald's did cash drops at certain times. I wanted to be in that area during the drops.

Before the days of security services, we did bank runs and diamond drops. The bankers or business owners would sit in front while I chauffeured them where they needed to go.

Whenever I ran into an issue, I approached Sgt. Jamison. He had become a respected advisor. I asked for his advice when I stopped the mayor's 18-year-old son for drunk driving.

"Frank, should I arrest the kid or just have his dad called to pick him up?" I asked.

A sensitive situation.

He looked at me, gave me this grin, then said sternly, "You have good instincts, you have been trained, you're smart. Do what you think is right. Fix it."

I took the kid home to Dad, who proceeded to beat his ass. I preferred letting the parents deliver the punishment. It also kept kids' records clean, which could have cost them entering college or job opportunities for making stupid, teenage mistakes.

For young speeders, I pulled them over, gave them the bright orange part of the ticket and said, "Put it on your sun visor with a rubber band and look at it when you consider speeding."

I took people home who had too much to drink. If they didn't kill somebody or reek of alcohol, I'd say, "Get in my car, I'll take you home and you can pick up your keys in the morning at the station."

I even gave some scumbags a break. I'd overlook an infraction, but then told them I needed some information. Quid pro quo. I rub your back, you rub mine. I'd let the minnow get away so I could catch the whale.

When making a pass around my territory, varying my route remained a priority. Don't know who's watching. Don't know who's listening.

If burglars know what time you're driving through, they'll plan break-ins and robberies around it. They also follow police scanners and listen to badge and car numbers.

Over time, you learn things. Unusual footprints in the snow. Broken glass. Barking dogs. Shining a spotlight on a glass window and it doesn't reflect back. That means the window has been broken.

The worst calls? Domestic cases. You never know what way those things will turn. The husband and wife may hate each other but when cops arrive, we're the bad guys. That's because when we show up, somebody's usually going to jail. It can get ugly fast and the victims and suspects are hard to separate.

In the days leading up to Christmas – when crooks wanted to play Scrooge and either burglarize homes or shoplift – we worked in teams, wore plain clothes and drove unmarked vehicles. Tony Blackstone became my partner during the holidays.

While driving around a plaza, we overheard a call of a domestic disturbance a minute's drive from our location. The other cops were about seven, eight minutes away.

Upon arriving in the couple's driveway, they became quiet

when we walked up and knocked on the door.

The husband answered and opened the door after we held our badges up.

We could sense the tension between the two but saw no marks, cuts or blood shed when we entered.

"We can leave if you promise to work your problems out," I said.

They nodded.

"If we have to return, one or both of you are going to jail," Tony added. "Understand?"

They kept nodding.

"Understand?"

"Yes," they said.

The other officers showed up.

"What happened?" they asked.

"Nothing," I replied. "No harm. No foul."

The guys said, "Good, no paperwork," and we continued our beats.

My sergeant, Conrad Williams, didn't throw any bouquets.

A call came on our radio: 112 to 150. His car to mine. He wanted to meet us at the corner of 91st Street and Riverwalk Drive.

I looked at my partner and said, "Fuck, here we go."

When we arrived, we could tell he was pissed.

"What the fuck are you doing running in with plain clothes? You're not doing your job right. You're supposed to watch the plaza stupid. What were you thinking?

Not one to clam up, I responded, "With all due respect, we could've had two citizens kill each other if we were there a couple of minutes later. The location was a minute's drive from the mall. That's not a situation we want to be in, either. I responded out of common sense. That's what we were doing, sir."

Now he thought I was being disrespectful. "I have half a notion to write you up," he said.

Realizing at that moment he had control over my young career, I backtracked and said, "Okay, okay, I apologize, I understand."

But once we left, I vented to Tony.

"Can you believe that fucking guy?" I said. "He's up my ass for no real reason. This guy doesn't like me."

Tony listened and said, "Cal, you did the right things. You were proactive and de-escalated situations – twice. Remember these experiences."

In the coming days, I learned about Conrad Williams' tenure with the Oldsmar Police: Day turns with weekends off; promoted to detective; demoted to second shift in a marked patrol car.

Most cops don't recover from that. But I also found out something else: Conrad Williams had a lot of friends in key places.

CHAPTER 3

Truckers & Truck Stops

**"Think of it as a big refrigerator
with a compressor, condenser,
expansion valve and evaporator."**

– Description of reefer trucks

Intrigued by my responses after hearing I worked for Thomas Funeral Home, Sgt. Jamison wanted to see just how much experience I had.

"Cal," he said. "What do you know about truck stops?"

"Well," I responded, "I worked at Universal Fuel Station the year before I started at Thomas Funeral Home."

"What did you do?"

"Pump ethyl. I was a lumper. Other things."

"Other things?"

"Yes, other things."

———

With 3 million truckers driving on interstate highways all over the country, I met a smorgasbord of personalities.

The majority of them passing through had horrible hygiene.

Most looked like they just returned from camping in the backcountry for two weeks.

The common image I remembered? A big, gruff, smelly, pot-bellied lumberjack who had cartoon-like flies circling over his head. When he opened his mouth, his stained teeth and gravelly voice from smoking two packs a day of Marlboro Reds and drinking whiskey straight left an impression.

His truck had the not-so-faint smell of urine and feces because he hadn't bathed with anything but a wet wipe for days while he kept a plastic milk bottle that he used to piss in while driving.

If an interstate driver annoyed him, he'd release said piss – called a trucker bomb – that would splatter on the driver's windshield.

I tried to stay upwind of truckers and their rigs as much as possible. I thought about offering breath mints but I didn't want to insult them and hurt my earning potential.

I learned ways to make money on the side legally.

If a trucker said, "I need a lumper," he wanted someone to lift heavy items off the truck for $7 an hour. Pumping ethyl earned me $1.25 an hour.

———

When Jimmy Hoffa ran The Teamsters Union from 1957 to 1971, many people called him the second-most-powerful man in the country.

Founded in 1903, The Teamsters went from 75,000 members to more than 1 million in 1951, thanks in large part to Hoffa. Many members were truckers. By the 1980s, 1,000 truck stops, travel centers and travel plazas had been built around the country.

Using "quickie strikes," secondary boycotts and other tactics to leverage union strength, truckers began to get paid well. Former Attorney General Robert Kennedy called Hoffa's teamsters, "the most powerful institution in the country aside from the United States government ... and as Mr. Hoffa operates it, this is a conspiracy of evil."

Even after Hoffa's reign ended, truckers made about $22,500 in 1979, which would be worth $100,000 today.

But the combination of Hoffa being arrested, then killed; the teamsters loaning pension money to the mob; and Kennedy's words reverberating after his death led to a public and political backlash.

The Motor Carrier Regulatory Reform and Modernization Act, more commonly known as the Motor Carrier Act of 1980, became a United States federal law that deregulated the trucking industry.

With Presidents Gerald Ford, a Republican; Jimmy Carter, a Democrat; and Ronald Reagan, a Democrat-turned-Republican, pushing for legislation, consumers benefited.

Their costs dropped by $8 billion each year.

They conserved fuel and their expenses for trucking transportation dropped.

While politicians said the trucking industry would benefit from greater flexibility and new opportunities for innovation, every-day truckers took a beating. Their wages plummeted.

Now they had to skimp; and this led to shenanigans.

I also learned ways to make money on the side illegally.

Truckers needed receipts when they bought diesel so if they needed 150 gallons, they'd tell me to bump the receipt to 200 gallons. With diesel at $0.55 a gallon, the company was billed $110. After the trucker paid $82.50, he received $27.50 back. He gave me $10 and kept the difference and it seemed all good to me. Being 16, a bit naive and new to the world of conning and scamming, it didn't seem like a big deal. Meanwhile, the trucker pocketed the money or used it for drugs or prostitutes.

Instead of paying me, some truckers offered gifts. One trucker opened his trailer and there were boxes of clothes, including ladies' coats.

"Jeezus, they're beautiful," I said.

My girlfriend Jan didn't like her coat – but her mom Margie Lou did. I picked out a beaut – powder blue crushed velvet, big side lapels, gold buttons, a belt buckle that went through loops on the coat. It came in a bag and box, just like they came from the store. Even better, it had no price tag – because it never made it to the store.

When I gave Margie Lou her gift, she screamed with delight and wore it everywhere. I swear she kept it until there were holes in the elbows. And she'd always tell everyone, "Guess where I got this? From Jan's Cal!"

Her husband Harold gave me a dirty look. Either he knew where I got it or he realized he had to up the ante.

The perks for pumping ethyl were just creative hustling by me to earn an extra few bucks, but it gnawed at my conscience. After some reflection, I realized I was wrong and never crossed that line again after I went to work in the funeral home. I decided I wanted to be proud of all my decisions in life going forward.

———

I also learned the mating calls of truckers to prostitutes. Prostitution is one of the world's oldest professions, and over the centuries, where the sexes have congregated has varied. Brothels, bars, ranches, red-light districts, truck stops. Before the truck stops, dirt roads, 50-cent chili, $3 hotel rates and "warm company" offered incentives to get a man to stop.

———————

Sgt. Jamison smiled. He didn't follow up on "other things."

"So you know your way around a truck stop?"

"Yes sir," I replied, a bit sheepishly.

In 1975, Oldsmar city leaders did something smart. They built the police station central to where most of the crime occurred.

Because the 105 Truck Stop became part of our district and it could be reached in less than 15 minutes from the police station, I often made it the first stop on my beat.

Truck stops are like small communities unto themselves. Within those communities, there are two different worlds; and within those worlds, you had the good, the bad and the ugly.

The good: Coming off SR 45, 62 and 68, truckers saw the 105 Truck Stop. The oasis had 25-30 diesel fuel pumps on the right and 10-car passenger islands on the left. A repair and maintenance center was in the back.

In the middle stood the control center. It resembled a bank with individuals working behind plexiglass where they could see every fuel pump.

Services offered included Western Union; money that could be wired; fax and copy machines, Comcheck or company checks; and basic hotel rooms.

Behind the control center stood a gift shop leading to a restaurant with a huge buffet and coffee bar. Great food.

The area also held shower rooms, a movie theater and video game room.

And lots and lots of cigarette smokers. You could cut the foggy air of tobacco with a knife.

Outside wasn't much better.

The diesel fuel smell almost choked you. Just 20 to 30 minutes and your hair and clothes smelled like diesel. The clean smell of starch and laundry detergent after Jan washed my uniform, shirt and pants quickly erased the odors.

Truckers had a tire buddy – a rawhide strap around the wrist, a wooden-handled stick and a metal shaft. The tire buddy checked for flat tires with a couple of sharp taps or it could break the nose of an intruder.

There are three main trucks commonly used for long-haul driving or over-road shipping: flatbed trucks, refrigerated (reefer) trucks and standard box trucks. These versatile trucks transport cargo that is bulky, such as construction equipment, cars or mobile homes.

Reefer trucks have the added benefit of having refrigerated units that can transport frozen meat, fish, vegetables, dairy, produce and pharmaceuticals. The units usually are located in the front of the trailer and the cables are connected to the tractor.

Think of it as a big refrigerator with a compressor, condenser, expansion valve and evaporator.

Truckers often sleep in their trucks so they keep their vehicles running all night, especially in the winter. Otherwise, they'd freeze to death. One frozen victim we found about a month after he died. I can't begin to describe the smell when we opened the door.

Some truckers who slept in their trucks bought shower tickets. If they didn't want female company, truckers put a bra on their antenna or driver window or placed a sticker on their window that read: No Lot Lizards Wanted. Lot lizards are affectionately known as prostitutes by truckers.

The bad: If truckers didn't put up any of those "Do Not Disturb" signs, they could almost count on an individual taking a quarter and knocking on their window at any time. Ladies and men of the night. Hookers. Prostitutes. Some men weren't fussy. All they wanted was a warm pair of lips to suck or welcome Mr. Johnson in.

On a cold night, the hookers had the perfect line. "Could I come in and warm up?" they asked not-so-innocently.

They offered a service. Like a burger place, these individuals were in and out – pardon the pun – and on to their next truck.

The ugly: Across the street from the 105 Truck Stop was an establishment called the 44 Magnum Lounge. This cesspool offered a level of debauchery and filth that tested one's depth of depravity.

Proprietors called their bars clubs with members having to ring a door and pay to gain entry.

Drugs would be transacted in bathrooms or party rooms. Crack cocaine had started to become an epidemic. There also was LSD, marijuana, heroin and an amphetamine called "Crank," which was like Red Bull times 10. The boost helped truckers drive extra hours.

Massage parlors. For sore necks, sore backs, sore shoulders, sore hamstrings and anything else that might be ... sore.

Shower rooms. Just hose the hookers down, wash them with mitts and use your imagination. Or theirs. The ladies often wrote their contact information on the bathroom stalls.

Glory holes. In the back two stalls of bathrooms, showers, video arcade booths or lounges, there's a hole cut out large enough for a man to fit his privates. He then had those privates serviced. In the lounges, there's an audience.

Besides the prostitutes, there also were homosexuals, transvestites and hermaphrodites, who possess both male and female sex organs. There was no telling who could be on the other end of the glory holes.

These people arrived for sex or drugs. One fed the other.

The convenience store sold cruisey magazines that told of hook-up spots in the city and rest areas or malls for gays as well as straights.

A barbershop or shoe-shine shop seemed legit but anything could go on in the back rooms – drugs, peep shows or card games.

Poker and three-card monte were most popular. If the prostitutes and pimps didn't take the truckers for a ride, the card games did.

And it got worse.

Often, we'd get calls from truckers saying, "I lost my wallet" or "Someone broke into my truck." Hard to do when many of these guys had their wallets chained to their belts.

What really happened? Pimps or the hookers themselves would lighten a trucker's wallet. A woman could use her mouth and hands simultaneously while a man's eyes rolled back in his head.

On a Sunday, I sometimes had to work from 6 a.m. to 2 p.m. I had just finished a shift a few hours earlier and I wanted to ease into my day with a coffee and a donut at D Squared.

So when I responded to a trucker in distress, I was short on patience.

"Don't bullshit me," I'd say. "Don't insult my intelligence. Do you want to tell me the truth or do you want me to take a report and send a copy to your employer?"

Sometimes, truckers wouldn't realize they had been robbed until they were 400 miles down the road. "If you want to file a report, you have to drive back and sign your signature on the incident report," I said.

They never returned.

———————

Whether it be exhaustion, laziness or a combination, truckers often didn't walk the quarter mile to use the public bathrooms. Or the showers. For days.

I can tell you that for a fact.

Guys literally didn't give a shit. Or care where they shit. Or pissed. Or threw up.

Many would open their door, step on the running board, open their fly and be a whiz kid.

To do No. 2, they'd get down on the ground, walk around their rig, find an area obscured from other truckers and drop their own load.

Toilet paper? Don't know. Don't care to know.

One night, we were in uniform and had to catch people in the act selling drugs. We called them out and they ran.

We chased them by, in and around trucks, about 50 of them lined up for the night. Some crooks made the dangerous move of rolling under moving semis.

It was dark without a lot of lighting and it had rained earlier so in our chase, I thought I had stepped in mud or puddles. Not so. When the crook got away – it happened to the best of us – I returned to my car and said to myself, "What is that smell?"

There it was - caca on my polished shoes. Shit. Literally.

The consecutive hours on the road for truckers are rough enough; but when they don't even walk a few hundred feet to a toilet, they're prime candidates for back issues, pilonidal cysts, heart attacks, diabetes, deep vein thrombosis, varicose veins, cancer and anxiety.

Anxiety. Making deliveries on deadlines. Sleeping in cramped quarters. Worrying about being robbed.

No wonder some of them looked for female companionship. Or just a wet pair of lips to find a warm home. A primitive call to nature.

————

Within a few months, I realized that most of the activity came in the dark. As a high school wrestling coach once told me, nothing good happens after midnight.

One night, I noticed this sweet-looking Mercedes Benz in the back area of the parking lot. Because I'm naturally nosey, I kept observing.

The driver didn't look like the snobby, sophisticated, three-piece-suit-wearing car aficionado. This guy had a flannel shirt, baggy jeans and disheveled hair.

What's a Mercedes Benz doing at a truck stop interchange?

I learned it's important to become friends with the dispatchers so I picked up smokes and McDonald's for them.

When I asked them to run a check on the Mercedes, they quickly complied.

"Radio, give me a 20-21 on a Florida registration with NTS5C8," I said.

The dispatcher had the ability to go into The National Crime Information Center – NCIC.

It was designed for rapid exchange of information between criminal justice agencies. Users access the NCIC computer located at FBI headquarters through regional or state computer systems or with direct tie-ins to the NCIC computer. The data is stored in 12 files: article, boat, Canadian warrant, gun, interstate identification index, license plate, missing person, securities, U.S. Secret Service Protective, unidentified person, vehicle and wanted person.

The car and license plate came up blinking 37. A hit! The code for a stolen car.

The Mercedes had been stolen six months earlier. Sgt. Jamison told me to take my cruiser and park in an area where I could see the car and room where the driver stayed. Then I waited and waited. With this theft being a potential problem, two other cars and three other officers joined me.

Early in the morning, a man came out with a female. I radioed their movements to alert the other cars – "Radio, 37 is going down."

The four of us ran to them, drew our weapons and identified ourselves. The man and woman raised their arms and dropped to the ground as we ordered.

This is the report made on the collar:

Dear Chief Myers,

Dispatcher Loretta Jefferson ran a check on a vehicle from Fort Lauderdale, Florida, stolen several months earlier. Officer Raven picked up the surveillance and staked out for four hours and stayed at his post until 5 a.m. He gave a statement of confirmation and returned to his shift at 8 a.m.

I later learned the Mercedes was worth about $50,000. The driver had been up and down the Eastern Seaboard with it.

Sgt. Jamison helped me get an award for my work. In the *Oldsmar Independent*, in the Local Roundup Section, the newspaper ran a short blurb on the arrest.

Sgt. Williams pulled me aside a few days later. Talk about giving a back-handed, half-ass congratulations combined with concern – I think – and a not-so-mild warning.

"Hey Hollywood, trying to make lieutenant in your first year on the job?" Williams said.

My smile disappeared and I looked at him awkwardly. "Sir?," I said.

"Look Raven," he said. "About the other night. The reason why I got on your ass is that you're too eager, you're too overzealous. You're new at this. Take your time. Assess the situation. Wait for backup. You were fortunate. That couple could've had a gun or knife. One, or both, could've attacked with those weapons. God damn it, I would fucking hate to call your wife and say, 'Ma'am, I regret to inform you, your husband is in the hospital – or the morgue.' You get where I'm coming from?"

I nodded.

He then shook my hand, but before leaving he said, "And don't be camping out at that truck stop. There's nothing out there but whores and horny truckers. Let them fuck each other up."

Those comments really pissed me off. I admit to being too eager but his half-ass approach bothered me. I never believed in cutting corners. I was still learning my way as a cop, Sgt. Williams was right about that. But I could always read people well, and I didn't need a babysitter. I felt I was being micro-managed. Sgt. Williams was becoming a thorn in my ass. It was becoming clear that he was about CYA.

When I shared the message with Sgt. Jamison, he bit his lip – literally.

"Follow your instincts," he said. "Be quick but don't hurry. Walk softly with Williams; but carry a big stick with the crooks."

———

While making my rounds at the 105 Truck Stop, I saw a poster in the control center about a missing person.

These are called BOLO sheets – Be On The Lookout.

The sheet, with a photo and description of a young female, read as follows:

Height: 5'4"-5'6"
Weight: 125-130 lbs.
Hair Color: Red
Clothing: Wearing heavy poncho
Last seen: 105 Truck Stop

"Can I make a copy of this?" I asked.

"Go right ahead," one of the tellers replied.

My instincts rarely betrayed me. I kept the copy on a stainless steel clipboard.

As I looked at her image over the coming days, it became ingrained in my mind.

I had a nagging feeling this person would be part of my police work in the future.

CHAPTER 4

Truck Stop Lingo

Brown Sugar: "Breaker 1-9, anyone looking for a horny commercial beaver out there on party row? Take it to the Double Harley for Brown Sugar. It'll be worth the trip."

Trucker: "Hey Brown Sugar, you got Gentle Ben on the Double Harley what's on the menu?"

Brown Sugar: "Gentle Ben 20-40-60. What house are you in?"

– Example of the way truckers and prostitutes connected on the CB

After only a few years on the job, my commendations and newspaper articles written about me started to build a nice resume.

A scumbag went into a 7-Eleven, locked the door and raped a cashier. I saw a description of him familiar to a guy I arrested for speeding just days before.

I passed the name and license onto detectives.

"This guy drives like an asshole," I said.

Sure enough, detectives picked him up when he appeared for his court hearing on the speeding ticket. I received an award for that.

I responded to a shooting in progress less than a mile from the police department. Upon responding, I could hear on my police radio the conversation between the dispatcher and a female caller, whose female friend and her son were being shot at by her estranged boyfriend.

As I rolled in, I saw the scumbag with a shotgun. I got out of the car, positioned myself behind the driver's side door, took out my 9 mm handgun and zoomed in on the boyfriend. As I moved out, I pointed at him and ordered him to get down. He turned the shotgun on himself and blew part of his face off. He survived.

In the shooting incident, the 17-year-old boy was shot in the heart and died instantly. I later found out that the suspect who shot himself was the brother of the woman who was violently raped at the 7-Eleven.

The boy's mother was critically injured during the shootout. While waiting for the ambulance, I used a towel to hold the mother's intestines in. She repeatedly asked about "Jackie," her son, and I didn't have the heart to tell her he was gone. Later, at the hospital, I met with the victim's family to make the official death notification. It turned out they were good friends of my parents, which made the situation even more difficult.

I received another call to go to a honky-tonk bar called Bobby's Place. A patron assaulted other bikers while causing damage in the bar.

Drunk and high individuals were dangerous because they felt no pain. A fellow officer said he once tased a guy three times before he went down.

Ned Johnson introduced himself to me with a slap to the face that knocked off my glasses. We started fighting and I'm getting tired and running out of gas. Finally, I heard the sirens approaching, gained the upper hand and cuffed him. But not before he nailed me in the shins with his steel-toed, biker boots.

As I put him in the cruiser, he kicked out the glass in the window. Knowing my name, he said in a raspy voice, "Raven, I know where you and your family live and I'm going to kill all of you."

Then he spat in my face. We had to hogtie his legs together to control him.

When we arrived at the police station, he threatened my family again. I looked at my shins. They still had dents in them.

On another night working special duty at McDonald's at 2 a.m. Some nights, cops would arrive just as a McDonald's employee threw out leftover food. The cops took the food, threw it by an illegal dump site and shot the big-ass rats that scrounged for food.

On this night, a highly intoxicated, drunk mutt started dropping F bombs and threatening the woman at the drive-thru window.

I surprised him when I said, "Shut up and stop the threats or you'll spend the night in lock up."

The guy said, "Fuck you," and drove out of the McDonald's. I'm behind him on foot, chasing the idiot, who hit a sign post and bailed out of the car. He ran behind other businesses and concealed himself underneath a recreational vehicle.

When I came around the front of the RV, the suspect pointed a small-caliber firearm at my head. Meanwhile, Roger Gleason, who watched the whole thing, came from behind and hit the suspect's arm, which allowed me to tackle the guy.

I later presented Roger with an award from the police department and the Fraternal Order of Police.

But one of the biggest collars I made came thanks to one of those deals I made with a small-time drug addict.

I pulled a repeat offender over, Munk – also known as 'The Rat' – for having a suspended driver's license and invalid plates. After having a "Come to Jesus talk" with Munk, I explained to him I could jam him up by hooking his car, issuing multiple citations and impounding it or he could walk home, obtain a new license and avoid fines in the hundreds of dollars. He saw the light.

The next day, Munk called and said, "I don't want to get in trouble but ..."

Now a confidential informant, he proceeded to tell me that he knew the two guys who had been burglarizing stores, including Valentino's Market. Apparently, they worked with a third-shift employee and forcibly entered the rear of the store.

We wired up Munk and he got the guys to talk about what they stole. Shortly after, we came with a search warrant and found all sorts of stolen items, including cartons of cigarettes, cash, beer, wine, and various other groceries.

Since we got them on a felony pinch, they got two to three large in the penitentiary.

Munk became one of my top informants. I wanted to help keep him off the rock, but he just couldn't stay clean.

Included in the attaboys came a card and newspaper clippings from Dorothy: *Cal, congratulations, I'm proud of you. C'mon over and I'll have rhubarb pie waiting this time. All the best, D.*

However, the reactions to my successes were mixed. The Oldsmar Police's old guard started to get annoyed with my honors. I could sense an underlying animosity and contempt among some of the cops.

Somebody wrote an angel's halo above my head in a picture that went with an article.

"Rookie's getting a big head," one said. "Maybe we need to pop it."

"Hey Hollywood," another said. "When you walkin' the red carpet?"

Now, you can tell the difference between ball busting and jealousy. It's really clear. And the old-guard cops made no secret of their feelings. Ironically, those same people never got off their asses.

I just smiled and ignored them.

Besides the press, word traveled fast at the truck stop.

As I grabbed a bite to eat, 105 Truck Stop owners Jim Dail and Greg Shriver came by. Good men. They grew up in Iowa, working as teens at one of the largest truck stops in the country. Christian men, they brought up their children in this community and gave back by sponsoring Little League teams and scholarship programs.

"Nice work the past few months," Dail said.

"That Mercedes arrest impressed me," Shriver said. "You take your job seriously."

"Thanks," I said. "Doesn't everybody?"

"No," they said in unison. "Are you going to do some 10 to 2 shifts?"

The 10 p.m. to 2 a.m. shifts were extra hours officers could work on vice detail. Called The Strike Force, the 105 Truck Stop owners along with the police department worked together on a schedule.

"It goes by seniority," I said. "The veteran cops have a

stranglehold on those jobs."

"Really?" Dail said.

Shriver added, "All they do is drink, eat and sit in their cars on our dime."

"Sometimes," Dail added, "I think the cops are getting their fingers wet."

"I can neither confirm nor deny," I said to their slight chuckles.

"Well, Cal, we just want you to know we appreciate all you do," Dail said.

Shriver added, "And we just may have to do something about that seniority shit."

Before they left, Dail chuckled and said, "Hey Cal, you figuring out that new language?"

I lifted up my list of CB terminology.

"Can I see that?" Shriver said. When I showed him the list, he scanned, smiled, took out a red pen and wrote A+ on it.

"We'll get you a bachelor's degree in CB Language," Dail said.

As the centuries and decades passed, sending messages varied in ways to elude the law.

Smoke signals. Papyrus scrolls. Sealed, rolled-up papers delivered by messenger or on horseback. Carrier pigeon. Radio. Television. Emissaries.

In the 1960s, 70s, 80s and 90s, the citizen band radio, or CB, became the preferred method of subterfuge.

Ham operators, or amateur radio operators, used equipment at an amateur radio station to engage in two-way personal communications with other amateur operators on radio frequencies assigned to the amateur radio service. These people need a governmental regulatory authority after passing an examination on applicable regulations, electronics, radio theory and radio operation.

CB operators don't need to do that. They can just get a device at a truck stop, assemble it, add an antenna and join in the conversation.

CBs became standard issue equipment on trucks. The original idea was to let truckers exchange information, like good eating spots, hot spots where police parked and reputable mechanics.

However, that devolved into truckers desiring other information – massages, drugs, alcohol and female and/or male companionship.

To maneuver around the police, truckers, pimps and prostitutes developed their own language. They also flashed their marker warning lights on their truck to indicate their location.

The CB code is a language unto itself.

I learned I needed to know everything about CB language. Thanks to my early days of pumping ethyl, confidential informants, a CB shop operator and helpful truck drivers, I educated myself. To keep up, I also listened and documented radio traffic constantly.

Prostitutes had about a half-dozen names – booger, coin-operated beaver, commercial company, sleeper leaper, working girl and lot lizard. A male prostitute for female drivers was called Buffalo.

Equal opportunity, right? Women truckers got lonely, too.

If a person wanted oral sex, he'd ask for a BJ or head. If he wanted oral sex and intercourse, he asked for half and half. Hold the sugar.

For years, TV shows and films used the term "good buddy." In truckers' terms, that meant a gay man who liked to pick up truckers, usually for free. Good buddies usually hung out at rest areas called pickle parks.

During their communication, the men would ask "Are you a top or a bottom?" or "Are you looking for a rusty trombone?"

Sort of like a plug and a socket.

Cocaine went by nose candy or snow.

Gas Station Heroin is a type of opioid. Black Beauties, or Biphetamine T-20, was the street name for a combination: Amphetamine capsule/tablet containing 10mg of amphetamine and 10mg of dextroamphetamine.

Marijuana had a number of names – herb, road dope, skunk, skunk weed, doobie, big fat Philly blunt or smoke.

Benzodiazepines, which slows down the nervous system, were known as bars, benzos, blues, chill pills, downers, nerve pills, planks, tranks and zannies.

There were dozens of other terms such as Big Road (interstate highway), Box (van-type truck trailer), Bulldog, Little Puppy (Mack truck), Coal Bucket (dump truck), Corn Binder (International tractor), Covered Wagon (trailer covered by tarp), Fist Bed (uncovered trailer), Freight Shaker (Freightliner trailer), K-Whopper (Kenworth tractor), Large Car (conventional truck tractor), Party Row (Far back truck stop parking row) and Pete or Peter Car (Peterbilt).

Some more of what was on my CB terminology list:

Rooster Cruiser: A truck with lots of extra, unnecessary lights and chrome just for show.

Suicide Jockey: A driver who hauls dangerous freight, like explosives.

Large Car: Owner-operator truck with no speed governor, can drive it like a car. Usually a long-nosed rig (hood).

Owner-Op: Driver who owns his own rig, as opposed to a company driver who drives a truck owned by a trucking company.

Pilot Car: A car or cars used to escort oversized loads. They often have long poles sticking up to the height of the load they are escorting to test clearances on bridges and overpasses.

UFO (Unidentified Four-Wheeling Object): A vehicle that's driving erratically or dangerously.

Bear: Police were called many variations of bear, such as Smokey (Smokey Bear), Bear In The Air (police in helicopters), Full-Grown Bear (state trooper) or Polar Bear (a white unmarked police car).

And then there are the CB radio channels, all with their own nicknames.

Channel 1: The Harley or The Basement

Channel 7: The JD (Jack Daniels) or Whiskey

Channel 19: Sesame Street or Take it to the Sesame

Channel 31: The Baskin-Robbins.

I had a CB in my car. On nights off, I could plug a cord into the cigarette lighter and my small antenna could pick up conversations since I was eight miles from the truck stop.

When I heard something bad was going on, I alerted the cops on patrol as well as security officers at the truck stop.

This made me the go-to guy for fellow officers on CB talk. Since I was still young, I had to be respectful. This also led me to being heavily involved with the National Association of Truck Stop Operators (NATSO), whose members included national truck stop chains and off-highway transportation energy providers.

Sadly, when things went wrong at the truck stop, the security officers often called me instead of the officers on duty.

But that's the job. Once it's in your blood, you're screwed.

———

CB language requires translation for the uninformed as the code names were designed to camouflage communications. Take for instance, this conversation:

Brown Sugar: "Breaker 1-9, anyone looking for a horny commercial beaver out there on party row? Take it to the Double Harley for Brown Sugar. It'll be worth the trip."

Trucker: "Hey Brown Sugar, you got Gentle Ben on the Double Harley what's on the menu?"

Brown Sugar: "Gentle Ben 20-40-60 what house are you in?"

The conversation above has a lot of elements to it.

First of all, prostitutes often worked out an arrangement with truckers to go from truck stop to truck stop. In return, the trucker often would get a blow job for free.

"Horny commercial beaver" means the prostitute is on her way.

"Double Harley" references Channel 11.

"Brown Sugar" and "Gentle Ben" are handles or names of the people talking.

House is the type of a truck, like a red Peterbilt or blue Kenworth.

"What's on the menu?" is asking what Brown Sugar is offering.

And the numbers (20-40-60) signify the activity and the price. So, to translate, it means a blow job for $20, sex for $40 and both for $60.

These are among the things I shared with the other officers. As you can imagine, it was like teaching a bunch of teenagers with their wise-ass comments and jokes.

———

I overheard a call on intercity about a young woman who had been beaten in Richland County and lay in critical condition in Mercy Hospital. She had been beaten, choked and left for dead.

Her name: Mary Masters, with a CB handle as Pepper.

As Richland County Sheriff Lance Briggs put out this information, my instinct was that I knew her in some way.

"I think we talked to this woman," I told the dispatcher. "Check the FI cards."

Field Interview cards are when officers talk with prostitutes. They usually aren't arrested but information is gathered on them, a photo is taken and they're often warned if they are caught again, there's a good chance they'll be arrested for criminal trespassing.

The dispatcher confirmed my suspicions. We had interviewed her five weeks earlier.

I raced to the hospital to see if she'd gain consciousness and be able to give a description of her attacker.

That never happened. When I arrived at Mercy Hospital, a charge nurse gave me the bad news: Mary Masters died.

Sadly, she left behind a young daughter.

CHAPTER 5

Poor Girls

**"I have a place, I have kids. If
I get them a babysitter, I gotta
make money so I gotta hook."**

– Rainbow, one of many prostitutes
interviewed by officer Cal Raven

Sgt. Jamison had a look of shock when I shared my youthful experiences that prepared me for a job in law enforcement.

"Callaghan, in my 27 years on the force, I have never, ever, ever met anyone who has been through as much shit as you have before being a police officer," he said. "We have guys with two or three years under their belt, and I don't think they've fucking seen all you've seen."

"That's good, right?" I said.

"Yes and no," Jamison said. "Yes, you're not surprised by much. No, that's a lot of shit to see before you're 21."

I squirmed, not knowing what to say.

"Cal, listen to me carefully," he said. "If ever a time comes where it gets to be too much, there are places where you can get help. I just wouldn't advertise it. Understand?"

I nodded.

"Based on what you told me, I gather you also have experiences with prostitutes," Jamison said.

"Not personally," I quickly said. "But yes, I've seen and heard a lot about that, too. How did you know?"

"Cal, everyone on the force knows there's a massage parlor shouting distance from Thomas Funeral Home. And if you've been around truckers long enough at the truck stop you worked, the word hooker or whore or prostitute had to come up.

"I'll tell you this. If you give those ladies their dignity, treat them with respect and ask them nicely, even when you arrest them, they can become some of your best informants. At the end of the day, women like to talk and they like to gossip."

It was probably a year later, but that conversation came back to me before I approached various "ladies of the night."

Many people call prostitution the oldest profession in the world. Look it up. Its history goes back to 24th century BC. Records mention prostitution as an occupation. It traveled from Greece to Rome to India to China and Japan. Put a finger on any land area and this type of business went on.

In Islam, prostitution was considered a sin but sexual slavery via concubinage in Islam was not considered prostitution. Semantics, even back then.

There are biblical references. There is art showing sexual acts. A 19th century argument made in North America stated that prostitution was a "necessary evil" and led to fewer affairs when a man's wife didn't want to have sex. I guess they didn't have cold showers back then.

———

The first women I talked to didn't give me much information. They didn't trust cops and I was new.

Having made a few collars and being young, my first thought was procedural with the prostitutes – field interview, take their photo, give warning. If I saw them again, I charged them with criminal trespassing. In order to get a soliciting prostitution charge, you had to be offered a sex act for a fee.

On the few times I did catch them in the act, the women would say something like, "Hey Callaghan, can't you make this go away? What do you want? Sex? A BJ? Both? Let's just go in the back seat, have our fun and I'll be on my merry way."

I politely declined.

We also used the disorderly conduct charge on prostitutes depending on their activities observed on the lot. If they robbed or shook down a truck driver for his wallet, they would be charged with strong-arm robbery or theft.

After I built a rapport and interviewed these women about their daily lives with men – and women – they did like to talk. They shared details that almost made me sick, but also gave me perspective.

Their stories actually made economical sense, despite the dangers, which led me to being empathetic. Their activities were solely to help them survive and provide for their kids, even though society looked down upon them. This newfound perspective led me to treat them like I did small-time crooks, and also made me realize they were people, too.

———

While they made it extremely difficult on themselves, these women had become products of their environments.

Many came from middle to lower-middle class families in the Midwest, which had seen a recession during the Carter Administration that lingered into President Reagan's first term. A number of businesses from steel companies to auto manufacturers struggled while truck drivers and farmers fell on hard times.

The trickle-down effect began. Laid-off parents turned to alcohol or drugs, if they hadn't already been doing it. Either way, they didn't or couldn't send their children to college or a two-year school; and if teens wanted to work, options were limited. Jobs like bartending, waitressing and working cash registers were taken by people who lost their better-paying jobs.

But the biggest crime parents committed was neglect. They didn't know what their kids did. Many didn't care. Without supervision, the girls – and some boys – either screwed around in school or dropped out. They turned to drinking, drugs and sex.

They often ran away from home or were kidnapped by people who became their pimps. They became part of sex rings. This is why there were hundreds of unidentified victims called Jane Does – and John Does – in the FBI's Violent Criminal Apprehension Program or ViCAP.

Pimps acquire and protect their girls and women, but in return, the pimps often receive 50 percent or more for their services. We never arrested the pimps because it's a difficult pinch to make. The prostitutes had to turn in their pimps; and if the pimps didn't get jailed, the consequences could be severe.

The only way we could get involved is through The Mann Act. Previously called the White-Slave Traffic Act of 1910, The Mann Act made it a felony to engage in interstate or foreign commerce transport of "any woman or girl for the purpose of prostitution or debauchery or any immoral purpose."

I interpreted this as human trafficking with the purpose of prostitution. We zoned in on it even more if the females were younger than 18.

Women could become prostitutes without having pimps but they ran the risk of customers not paying them, beating them, raping them or killing them.

———

That's what happened to the Jane Doe that I had made a copy of on the missing-person poster.

In Lawson County, a farmer found her in a ditch by a cornfield, about two hours from 105 Truck Stop. The woman, 21, about 5-foot-5 and 125 pounds, had her auburn hair in braids. She had been dead for a couple of days. Nicknamed "Poncho Girl," she was barefoot, beaten and strangled.

A known prostitute, she also had drug issues. Pollen tests showed she had traveled to the Southwest part of the country. I didn't know it then, but Poncho Girl was Victim No. 1. Mary Masters became No. 2.

———

After I made a couple of visits and showed I wasn't hellbent on arrests, the women let their guards down. Or should I say mouths.

When I tried to have a conversation, some of the women mumbled.

When I asked them questions, I couldn't understand what they said.

Showing my frustrations, I said, "Can you speak up more clearly?"

Much to my surprise, they proceeded to take condoms out of their mouths. When giving blow jobs, they were ambidextrous enough and fast enough to put them on a man's penis before giving oral stimulation. Gift wrapped protection for both sexes.

I then met Yvette Mendez. When we first talked, Yvette had a succinct response to why she worked the truck stops.

"Faster money," she said as she took a drag of her cigarette. If she hustled and was lucky, Yvette said she could make $800 in eight hours as opposed to $200 to $300 if she worked the Oldsmar streets or in part-time jobs.

While she had to go to the hospital for stitches, was raped and nearly killed, she said the worst was servicing truckers who had the hygiene of a sewer rat.

"Dingleberries and duck butter," she said.

At first I thought she was either fucking around with me or talking about a kid's cereal but then I soon found out the harsh truth.

Located in the X-rated section of the CB manual, dingleberries are small pieces of dried fecal matter clinging to anal hair or small shit balls on a truck driver's ass hairs that have a tendency to fall off during a blow job or rim job.

A rim job is a vague term for an extremely specific sex act — like licking and sucking a man's butthole. This can be incredibly, awfully, grossly, nasty if the man has crotch crickets (public lice). Lice is not nice.

Duck butter is a slang term referring to bodily fluids,

particularly sweat, semen, smegma, or other secretions around the genitals especially on an uncircumcised male.

As I listened to Yvette share these stories, I almost vomited. Remember, I'm the guy who has seen dead, bloody and mutilated bodies as a teen.

As I processed this information, Yvette said she wished the police wouldn't let her out of jail so fast. Why?

"If they let me stay in for 90 days, I could get rid of my crack habit," she replied. "I've been in jail more than 50 times; and I'm always released in less than a week."

Before she waved goodbye, Yvette said, "I worked two nights here before and I'll be seeing you again soon."

Next up? Rainbow. I asked in frustration, "Why the fuck are you doing this?"

Again, a simple answer. "I have a place, I have kids," she said. "If I get them a babysitter, I gotta make money so I gotta hook."

She said most jobs of being a maid at a low-budget hotel, cashier, waitress or topless dancer hardly can pay the bills. And they're a lot more hours of work.

"Doesn't it hurt your dignity?" I asked.

"Dignity and ego are one thing," she said. "But surviving, that's something completely different."

A lot of them would say, "Hey Cal, at least I'm gainfully employed and not sucking up welfare."

As I listened to the ladies, I realized most are not stealing, not robbing. They're just trying to keep their heads above water. And this may sound bad. They are servicing a need. A need man has had for thousands of years. The idea of legalizing prostitution has been talked about, but outside of Nevada, it's illegal. In Maine, selling sex is decriminalized but buying sex is illegal.

Some of the ladies cried. "I don't want to be here," they

sobbed. "But what am I going to do?"

While I didn't accept their offers of blow jobs, my empathy turned to sympathy. They were somebodies treated as nobodies.

One night, reality hit me in the face. I'd give some of the ladies a few bucks and say, "Get something to eat and get out of here."

They'd respond, "Cal, where am I going to go? Go to the next truck stop? Go down two exits where I'd be in Indiana?"

I didn't have an answer.

The best thing I could do was keep talking to them, keep showing them respect and maybe they could give me some leads. As Sgt. Jamison said, "Women like to talk and they like to gossip."

———

Talking to the ladies over the last few months had bummed me out.

Then I received a call from my children Janet, Laura and Clayton.

"We miss you daddy," they said.

"Stop catching the crooks and come home," Janet added.

"Jan, did you teach her the word crook," I asked.

"Oh, she soaks things in like a sponge," she said. "Be careful out there. The weather is getting bad."

An early November snow started coming down. The temperatures had dropped unexpectedly.

My partner Tony Blackstone and I drove to the 105 Truck Stop for our 10 to 2 shift. We wanted some coffee but the machine was broken.

As we listened to the CB, we heard drug dealers offering

an eight ball or one-eighth ounce of cocaine.

Tony rolled down his window and said, "Cal, don't do it, don't do it."

I said, "Watch this."

I got on the CB and said, "Hey anybody looking for the real good stuff?"

"How do I know you're not a cop?"

"How do I know you're not a cop? Get out of the truck, go in front of the vending machines, punch or rock the Coke machine twice, then turn around, put your hand behind your back and jump on one leg. Then meet me by the phone booth."

We watched the sucker make tracks in the snow.

Just before he got to the vending machines, I went on Channel 19 where there's a big audience and said, "Watch what this nut case does by the vending machine."

After he did his act, hundreds of truckers in their vehicles started blowing their air horns, much to his embarrassment.

As he ran back to his truck, flashing the bird to everyone in sight, he jumped in only to hear his fellow truckers bust his chops.

"Hey Rocky."

"Hey Hopper."

"You do the Hokey Pokey."

"We have snowflakes."

"Encore. Encore."

For the next hour, we laughed and laughed. The night went by a lot quicker.

———

As quickly as we picked up four inches of snow, it melted away, thanks to temperatures that had warmed back up to the 50s.

Just enough time for police to discover the body of 23-year-old Sally May Thompson. Victim No. 3. The dark, red-haired, 5-foot-3 prostitute was found about 100 miles from us in Johnson County. Dead about two weeks, the blunt force trauma to her head was so severe, you could literally see the traumatic brain injury.

I decided to wait until after the holidays before showing the girls photos of the victims to see if they'd be more open to talking.

Part of me thought putting them in jail – even for a few days – would give them a chance to have a few good meals, give their bodies a break and let them think if this is something they wanted to continue doing.

Yes, their options were limited. But any option has to be better than having a rope wrapped around your neck and the air squeezed out of you, doesn't it?

Anything has to be better than being beaten so many times your head breaks open, doesn't it?

Any choice they make has to be better than going into a truck and risk being killed.

Doesn't it? Doesn't it?

Miles away in Northeast Arkansas, Bert Driller filled his beat-up, 1975 Ford pickup with suitcases full of clothes, snacks, drinks, toiletries and any valuables he had. Despite hearing the sobs of girls in the background, he continued packing.

Driller could ignore crying – and what most people said; but there was one voice he couldn't ignore: Richard's.

Driller couldn't figure out if that voice belonged to his twin brother who died during childbirth, his father or something else. It reminded him of how the dummy 'Fats' mentally controlled the ventriloquist 'Corky' in *Magic*, a 1978 film. That film struck a nerve with Driller.

Whatever the voice was and wherever it came from, it seemed to have a grip on Driller.

Just two years earlier, the voice spoke to Driller so he ended his marriage with Ann Leigh Coffman; and in the process he ended her life. He wrapped a nylon rope around the red-haired woman's neck and choked her after they had sex. Forced sex.

Few people knew of the couple's marriage in Arkansas; and by the time her body was discovered in a Texas river, there was little evidence after the bobcats and gators got through with her.

When authorities asked about his missing wife, Driller just told them that he had been on the road for two weeks. He said the marriage was on the rocks; and when he hadn't heard from her for days and he returned to an empty house, he figured she just left.

As he returned to the house and zipped his fly, Driller looked at sisters Terri Jo and Ashley Judson and said, "Not a word. Ever. Understand?"

The girls, not even in fourth grade, nodded.

"I'll be back to see if you two kept your promise."

Driller had met their mother, Alice, on the rebound after her ex-husband left two years earlier. Lonely, she and Driller spent a few nights together. She trusted him enough to babysit the girls when she left for a couple of hours to run errands. Terrible mistake.

The voice's appetite had shifted from older women to younger girls; and Driller complied to its desires.

Terri Jo and Ashley held each other, shaking. Hearing the sound of his pickup driving away eased their anguish briefly but they still felt a piercing, internal pain physically.

The idea of Driller returning petrified them; but fortunately, their mother arrived 30 minutes later and could see the tears running down their faces and their bodies quivering with fright.

CHAPTER 6

The Cops' Fine Line

**"Sometimes the cops
are the robbers."**

– Patrick Raven

A few weeks into my job, Dad and I sat down with dad's friend Barry Witkowski in Costello's Restaurant. It had a reputation for being a mob hangout but the food was so good, we overlooked it.

After Barry and Dad congratulated me, they got down to business.

Having owned a construction company for decades in Oldsmar, Dad had a few experiences with the local police. He also bailed out buddies and employees who got drunk and belligerent, which got them put in lockup for the night.

"Are you really sure you want to do this?" Dad asked.

"Dad, you know I was raised right," I said. "I'm going to do the right thing."

"I don't think you understand. It's not you who I'm worried about."

"Well …"

"The thieves, wife-beaters, con men, mob and that Godforsaken, devil-incarnate 44 Magnum Lounge is bad enough," Dad clarified in a sharp tone. "But then you have to deal with the system. The judges, prosecutors, defense attorneys, even guys in your own police station. Sometimes the cops are the robbers."

I paused, then responded, "You know, I have this sergeant. Williams. I can tell. The guy doesn't like me. He reamed me out for no reason."

"Cal, you're a go-getter. Williams plays it safe. I have some cop friends who say he's up for chief. That may not be good for you."

"Yeah, I know. He's got friends, Dad. He's got a lot of friends."

"Yeah," Witkowski said. "Be careful."

Conrad Williams didn't plan on being a police officer.

Always good with his hands, he went to trade school and became a handyman. He could do just about any job related to building a home.

But when the Illinois economy struggled, Williams jumped from place to place. He also had a hard time with handyman gigs because he didn't have people skills to close deals. The worst came when he couldn't afford to finish building his own home he started from scratch. He had to claim bankruptcy.

Down on his luck, Williams reached out to a high school friend, Travis Simoneau, who started to build an insurance business.

Simoneau partnered with Williams on a side business called Local Home Packages. The idea was that homeowners could get rebates on home improvements and increase the value of their homes when they bundled all their insurance needs – home, car, boat, even life. The rebates and deals weren't that great but homeowners believed the smooth-talking Simoneau. Williams, who had steady work, then took his friend's advice, and gave himself a second income by going to the police academy, graduating and becoming a police officer.

Williams' father Jerry, a successful executive with one of the top automakers, started making generous donations to the Oldsmar Police Department so it could buy equipment not covered in the township's budget. This not only helped get his son on the force but also got him a 6 a.m. to 2 p.m. shift.

That's why Conrad Williams welcomed day turns with weekends off, which worked perfectly for his handyman jobs.

When he started shortchanging his detective duties, word got to Chief Dustin Myers. After personally seeing Williams pass on doing interviews for a case to a colleague so he could remodel the interior of a client's home, an irate Myers demoted Williams to afternoon/turn sergeant in a marked patrol car. Williams might have gotten a slap on the wrist under ordinary circumstances, but Myers caught him red-handed because the client was the chief's next-door neighbor.

Simoneau told him not to worry about the demotion. "If you're interested in being a chief, you can say you have the qualifications of road duty," he said.

Williams' father also stepped in again. His influence helped Simoneau become a township trustee. When a second trustee position opened up, Simoneau recruited banker Walter Hutchins.

They combined to help Conrad Williams become a detective, then administrative assistant. Watching Williams pull the same stunts but unable to discipline him, Myers retired early and Williams succeeded him as chief.

He then promoted his buddies to positions they really didn't deserve while demoting or pushing out accomplished detectives and long-time, talented lieutenants who he felt snitched on him. Ironically, a couple of the snitches became Williams' allies when they saw the office politics playing out and decided they'd play along and kiss-ass to get ahead.

So, what the new chief created was a group of unqualified detectives, captains, lieutenants and sergeants as well as opportunists. Meanwhile, about a dozen good cops and sergeants considered their options while keeping their heads down.

This is what I joined – a disjointed police force, short on proactive, aggressive policing using state-of-the art investigative procedures and long on favoritism and cronyism.

Because I worked hard for my first four years on the job to prove myself, along with plenty of chances for extra work through the police department and my eagerness, I regularly worked 70, 75, 80 hours a week.

I put in those hours because I wanted Jan to stay home with our kids – Janet, Laura and Clayton. Working the 2 p.m. to 10 p.m. shift also allowed me to wake up with the kids, help feed them or take them to lunch on Saturdays or days they had off from school.

The main agreement we had while working special details for private businesses and community events was we had to work at least four hours on the shift.

I did everything to provide for my family, working church festivals, department store security, fast-food restaurant security, high school football game traffic and road construction where I walked behind crews laying down tar on the roads in 90-degree heat. With my kevlar vest on, I must have lost 10 pounds on those days.

On the rare day off, I often slept most of the time.

We did make ends meet and we went on the occasional vacation, but we had one car and a modest three-bedroom, Cape Cod home with 1,960-square feet, basement and a small backyard. Fortunately, the school and a park were a short walk away. A small backyard also helped because Jan mowed the lawn most of the time.

When I told Jan of my plans to be a cop, she totally backed me. Her family worked in construction, steel mills, corn production and the Sta-Rite company, which produced water pumps and pressurized water storage tanks. Often, her cousins and brothers would get laid off for three months at a time, maybe more.

While I worked like a mule, I'd see other cops living in bigger homes with bigger lots and having boats on the side of their house.

They had kids, their wives stayed home, they were just a few years older. How did they do it?

Rich family, perhaps? An inheritance? I convinced myself that I could reach their status by sticking with it and getting promoted to detective.

I'd soon realize other factors helped their status.

Among our duties in the last few hours of my shift, I would drive by local stores and make sure I didn't see any suspicious activity.

That would include loitering, kids hanging out close to 11 p.m. and individuals giving an indication they thought of burglarizing a place. They'd wear a dark jacket with dark pants, dark shoes.

Steven Mallard, the owner of The Shoe Store, is someone I knew well. We graduated the same year. Whenever I'd go in to buy a pair of sneakers or shoes for my growing children, he'd quickly say, "Blue money is no good here." I often protected his store by doing night patrols on a frequent basis.

Blue is the police color. It goes back to the mid 1800s. One of the main reasons is functionality. It's easier to clean and maintain blue than a lighter/brighter color as it hides stains and marks.

Even so, I found it difficult to keep my uniform clean; but I have to admit, I didn't mind getting my hands dirty. In fact, if I came home with a clean uniform, I'd feel a bit guilty, like I had just coasted through the day.

Even when I protested Steven's offer, he'd wave his hands, get serious and say no.

I felt guilty about the free shoes.

And if Mallard belonged to organized crime, the mob, I'd owe the syndicate the rest of my police life. Maybe even the rest of my whole life.

And once they get a piece of you, they get a piece of your ethics, they get a piece of your heart and they get a piece of your soul.

Dad worried about that, too.

Like in spycraft, it starts small, with a coffee and conversation. The mob guy talks you into having breakfast. He pays, of course.

Then he and his wife are taking you and your wife to a concert, dinner or dinner and a show.

You get introduced to his friends. Maybe you play cards and you win. Or you lose. Either way, they start asking for favors.

Look the other way on a drug deal. Look the other way when a jewelry store or Walmart or Costco is being burglarized – or a truck itself is taken. Take your time when called to a raid.

Soon, you find an envelope of cash in your police car around Christmastime. You discover it comes from a butcher – because the mob guys told him to. Or you go on vacation and find your hotel room or tickets to rock concerts and Las Vegas shows are comped.

They buy things for you. In return, they also own you.

———

In the old days, racketeers had a black book or notepad where they kept a list of people on the payroll. Those included cops. Instead of by name, their badge often was written in reverse. This led to the phrase "being on the pad."

Some guys on the pad rationalized it by saying the police department doesn't pay enough. Others don't realize the hole they're in until they're buried. And others like a taste of the high life and are dirty cops.

And it's not just the cops who were robbers like Dad said, but other people in law enforcement were on the take.

In my second year on the beat, I nailed a guy, a prominent businessman in the community, on a driving under the influence (DUI) charge. He also caused a car accident that injured the other driver. I saw that person freed on a technicality because someone had lined the judge's pockets.

Mentally, as a guy in his 20s, I had a hard time dealing with the blue wall of silence, the politics and the unknown of who may stab me in the back and who was on my side. The lines started to get blurred.

You didn't want to come across as too much of a boy scout with the cops because you didn't want them thinking you were a rat for the chief or working with internal affairs.

But you also didn't want to be owned.

Within a few years, I got to know the good cops. There were a few I could count on.

Frank Jamison. A great mentor, he always kept me on the right path.

Tony Blackstone. We looked out for each other and we had built up a good rapport in the few times we worked together. Whenever I had a question, he offered good suggestions.

I also could count on Pete Devita, Danny O'Brien, Ron Buffett, Rocky O'Rourke and Tim Gates. Because Pete was a great guy and cop, I tolerated his annoying cigarette smoking. We always used the same patrol car and his shift was just before mine.

When June Briscoe became the fourth prostitute killed in the last four years near an Illinois rest stop five counties away, the guys who cared started comparing notes.

I also made more headway with the ladies of the night because of Yvette Mendez. Even though I arrested her more than once, she respected me because I respected the other women. I also respected her. When she gave me a couple of good tips, I looked the other way with her indiscretions when I could.

When I approached other women, they told me, "Normally I wouldn't talk to a cop but Yvette said you're on the up and up."

The women also had the extra incentive of catching a killer who may be in their midst. Like the other victims, June Briscoe was young. Like the others, she was beaten or strangled. And like the others, her body was dumped less than 250 miles from where they spent time – the 105 Truck Stop.

Corporate officials quietly monitored the situation and talked with 105 Truck Stop owners Jim Dail and Greg Shriver. A story in the Chicago Tribune unfairly ranked the 105 among the worst truck stops. Most of the illegal activity, prostitution and related crimes occurred across the street at the 44 Magnum Lounge.

Local business at the truck stop had already started to decline.

June Briscoe's death wasn't going to help.

My discussions with Dail and Shriver heated up. They wanted to put some teeth behind truck stop security.

"We're going to be more proactive with those who work for us from 10 p.m. to 2 a.m," Dail said.

Shriver added, "Cal, we want you to head the new security detail. Put a team of your guys together who really are going to get things done. Not just the guys who drink our coffee, eat our donuts and make a cursory tour."

I asked, "When do you want to start this?"

"January," Dail said, which was only a few months away.

Shriver added, "This will give you time to put your crew together and it'll give us time to put a plan together."

———

By age 26, my fifth year as a cop, I had earned respect with some key arrests and also by training guys on coping with the activities and goings on around the 105 Truck Stop and the 44 Magnum Lounge. That training included sharing my self-made CB Language Manual, which led us to rooting out some sex rings.

With me being in charge, I had decisions to make.

The slacker cops, they were out.

I also thought that I needed to know the guys more.

So when they asked about going out for a few beers after our 10 p.m. shift ended, I started attending a few of the gatherings.

You know, when you put a handful back, it's a bit like a liquid lie detector.

Some guys you know are in it for the right reasons. They are the ones who want to do the right things and want to keep the bad guys off the streets. One guy said he worked the extra shifts so he could send his daughter to college.

Others unknowingly hinted that they were on the pad based on a boat they "got a good deal on" while others winked about a car they bought with all the extras for the base price. And they made comments, like Williams did, about the prostitutes.

A common chorus refrain: "Why should we worry too much about these hooker killings? Survival of the fittest. Maybe some of these filthy bitches will get scared off."

Then they'd laugh. You could gauge the laughs. The ones who laughed the hardest, I had no use for.

After a couple of weeks, I knew who I wanted.

———

I woke up one December morning with a cold, runny nose, chills and diarrhea so I called in sick.

With Oldsmar being hit by a blizzard and schools closed, there wasn't going to be a lot of activity.

With this being a Friday and having the next two days off,

I figured I'd try to heal up before the holidays. Didn't want to give anybody my bug.

Jan is like a nurse in getting me to feel better. Tried-and-true vapor rub on the chest. Hot teas with spices. Chicken soup with veggies. Hot toddies with two ounces of Irish whiskey, one teaspoon of honey, a squeeze of lemon and boiling water.

I started to feel better so I moved from the bed to the couch and wrapped myself up like a tamale.

"Anything good on the tube?" I said as I turned on the TV.

"Just the soaps, dear," she said.

Just then Days of Our Lives appeared. I stopped to hear a voice say, *Like sands through the hourglass, so are the days of our lives.*

"You know," I said. "Dorothy loves these guys. Bo and Hope, Bo and Hope, Bo and Hope. The rebel and the princess. He kidnaps her and then they get married and have a kid. He becomes a detective."

"Honey, you sure you're not watching it with her?" Jan joked.

Hope appeared on the screen. "Whoa," I said. "Easy on the eyes."

Jan shook her head. "I like Wayne Northrup," she said. "He's trying to solve a murder."

Hope entered a room and she found Bo and Wayne talking about a case. They had files in front of them.

"Look at the ligature marks on these four victims," Wayne said. "All in the neck area. Almost looks like the same rope."

"All in communities within 20 miles of Salem," Bo added. "Do you think we have a serial killer?"

"Maybe. I don't think they were killed in those towns. I think they were killed here. We have a strangler. The Salem Strangler."

The show went to commercials.

"Cal, you have that funny look on your face," Jan said. "What is it?"

"I don't know, I need to check something," I said.

I went to my office where I had made copies of police reports. I looked at them again.

I then called Tony Blackstone.

"Cal, I thought you were home sick," Tony said.

"Feeling better. I was watching ... I was thinking, do you have the photos of the victims?"

"Yes right here in a file."

"The choke marks. Are they similar?"

"Yes. You know, the angle where they're choked is awfully similar. It's almost like the guy is 6-2, 6-3. Are you thinking what I'm thinking?"

"SK? Yeah."

———

Adrenaline is an amazing thing. That and Jan's care had me back on the beat.

After sleeping about 30 hours on Friday, Saturday and Sunday, I'm raring to go. A few more calls with Tony Blackstone and we came up with a plan.

Devita, O'Brien, Buffet, O'Rourke and Gates would run this by the newly minted Chief Conrad Williams. Just as Dad predicted.

Chief Williams had been on the job about three months. Most people would use my idea as a great opportunity to make an impression, rally the troops, work with other agencies and find this nut job.

Not Williams.

He blew up.

"So who are you, God damn Ebenezer Scrooges?" he barked. "What do you want me to do? Go on TV tonight and say, "Merry Fucking Christmas. Happy Fucking Holidays. We think we've got a serial killer loose for those of you thinking of caroling over the next few days.

"Let's just kill Christmas shopping for our struggling businesses, keep people out of the restaurants and bars on New Year's Eve and put God damn coal in all of their stockings."

I cut in.

"Chief, let's put a plan in place over the next couple of weeks."

"Everyone else leave! Raven, stay. Now."

Guys slapped me on the back before leaving while looking away from Williams.

He didn't notice as he messaged his assistant on the phone to bring "the guys" in.

When they arrived, Williams, arms folded, looked at me. "So Mr. Plan, please explain."

As I spoke, I looked into the officers' eyes. I could see the disinterest, apathy and lack of empathy. Many glanced at Williams and fed off that. Of course, if he endorsed my plan, they would've said, "Yeah, yeah, let's do this."

But they didn't even listen.

"You want us to do this tonight?" one said. "It's almost Christmas for God sake."

"Is this our big resolution? Find the boogeyman?"

"Don't you need five or six to have a serial killer?"

I quickly replied, "They're coming."

Williams dismissed everyone, except for me again.

"Raven, haven't you grabbed enough headlines by now? Stick to the streets, not the truck stops."

He and I were about to butt heads like two rams.

———————

With the community quiet after Christmas, and on a day I'm off, police cars from around the state parked in the lot.

I know because Tony Blackstone gave me a call. And Ron Buffett. And Rocky O'Rourke. So I took a brisk walk and sure enough, patrol cars came from 12 different Illinois counties.

So much for an undercover meeting. And Williams didn't invite me.

Johnson County Sheriff Bill Jarrold headed the group.

"Let me get to the point," he said. "These four killings in our state. Is there a pattern?"

"What do you mean?," Peoria County Sheriff Allen Jones said.

"Is there a serial killer, God damn it? Do I have to spell it out?"

"No, I don't believe it," Williams said. "Isolated cases."

"Even though most of these prostitutes worked out of the truck stop in your district?"

"We had an issue with prostitutes a couple of years ago and cleaned it up. It'll get cleaned up again."

"Is Raven part of that group? I saw his name in some stories."

"No. I have my own men."

"But Raven has been getting things done."

"He's a grandstander. I don't want him in the loop."

Jarrold paused, then asked, "You don't like this guy?"

Williams stared at Jarrold but when the glare was returned, he looked away.

"It's your backyard, Conrad. If it's isolated, fine. But we get a few more dead hookers linked to the 105 Truck Stop, it's coming back on you."

In Little Rock, Arkansas, a man is supposed to be in court but doesn't appear.

"Is the defendant here?" Judge Connolly asked.

"No judge," county prosecutor Dub Marshall said.

"Counselor, where's your man?" the judge asks.

"Don't know your honor," public defender John Dixon replied. "He's just disappeared. I called the truck company he worked at. They've gone out of business."

"Judge," Marshall said. "The charges are serious. Two counts, sexual molestation with a minor."

"This happened?"

"Four years ago."

"Four years? Have you called the man's family, friends?"

"Yes, your honor," Marshall said. "They don't like him but they haven't seen him for at least two years. The man simply disappeared. Gone. Like a fart in the wind."

"Men, this is not good; but we have to dismiss the case for now. Mr. Dixon?"

"Yes, judge."

"If you see him or hear from him, let Mr. Marshall know. And if he is in my courtroom, even if it's a parking ticket, we will open up his entire case history."

"Yes, judge."

"By the way, John. What's his name?"

"Bert Driller, your honor. Bert Driller."

CHAPTER 7

Conflict Intensifies

"We work for God."

– Highly decorated New York City
homicide detective and speaker Fred Fry

105 Truck Stop owners Jim Dail and Greg Shriver weren't joking. They said they wanted to have me run point on their new security detail in January; and it was just hours into the new year when they made the formal offer. I accepted.

They told me I received the offer after our conversations and the number of arrests and convictions I made around the truck stop as well as my district. They also liked the aggressive, proactive, innovative approaches I used, and most importantly, ideas I shared in our meetings, which included implementing a new-and-improved strike force as well as a security operations program that could be used by the 105 Truck Stop and its partner truck stops across the United States and Canada.

I also received a nice letter from Trucks Stops America corporate owner Lawrence Baycroft.

"We would've done Jan. 1, but we went to California to watch Iowa in the Rose Bowl," Dail said.

Shriver added, "Brutal start. Nice comeback but just not enough."

I'd have a team of men who rotated and worked the 10 p.m. to 2 a.m. shift every day. Dail and Shriver said "the big dogs," those with TSA Corporate, would pay me to attend various seminars and conferences and they'd put me in contact with those running NATSO – the National Association of Truck Stop Operators.

In addition, I also would connect with RISS - the Regional Information Sharing System; ROCIC (Regional Organized Crime Information Center) in the Southern states and MAGLOCEN (Mid Atlantic Great Lakes Organized Crime Law Enforcement Network) through our Oldsmar Police Department.

Chief Conrad Williams bristled when he heard I received free flights and expenses to attend these advanced learning seminars through Truck Stops of America. Honestly, I think if he or his guys had been asked to attend the conferences, they would've turned it down. But with a young man getting these opportunities, Williams' jealousy radar went up to an 8.

It also irritated him to no end that I would decide who would work the special detail at the truck stop – and who wouldn't.

So, he exacted his own measure of revenge.

"Raven, if you attend these non-NATSO trainings, you have to use your vacation time and pay for the conferences," Williams said. "And I won't let you use a patrol car for travel. Can't be giving preferential treatment to a 27-year-old cop."

As a young police officer, I chose to think outside the box and tried to increase the professionalism and productivity of a department that needed change desperately. The men I picked - Tony Blackstone, Pete Devita, Danny O'Brien, Ron Buffett, Rocky O'Rourke and Tim Gates – committed to that mindset.

In making these decisions, I stepped on the toes of a number of the veteran cops threatened by my initiative. They talked about "somebodies and nobodies." Even though I had this position, they reminded me that I was a nobody within the department, and that they had RHIP (Rank Has Its Privileges).

I wanted to tell them they hid behind their ranks.

I learned in the law enforcement and criminal justice communities, the rank structure is etched in stone. Ignoring it, even with the best intentions, can prove detrimental at best on a personal and professional level, stripping one of dignity and livelihood.

The thin blue line was window dressing. Behind the blue curtain lived a world of distrust, infighting and cliques. Fistfights, backstabbing and ratting are common occurrences. Lying, creative writing by superior officers on police reviews – that could negatively or positively affect cops, creating favoritism – and selective disciplinary action are routine acts. And if you make a mistake, even with the best intentions, they'll put you on the shelf, undermining and discrediting you in hopes of pushing you over the edge.

Exhibit A: Sgt. Frank Jamison. His desire to do the right thing, not the easy thing, and mentor me and others likely kept Williams from promoting him to lieutenant.

This is part of the ugly policing underbelly that few outside the job know exist.

They don't teach you about this in the academy and once you hit the streets, you're blindsided by this subculture with nowhere to turn.

I started to become part of a disturbing trend in police departments – Intentional Infliction of Emotional Distress (IIED). In laymen's terms? Bullying.

In a 1976 Illinois case – Public Finance Corp. v. Davis –

the court discussed the elements that a plaintiff must prove to receive damages for IIED. It said a plaintiff may recover damages for Intentional Infliction of Emotional Distress if he or she can prove that:

a) the defendant's conduct was extreme and outrageous;

b) the defendant intended to cause or recklessly or consciously disregarded the probability of causing emotional distress;

c) he or she suffered severe or extreme emotional distress; and

d) the defendant's conduct actually and proximately caused emotional distress.

After my wife and I considered legal action, we consulted attorney Thomas Elkington, a former cop.

The first day, he and staff members got real excited when I told them what had been transpiring with me the past few years. "I think we've got something here," Elkington said, as he moved his hands and arms around.

The next day, he and his staff had a completely different tone.

"I don't think this is going to work," Elkington said. "After another review, we don't think we have enough here. Also, if you have any goals of being a sergeant, lieutenant or even chief, this would eliminate that."

He continued, "What you've done here Mr. Raven is show you're a great cop. Not good, but great. It would be career suicide to consider legal action. And if you lost, what would you do?"

Elkington's change of direction really upset Jan and I. We felt jammed up. The thought of not being a cop anymore scared the hell out of me. I had been on the beat for about five years, but I was a loyal and hard-working police officer.

And the idea of doing something else also gave me agita.

———

In my first months as security manager at the 105 Truck Stop, I implemented a comprehensive strike force of off-duty police officers working in plain clothes in groups of 2-4 officers to combat vice activities at one of the largest and busiest truck stop interchanges in the US.

But that didn't prevent a fifth victim – who spent time at the 105 Truck Stop – from being killed, this time out of state.

Jada Arlington, 28, killed on I-62 near Ohio, off Route 4. Same characteristics. Beaten to death, then strangled.

I wanted to reach out to fellow detectives to voice my concerns. With my Christmas Eve lambasting by Chief Williams showing I'd receive no support from him, my friends in the department said, "Be careful Cal, be careful, he's up your ass, he's watching you like a hawk."

However, the Irish in me wanting conflict, I approached Williams who said, "You know what to do. Form 7."

Form 7 is a written report that is given to detectives.

"Guys, something stinks here," I said.

The response? They didn't give a shit.

Their comments included:

"Why are you spending so much time down there?"

"Mind your own business."

"Just a few bitches taken off the streets permanently."

"Catch someone who's DUI."

"Catch a real crook."

I guess none of these men had daughters. Their roadblocks wore on me.

Dail and Shriver sent me to my first conference in Cleveland – five days of intense training at Deerfield Academy, one of the best private research universities in the country with an outstanding criminal law program.

The training focused on forensic evidence, what to look for in homicides and the different types of homicides.

Before the conference began, organizers mailed us a brilliant book – Crime Classification Manual: A Standard System for Investigating and Classifying Violent Crimes. By John E. Douglas, Ann W. Burgess, Allen G. Burgess, and Robert K. Ressler. They worked with the FBI's National Center for the Analysis of Violent Crime.

My key takeaways from reading the book and attending the conference included:

1) How to do a victimology report.

2) When called to a crime scene it needs to be pristine until the crime scene unit arrives to process it. Place yellow crime-scene tape around the entire scene and maintain a log of every individual who enters and exits the crime scene. Take photos from various angles and locations with descriptions and note the direction that is depicted in the photo.

3) There's a checklist of more than a dozen things to do when investigating a criminal death scene.

4) **The various classifications** of homicide-murder:

First-degree murder: An intentional killing that was premeditated and deliberate. Regardless of intent to kill – this is known as the felony-murder rule.

Second-degree murder: An intentional killing that was not premeditated. This can include impulsive acts of violence or killings that occur with malice but without prior planning.

Third-degree murder: A category that varies by state but generally covers unintentional killings that don't fall into other categories, often involving recklessness. Only a few states have a third-degree murder charge.

Manslaughter: A category of homicide that does not involve malice aforethought, meaning the intent to kill is not present.

Voluntary manslaughter: An intentional killing committed in the heat of passion after being adequately provoked.

Involuntary manslaughter: An unintentional killing that results from criminal negligence or recklessness.

Negligent homicide: Causing a death through criminal negligence, though the intent is not to kill.

Justifiable homicide: A killing that is permitted by law, such as in self-defense.

State-sanctioned homicide: Killings carried out by the state, such as capital punishment or lawful military actions.

5) There are two crime scenes – where the crime was committed and where the body was laid.

6) Serial homicides can be classified into types based on motive or behavior, such as visionary (responding to delusions), mission-oriented (targeting a specific group deemed "evil"), hedonistic (killing for pleasure or thrill), and power/control-oriented (seeking dominance over victims). Another system classifies them as organized, disorganized, or mixed based on the offender's behavior and planning.

7) Killers are like sharks. The sharks hang back and observe from a not-too-close, not-too-far base, and hunt strategically. Like sharks, they prey on the young, weak and those by themselves.

8) Police officers need to work off of solvability factors and victimology comparisons. It's best to start with a victim's background – were they a hooker, what bars did they go to, who did they hang out with, did they have children, were they pregnant?

9) Even killers can be compassionate in their demented ways. Some will cover up the faces of those killed, wrap them up or leave an item behind. These killers usually knew their victims.

10) Even though you're a police officer, you have to think like a killer when trying to catch these guys.

Among the speakers was the highly respected – and highly paid – Fred Fry, who talked to a group of 50-60 people on homicide investigations.

Fred became commanding officer of Deerfield's Homicide Task Force and was promoted to lieutenant commander the next year. He analyzed thousands of homicides and he started writing books and papers.

Fred had a sheet, which started at the top with the Fifth Commandment: Thou Shalt Not Kill.

Underneath was the oath of practical homicide investigation:

> *Homicide investigation is a profound duty. As an officer entrusted with such a duty, it is incumbent upon you to develop an understanding of the dynamics and principles of professional homicide investigation. Practical homicide investigation suggests that "things be done right the first time" and "knowledge is power." Knowledge which has been enhanced with experience, flexibility and common sense.*

Fred also handed out bumper stickers that said, "We work for God." He elaborated, saying, "We don't work for chiefs or captains."

With most people staying at the Cleveland Tradewinds, I tried to buddy up to Fred. It worked.

When I asked if we could have dinner and cocktails in the accompanying restaurant, he agreed.

While he's a great speaker, Fred sat there during our meal and listened as I shared my frustrations.

"How do I communicate this to the brass?" I asked. "How do I convey this is a problem without getting my head chopped off? How do I spur interest, not disinterest, and explain how this serial killer could bite us in the ass."

First, Fred made our jobs seem like a higher calling. "We represent the dead," he said. "The sad, poor people who can't represent themselves."

But, like Frank Jamison and others in my corner, he said I had to be tactful and factual.

"Don't turn into a misfit or hot dog or a Mr. Big Shot," he said.

Thank God somebody listened.

And somebody else wanted to listen, too.

———

Started by the Justice Department, RISS has six regions throughout the United States. MAGLOCLEN is one of those regions. There are 17,000 member agencies in RISS.

It's mandatory that members of these regions exchange crime information – surveillance photos, prostitutes ripping drivers off, license plates, missing persons, runaways, felonies.

I sent information, which included CB handles and terminology, that went in the MAGLOCLEN monthly publication. That took pressure off Frank Jamison. He then recommended that I be our department's representative to JT Hamilton, the director of MAGLOCLEN.

We found MAGLOCLEN extremely helpful with stolen property. A lot of these scumbag crooks blended right in with the truckers with the way they dressed and looked. They also were here today, gone tomorrow with their larceny.

The more we learned, the more valuable RISS and MAGLOCLEN became.

———

One of the key requirements of a chief of police or sheriff is to keep a lid on the trash can. They can't let the shit spew out. But at some point, you have to empty the trash.

When you compress and compress the shit, you create pressure, a buildup that can explode and create a mess.

And that's what Williams started to experience.

Barb Hahn grinded every day as a reporter covering the police beat for the *Oldsmar Independent*. Every day, she came to our precinct and read the various police reports, which are public record.

She noticed the field investigations of the women we spoke to who later died.

When Williams either avoided Hahn or offered little insight, she reached out to me. We spoke on the phone for about 30 minutes.

She first wanted to know about Jada Arlington. She peppered me with questions as any diligent reporter would do, then she asked about other victims.

"Did she spend time at the truck stop?"

"Yes."

"Were they all prostitutes?"

"Yes."

"Did the other victims spend time at the truck stop?"

"To the best of our knowledge, yes."

"Did you interview them?"

"Some, not all."

"What did you arrest them for?"

"Some criminal trespass, some solicitation."

"Where is the investigation?"

"Still in its infancy. We are gathering information. Hoping more people come forward, looking for more leads. It's difficult but more women are starting to open up with information."

"Why are they opening up?"

"They're scared. They realize they're vulnerable."

And then she asked the money question.

"Cal, do you believe this is the work of a serial killer?"

"Without a doubt," I said.

––––––––––

The next day, the headline of the front page of the *Oldsmar Independent* read: Without A Doubt.

With the accompanying subhead: Oldsmar Cop Believes Serial Killer Behind Interstate Killings.

I usually went through the back door of the department so I didn't notice the commotion in the front.

"I don't know what you said or did but there are all these TV crews in front of the station," receptionist Ann Matheson informed me.

My first thought? "Holy shit. I'm gonna have alligators up to my eye balls."

The police station's media relations person walked me out front where I faced the cameras.

When asked for an opening comment, I said. "I can't discuss the situation until Conrad Williams allows me to."

Jamie Conom, a veteran TV reporter, replied, "Why did you talk to Barb Hahn?"

The best I could offer was, "Good question. She asked me questions, I thought I was giving her background information."

"Did she say this was for background information?"

"No."

I could hear all the clicks from photographers taking photos. I began to feel ill.

"Has the chief spoken to you?"

"No, but I'm sure he will."

The PR guy saved me. "No further questions."

I quickly walked into the station.

While supporters shook my hand and gave me attaboys for coming forward, others busted my balls derisively.

During roll call, the intercom went off. "Raven, report to the chief's office."

I felt like puking.

Williams, who hid from the media, literally shook as I entered his office.

"Who in the hell do you think you are?" he yelled. "You're a lowly patrolman, a beat cop. You're not supposed to be talking to the press."

I stayed silent.

My mouth was too dry and my throat too tight to say anything. I figured the less I said, the quicker I'd be let out. But part of me wanted to say, "If you spoke to the media, gave them something, they wouldn't be coming to me and we wouldn't be having this conversation."

But being proactive wasn't in Conrad Williams' mindset.

Just then, his phone rang. I heard the voice on the other end.

"Yeah?"

"Uh, chief, they've found another body of a dead woman. Found in Ohio about two exits from where they found Jada Arlington. She had identification on her that she spent time at the 105 Truck Stop."

The color left Williams' face. He looked at me with a combination of rage and guilt.

"Goddamnit, one comment to that asshole of a reporter, one more anonymous source in her story, and you can brush off your resume. At the least, suspension. Are we clear?

"Yes."

"Are we clear?"

I nodded.

———————

The next day, we had physical defense training. Afterwards, guys came up to me with pretend microphones while rolling pretend cameras. Behind them, some chanted, "Raven! Raven! Raven!"

Actually, it felt much better than awkward silence. They also offered to buy me beers afterward.

My story was placed on the bulletin board. A few hours later, I saw scraps of paper left with thumbtacks after it had been ripped off.

Thankfully, an uneventful day on the beat. As I walked home, mentally exhausted, a car pulled into my driveway. A voice called out, startling me. It was nearly 10:30 p.m.

"Raven?"

I could see it was Dennis Dahl, one of the township trustees.

"You got a few minutes?" he asked.

Dahl, a retired cop, had been among those quietly giving me support.

"Cal, I just want to tell you, the community and the board is getting restless with Williams," he said. "They didn't like that he put you in a position where you spoke to the press, then he fed you to them after the story broke."

I just nodded.

"I heard he also blew up at you just before Christmas," Dahl added.

"Christmas Eve," I said. "I definitely turned to the spirits during the holidays."

"Hang in there. I also wanted to say you will not be suspended. Wayne Keller and I will back you. Jim Hole is neutral but in a pinch, he'll also back you. Cal, you're one of our own. You grew up here, like me. Whatever you learn, tell me instead of the captain. Continue doing your job but be as discreet as possible, especially when it comes to talking to the press. There is something called deep background. You only give information that way. No quotes. Not as an identified source. Not as an unidentified source. Do you understand?"

"I wish I knew that about 48 hours ago."

Dahl chuckled. "Cal, this may be for the best," he said. "Williams needs to address this. I heard there was a secret meeting and he told them these are isolated cases. Bullllllllshit."

"Yep. Heard the same thing," I said.

"Cal, one more thing," Dahl said. "Be careful how much time you spend at the 105 Truck Stop. Williams' people are watching you. They're waiting for you to slip. They're watching everything. Be careful."

As I walked into my house, I felt better in some ways, worse in others. All these thoughts ran through my mind:

- I'm trying to do the best work I can but I'm being followed for that?

- While I do paperwork, other guys are smoking cigars and cracking jokes.

- My captain clearly knows I'm right but he hates me for it.

- And women keep getting murdered.

That night, I tossed and turned and tossed and turned. I had a nightmare of having another press conference with the media.

This time, I didn't have my pants on. I tried to run and hide but the doors were locked.

———————

In Texas, Bert Driller engaged in a back-door card game with a businessman, a retired banker and a judge. He had befriended the men by fixing various problems in their home for a fraction of the cost of a handyman.

He killed them with kindness.

He humbly took them up on their offer of a card game after he told them of money he won in the lottery and lavish expenditures of a convertible, a Harley motorcycle, a boat and an RV, most of which was in a California time share.

They figured a fool and his money soon parted. What they didn't know is that he lied to lure them. He also had won some high-stakes poker games. Excellent at spotting gamblers' tells, he won much more than he lost.

As the night wore on, the businessman and banker dropped out after each losing $10,000. That left the judge, who was into Driller for about $20,000. Their cigar chomping, smiling, back scratching, eye-glass moving, shirt-itching ways weren't lost on the card shark, who "couldn't believe his luck."

The judge, his ego bruised at being bluffed and outplayed by someone of lesser intelligence, couldn't let it go.

"One more hand," he growled. "I win, we call it even. You win, I owe $40,000."

"Deal," Driller said.

There was a pause. The judge looked at Driller.

"Deal," he repeated.

The judge had four cards he liked, all hearts.

But they weren't in sequence.

"I'll take one," he said.

He drew a seven of hearts. A flush.

Driller could hardly contain his excitement. Three sixes and two nines.

"I'm good," he said.

The judge had sweat beads the size of raindrops. His shirt suddenly was soaked and he pitted out.

Adding to the drama, Driller said, "Judge, you can go first."

Looking at him with contempt, the judge put down his cards. "Flush," he said weakly. "How about you?"

"Good hand judge, good hand. But mine is better."

He laid down his full house. The judge vomited in his mouth. He swallowed, got up from his chair, then said, "Meet me in my chambers, 8 a.m. The back door will be open."

As the judge and other men left their seats and turned away, Driller quietly finished his drink of cola. He had been accumulating sixes and nines throughout the night and put them in his left sleeve. People notice when face cards are missing but not those.

Earlier in the night, Driller sensed the last hand would be played around 10 p.m.

While taking a break earlier, he went outside where he told a friend to set off firecrackers at exactly 10.

The diversion was all Driller needed to switch the hand he had been dealt with the one in his sleeve.

———————

The next morning, Driller went into the judge's chambers humbly, his head down.

"What's wrong, you just won $60,000," the judge shouted.

"I know and I feel bad about it," Driller said. "Maybe we can help each other out."

Intrigued, the judge said, "I'm listening."

"Well, I got in some trouble in New Mexico. I was working there. A couple of DUIs. Speeding tickets. I was only going

85, maybe 90. Well, I didn't have the money to pay so I skipped the hearing. I swore I'd never drink again. Haven't speeded either."

"What's your point?"

"I need a name change. You can have your $40,000 back. Can you help me?"

The judge pondered his dilemma. He had helped a few friends with similar requests before to wipe out other gambling debts.

"All right. Driller, you get a new social security number and do any other paperwork needed and I'll sign it and get it notarized. Have you been in jail?"

"No sir."

"Good. Otherwise, you're shit out of luck. I'll do this but you better not burn me."

"No sir."

"OK. What would you like your new name to be?"

"Something simple. How about Bart Gein?

"Meet me back here in two weeks."

As soon as he shut the door and walked home, Driller had a big smile.

Two weeks later, Bert Driller became Bart Gein. He gave his firecracker buddy $1,000, picked up his papers, put them in a folder and walked to his vacant rental unit. With the unit paid off, he jumped into his pickup truck laughing.

With a new identity and $19,000, he was free to do as he pleased.

CHAPTER 8

Fears Realized

"Snitches get stitches."

– Mary Beth Peters

When I woke up and walked to the kitchen for breakfast, Jan's concerned countenance permeated the room like the smell of dark roast coffee.

Not wanting to hear any more bad news, I looked at her sideways, forced a smile and said, "Honey, I hope you have something good to share."

"Well, not really," she said.

My smile left.

"Cal, do you remember anything about last night?"

"No, why?"

"You flailed your arms and legs and uttered things in your sleep," she said. "Thank God, I didn't get elbowed. More of your typical nightmares. They're happening more often."

It reminded me of my sleepwalking moment while working at Thomas Funeral Home.

I then told her about my day. She knew of the Oldsmar Independent newspaper story where I was quoted a number of times, including when I said, "Without a doubt," when asked if there was a serial killer. Then I shared the reaction of those who supported me, those who gave me a hard time and then my meeting with the captain.

"Sounds like the deck is stacked against you," Jan said.

As I was about to answer, the phone rang.

It was Frank Jamison who asked, "Cal, just wanted to let you know that the cops identified the dead woman. Mary Beth Peters. Does that name ring a bell?"

Mary Beth Peters.

Sleeping Beauty.

The first time I spoke to her, she had this confused look, which made me think she was more mentally challenged than drugged up. I cited her for trespassing.

Plus, she wore these neon yellow pantyhose. Her husband also pimped her.

When I asked her why she did this, Mary Beth said, "I know it's dangerous, but it's not a choice. My husband is making me do this. I'm doing what I have to do."

Six weeks earlier, I had arrested her. She wore those same yellow pantyhose. Mary Beth also looked heavier, particularly around the midsection.

"You've gained some weight since the last time I saw you," I said.

"Yeah, I'm pregnant," she said.

"When is the baby coming?"

"Another five months."

I remember the night. Windy, rainy, hail, looked like a tornado was headed our way. Not the conditions for a pregnant woman.

I offered Mary Beth the same deal that I did with other people: Give me some information and I'll let you go.

When she heard the offer, she shook her head and stuttered a bit. Maybe the weather caused that. Maybe not.

"No, no, no," she said. "I di-di-don't, don't have anything but, but, but if I do, I'll get back to you," she said.

I've had a string of people make those kinds of promises, then disappear.

"Gotta give me something. Help yourself out or I gotta take you in," I said.

When she kept shaking her head, I handcuffed her and took her to jail.

When we took Mary Beth to booking and fingerprinted her, I tried one last time to get her to talk. She came across disoriented but she did have something interesting to say.

"I have to be careful what I give you and who I give you," she said. "Snitches get stitches."

With that, I left.

The next morning, her pimp husband bailed her out. The next afternoon, she disappeared.

"Frank, how was she killed?" I asked.

"Same as the others," he said. "Head bashed in. Strangled."

Frank then paused.

"Anything else?"

"Yeah. Couple of things. Cal, did you know she was pregnant?"

"Yes," I replied.

"Also, a coat was placed over her head. And she was wrapped in a sleeping bag."

I made a mental note, then closed with Frank by saying, "I need to see the police report."

"I'll get you a copy."

I went into work early and Frank handed me a manilla envelope.

As I read the police report, these were the highlights (or lowlights):

– Blunt object to the top of the head. Deceased inside sleeping bag.
– Found in a creek.
– Reported missing May 9 at 1300 hrs. by her husband.
– Last seen May 8 at 2130 hrs. She was dropped off by her husband at Hoosier Truck Stop in Indiana.
– Was to secure a ride with a truck driver in the A.M. of May 9 and meet her husband at the 44th Street Cafe.
– Deceased used the CB handle of "Cinderella" as well as "Sleeping Beauty"
– Blunt trauma to the top of the head. 12-13 blows.
– Discoloration around the left eye.
– Struck in the face before death.
– No ligature marks were found around the neck.
– Wrapped up in a blue bed sheet.
– The outside of her green jacket had covered up her face.
– Deceased inside a zipped, yellow sleeping bag. The sleeping bag was tied at the top.
– The sleeping bag, with deceased, was found lying face down in a shallow creek.
– The water was 4 inches deep.

I let the words of the report sink in while I began my beat. After my 2 to 10 shift ended, I started my 10 to 2.

I saw a few ladies congregating.

Good timing.

As I approached, they didn't scatter. I sensed they wanted to talk to me. In a way, we're on the same team. We needed information and they had "theories."

In a role reversal, they questioned me, and the questions were fast and furious:

Is the killer a terrorist from another country?

Did the killer use the nickname Fire Breather?

Is the killer a woman?

Is the killer a man? Mary Beth had been scared of a guy, someone she serviced before, someone who slapped her around. That could explain the first slap she took.

"She didn't want to go back out there," Yvette Mendez said. "She was having morning sickness. But her husband kept putting her out there."

And then Yvette remembered a name.

"She said something about Goldberg, Goldman, Goldstein," Yvette said. "Then she said Mary Beth liked James Bond films."

Having watched every Bond film, I said, "Could it have been Goldfinger?"

"Yes," Yvette screamed. "That's it! How did you know?"

"He's a villain in a James Bond film."

Yvette gave a blank stare.

Guess she didn't have much time to watch movies.

As I walked away, another prostitute had a throwaway line.

"Talk to her pimp," she said.

"Her husband?" I asked.

"No, her pimp," she said. "What husband would put his wife out there, five, six months pregnant? She was his meal ticket and he was going to milk the cow as long as he could."

"They had this weird relationship," another said. "After she put in the work, she said he brought her gifts, like flowers, strawberry lip balm for her lips."

"Pardon me?" I said.

"Yeah, you heard me, lip balm," she said. "Strawberry was her favorite. Some of us need it, you know, after we, uh."

"I understand," I said, frowning.

The police report also mentioned there was a tube of strawberry lip balm 20 feet from Mary Beth's body.

———

I remembered listening to a profiler at Deerfield Academy talking about killers giving clues on whether they knew – or even were close to – their victims.

"Killers who don't know their victims dump bodies," the speaker said. "Killers who have an attachment or know their victims may in some demented way show some care for the body. They'll either wrap the victim up or cover them or put their face down so they don't have to look at them in the face when they walk away."

I turned back to the ladies.

"Have you seen Mary Beth's husband?" I asked.

They looked at each other. No one had seen him in a week.

"I think he's in Pennsylvania," one said.

While convinced that a serial killer had murdered the first five women, I had my suspicions with Mary Beth, No. 6. I pondered these thoughts:

While researching some of their ideas and leading me on a few wild goose chases, the prostitutes also made some valid points.

There was quite a time lapse between the time Mary Beth met with the trucker and the time her husband and pimp called the police.

Did Mary Beth usually spend more than one hour with any of her clients?

Did she spend hours with a trucker for the right price?

The fact she wasn't strangled differed from the serial killer.

The way Mary Beth had been disposed of was different than the other victims.

These are all questions I needed to ask Hassan Francois, Mary Beth Peter's husband, pimp and possible murderer.

———————

As soon as I went into the police station the next day, Labor Day, I told Tony Blackstone about my theory.

"Are you sure?" he asked.

"Sure enough that I think we should bring the pimp in for questioning," I said.

"Careful, Cal. You keep playing with fire. Whoever you tell is likely going to tell Williams. Let me see what I can do."

"Ok," I said.

During roll call, Frank Jamison informed us that, "Word from the top has come that you make just one pass around the 105 Truck Stop. Understand?"

He looked right at me as he said those words.

Before I started my rounds, I received a call from Dail and Shriver.

"Cal, I think I saw the dead woman's pimp," Dail said.

"Are you sure?" I said. "See if you can confirm it with any of the ladies."

"They usually don't get here until dark," Shriver said.

"Try anyway."

I raced over to the truck stop and met them. While I circled the lot, they moved to different entrances. We communicated by something new, a cell phone, called a bag phone. Compliments of the 105 Truck Stop, along with a truck stop vehicle during our special duties. It helped me do my job better and by association, the police department also benefited. However, Williams and his guys thought I was receiving gifts.

I found the irony rich.

I soon got a call from dispatch.

"150, what's your 39 (location)."

"105 Truck Stop."

"Need you to get over to the South side. Possible burglary.

When I arrived, I asked what they wanted me to do.

"Backup," the dispatcher said. "Wait for instructions."

While I parked the car and waited, Frank Jamison went into the dispatcher's room.

They're watching you! The detective I talked to said you're hot. They won't pick up the pimp at his home. Said you didn't follow orders in roll call.

I waited for a good hour. Finally, the dispatcher sent me to another area. Then another and another.

My whole day was like that. And the next day. And the next week. They were sending a message.

I started getting a half dozen calls asking about my location. If I radioed in from town, I usually wasn't bothered or sent to some lame-ass location, like a broken mailbox report. But if I said the truck stop, I was sent to another area.

When I asked some of the newer dispatchers why they asked for my location, I got a standard, "We were told you had to go to a specific area away from the 105 Truck Stop."

But when I talked to one of the guys I brought McDonald's for, he gave me a different story when we talked after work.

"Cal," he said. "The supervisor is telling us, 'If Raven is at the truck stop, give him shit and send him someplace else.'"

I also noticed women being friendlier to me than usual; and I didn't recognize some faces. My instincts told me that: 1) they may have been undercover cops brought in; or 2) the real hookers may have been paid to set me up.

I also had this weird sense I was being watched. Dail and Shriver confirmed this when they talked to me once before my 10 to 2 shift.

"Cal, we haven't seen you around much," Dail said.

"Guys, I swear, every time I drive by on my routine, I get a call from dispatch, sending me someplace else."

"Maybe that explains guys with binoculars," Shriver said.

"Binoculars?"

"Yeah, every now and then, we see guys in their unmarked cars with binoculars checking out what's going on. If they see us watching them, they quickly move on."

My gut did back flips when I heard that. Big Brother is watching. In 1949, a book came out called 1984 where the ruling party watches a low-level politician through telescreens; everywhere he looks he sees the face of the party's seemingly omniscient leader, a figure known only as Big Brother.

No wonder I started to feel paranoid.

To put a capper on it, I saw Wayne Keller at one of my daughter's school events. Another of the trustees in my corner, he quietly said, "Cal, somebody is following you late at night. One of the cops told me."

It's almost like they wanted me to know I was being followed. They also wanted to know if I was double dipping.

Double dipping, it's a tricky deal, especially if you're being watched. If I went over to the truck stop during my routine patrol – something I always did – I could be accused of doing work for Dail and Shriver.

If I talked with them during the afternoon on my shift, that could be considered double dipping; and if I did 9:30 p.m. paperwork for my regular job at the truck stop, that could be considered double dipping.

All that put me on edge.

The only good thing that happened is that my uniform didn't have any dirt on it, my shoes didn't even have a scuff mark. That's what happens when you don't have to respond to a situation, much less leave the car.

I told the 105 owners, I needed to take the night off.

"Any luck with the pimp?" they asked.

"No," I said. "They won't pick him up. I'm persona non grata."

"Not to us," Dail said.

Shriver added, "Hey, maybe it's best. Let's give the pimps and prostitutes a false sense of security. Next week, we will corral them."

"Good idea," I said.

It didn't help when I walked home, I felt like someone was following me.

When a trash can fell over, that really unnerved me and had me putting a hand on my 9 mm semi automatic.

I ran through a neighbor's back yard only to trip on a kid's toy and bang into a recycling bin. As the lights came on, I looked around and saw either a possum or raccoon scurry off.

"Who's there?" my neighbor Jeff Julseth said.

"Just doing some neighborhood watch," I joked.

"Oh Cal, good to see you, I feel safe now," he said.

———

When I got home, I took off my uniform, put on some shorts and a T-shirt and went straight to the liquor cabinet.

In the first few years, my normal routine after work would be to have a couple of pepperoni rolls and two short-neck bottles of Blatz beer and watch The Tonight Show with Johnny Carson. His monologues at the start of the show always made me laugh.

On this night, I mixed it up.

No food. I had some whiskey neat with my beer.

Replenishing my beer and the glass, I flipped to a Chicago White Sox game on the West Coast.

The White Sox were in the running for the playoffs so I made a personal bet.

If Lance Johnson got a hit, I'd take a drink. He hit a triple.

Next batter. Scotty Fletcher. If he brought Johnson home, I'd take another drink, Fletcher hit a sacrifice fly.

I switched to the Cubs. They also were on the West Coast.

I refilled my glass.

The Cubs weren't doing as well as the Sox but Ryne Sandberg was playing great again. The Cubs trailed 5-4 in the eighth. Sandberg up. Bases loaded. If he hit a homer, I'd finish my drink.

"Here's the pitch," Cubs announcer Haray Caray bellowed. "There's a drive down the left-field line. It might be. It could be. It is. A home run. A grand salami. Ryne Sandberg has done it again. Cubs lead 8-5. Holy cow!"

Down the hatch. That took the edge off.

Now, I could've stopped there. I didn't.

Meanwhile, I thought about Mary Beth Peters. I saw her as vulnerable, manipulated and with child. What she went through made me cry.

Then, I passed out in the recliner.

———

Bert Driller liked being back behind the wheel with a new alias - Bart Gein.

He laid low and allowed the heat to cool off.

Now, he had a new name, new look, new money. Heck, why not find a new place to live. How about Tennessee?

He had gone to trade schools years earlier to become a handyman. Now, he wanted to drive reefer units. His ability to control the gauges or make sure the units had enough freon came naturally. His HVAC training came in handy in his new role as truck driver of refrigerated goods.

With his new identity, Gein quickly got a job because of his clean look; he didn't haggle about his pay; he worked the longest hauls; he could do minor truck repairs; and he had no prior arrests with his new ID.

To blend in and look more like the other truckers, Bert Driller grew his hair long and added a beard and tattoos on his shoulders and arms. Already fat, he also put on a few pounds and downgraded on the hygiene.

However, Bart Gein was the lady killer, literally. He got a haircut, shaved, bathed, trimmed his nails and put on clean clothes. He never went to the same barber.

Once he had his new look, he and Richard were ready for action. They were on the prowl.

Once the predator found his prey, it was back to Bert Driller. He found that by gorging on salmon, eggs, legumes and spinach and snacking on nuts, seeds, berries and citrus while taking part in cross-country hauls, he could regain his beard and long hair in two weeks.

Two personalities. "I like the changes," Richard told him. "I like the looks."

Now, he was on his way to the East Coast.

CHAPTER 9

Proactive Measures

"Suck it up. This is politics."

– Frank Jamison to me when I was
bypassed for a promotion to detective

March days can be tricky in the Midwest because there are some warm weather days that melt the snow, creating soft, muddy grass, puddles in pot holes and dirty snow banks.

On this day, I didn't slip and fall while walking to work. I didn't get splashed by a driver running over a puddle or through standing water; and I didn't have to step in one of those snow banks on the way to crossing the street.

Roll call went quickly, then the guys were eager to get outside for some fresh air.

Because temps were in the high 70s, I put on the air conditioner in the car.

I proceeded to get hit with a blast of cigarette ash – all over my face, uniform and pants.

This wasn't the first time I got nailed with remnants of Pete Devita's Camel Non Filters.

Day after day, I had to deal with Devita's filthy smoking habit. Now it was time for revenge.

We made a drug raid. Besides bagging cocaine and heroin, we also found 15 bags of condoms; a couple of red pills designed to "inflate" a man's tool; five nudie magazines featuring the redhead of the month; two pairs of handcuffs – not police issue but close – and three dildos.

We took some "evidence." One dildo had the thickness of bratwurst and the length of a footlong wiener, except it was a dark green.

On a rare off day, just before Devita's shift, a couple of guys and I duct taped the green dildo on the trunk of the police car.

The guys and I then tailed him. The windy day moved that dildo around like it had convulsions.

Almost immediately, it caught people's attention. We could see Devita moving his head back and forth. People had to be smiling or laughing at him. As a woman crossed the street while he waited at a red light, she shamed him with her fingers.

When he saw the woman, he got out of his car, walked to the rear, saw the dildo and stepped back, part startled and part embarrassed as his face instantly turned red and he yelled, "What the fuck?"

He went back into the car, drove for a bit, then parked in a lot. As he got out and went to remove the dildo, we had taped words on the trunk that read: I have a 'hard' job.

As he took off the tape, we passed by, honking the horn. He yelled a lot of Italian words at us, followed by the word "cocksucker."

At the same time, Father Hallahan drove by, heard what Devita said and turned our way. The priest then rear-ended a car, which had stopped for a red light.

———

In Oneonta, N.Y., authorities gathered around a woman who had been dumped outside a rest stop. They identified her as Patty Belinda Dowling. Victim No. 7.

My friends at MAGLOCLEN and RISS sent me information on the death. This woman had a cloth stuck in her throat and was strangled. No clothes on, jewelry stolen.

When I showed Yvette Mendez a photo, she did the sign of the cross and said, "Yes, she was here. I don't know if the other women knew her. She kept to herself and seemed out of it."

I'm not sure Conrad Williams knew about this death or even cared. He seemed more interested in an upcoming announcement – where two officers would get promoted to detective.

Six years on the job and I thought I had earned a promotion. I hoped it might be my time. I had made some felony arrests, received recognition and had enlightened the department on dealing with criminal activity at the truck stop and using CB language. I also had to tell cops basic common sense stuff like turning off their radar unit before entering the area, so they didn't tip off the truck drivers and prostitutes, who had fuzz busters. They had radar detectors in their vehicles, which beeped or buzzed when police roamed the area.

As always, I was prepared. I had a printing company update my resume and bio to include the arrests, seminars and conferences I attended. I was told my monthly activity reports – everything from summons to solving burglaries to parking tickets – had surpassed any of the officers.

At the end of the day, it didn't matter.

"As many of you know, we've had two openings with retirements by two of our detectives, Romano and O'Leary," Williams said. "Today, I'm proud to announce that we have promoted Jacob Jefferson and Dominick Coosimano to detective."

Williams never looked at me. As his guys gave a hearty cheer, other cops clapped lightly, looked at me and shook their heads.

Lt. Matthew France and Lt. Jordan Kelly, Williams' right-hand men. As he spoke glowingly of the two, I heard a faint "Bullshit" from the back of the room.

Jefferson and Coosimano were known as Dum and Dumber. They had let crooks get away with shoddy paperwork, crime-scene tampering and general incompetence.

"Two members of the Breakfast Brigade," Tony Blackstone said to me of Williams' inner circle who met in the morning at Cassie's Place. "Sorry Cal. It sucks."

Frank Jamison looked at me sternly and said, "Suck it up. This is politics."

He knew. More than 20 years on the job and his prospects for getting promoted decreased by the year.

An Army veteran, he spoke his piece, like me. He did his job, like me. He lived by a code, like me.

But it just didn't matter.

It felt like a gut punch.

I still had a 2 p.m. to 10 p.m. shift to work. Before I hit the streets, I saw a sheet on the bulletin board, which came off as another slap in the face. It read:

> *Dear officers,*
> *Starting on Monday, the following officers will be part*
> *of shift changes.*

I scanned for my name:

> *Callaghan Raven will work the 6 a.m. to 2 p.m. shift,*
> *focusing mainly in the South District.*

So instead of me being more involved with the interstate killings, Williams tried to do everything he could to have me less involved.

The shift went by quickly with light activity. I spent a lot of time that day mentally preparing for my new normal. Even though the 6 a.m. to 2 p.m. duty is much easier than 2 to 10 p.m., it just felt like a demotion.

But it was going to be a big adjustment. My main hours now would be 10 p.m. to 2 a.m. at the truck stop, then trying to nap before my 6 a.m. shift. If I didn't get that sleep in, that would be one long-ass stretch. I could be killed by being in an accident or not being alert enough to respond in the afternoon.

When I came home that night, I looked like I had been run over by a truck.

Jan knew it. She smiled, took my hand and led me to the couch.

I bent down on her lap and bawled.

She gently stroked the back on my head and kissed me on the neck.

When I told her the news of Jefferson and Coosimano getting promotions, she cringed. "Gloria and Gina are going to be bragging about their husbands and it's going to be unbearable," Jan said. "I'm already dreading the Christmas party. You know, they're two dim bulbs."

"Hard to be bright when there's not a lot of juice going through their brains," I said.

We both laughed. I gave Jan a big hug and kissed her forehead.

"Thanks," I said.

"Anything else?" she said. "No more bad news, please."

"I got moved to the 6 to 2 shift."

Jan's eyes lit up. "That's great," she said. "Less time at

the truck stop. You know, I hate that place almost more than Williams does."

"I know but that's where the action is. And that 10 to 2 shift, then 6 to 2 is going to be really tough."

"Well, you always can stop the 10 to 2 and I can work part time."

That got my Irish blood boiling and I said, "You need to be home raising our kids. The right way. And I've got to find out who killed those girls."

"OK, Callaghan Raven. I know this means a lot to you. And Jim and Greg are good men. They need your help. As far as the timing goes, can you do 12 to 4 or 1 to 5? Whatever, it is, figure it out."

I smiled. "You sound like Frank," I said. "I think I'll have a drink."

"What can I make you?"

"A double whiskey. Neat."

"How about something to mix that with?" Ginger Ale?

"The sugar will keep me up."

Jan frowned as she made my drink.

———

The holiday season went by quickly as the days blended together.

I normally loved to load up on turkey, potatoes, stuffing and Jan's traditional green beans with almonds and bacon for Thanksgiving but I had a moderate plate. And quite a few beers with a wee bit of bourbon.

I talked to my parents briefly, then fell asleep – almost intentionally – while watching the football games.

I went holiday shopping with Jan and the kids but went through the motions.

"What would you like for Christmas?" I asked. "Why don't you pick some things out and I'll wrap them?"

Sensing my mood, Jan smiled and said, "That's a great idea. Why don't I do the same with you?"

When we told the kids of our plans, they were fine. Son Clayton, now 6, was a natural skeptic. He knew who Santa was shortly after last Christmas when he asked a bunch of questions we couldn't answer.

"How does Santa drop off presents in Ireland and Oldsmar on the same night?" he asked.

"Supersonic sleigh," we said.

"But there's like 5 billion people in the world. How's he gonna pull that off in 48 hours?"

"Supersonic reindeer?"

"Yeah, right. They still gotta take time to eat and poop. They're gonna graze in California."

"What would you like us to say?"

"Just come clean. Isn't that what you say to the hookers, dad?"

I bit my tongue.

———

As we went from store to store, Jan picked up a dress she wanted to wear for the Christmas party. She also picked out some stylish black boots, chocolates with raisins and hoop earrings.

"I like this idea," daughter Janet said. "Can we pick something out?"

Jan said, "Wait until San... Cal, what do you think?"

I nodded with a slight smile.

She then whispered, "Is it costing too much?"

"No, no, no," I quickly said. "I want to see their reactions."

"Cal," Jan replied. "What do you want?"

"I don't know," I said.

 "A dress shirt? New gloves. Some of those nuts you like?"

I paused. My Irish guilt took over. "I don't think I deserve much," I uttered.

Jan looked at me with a deep, empathetic look. "Cal," she said, her voice breaking up.

When she started to cry, my eyes watered.

Jan regained her composure. "OK kids, what do you want? Burger and fries or something else?"

"How about Chinese?" Laura said. "I'd like some Kung Pow chicken."

"Yes, I'd like that," Jan said, wiping her eyes as we walked to The Rising Sun Buffet.

———

The Christmas party went as expected – dreadful.

Jefferson and Coosimano did shots with Williams and his guys. As their wives bragged about their new dresses, rings and January trip they were taking to Cozumel, Jan rolled her eyes and took a big swig of her drink. She then looked at me and toasted with her glass.

I returned the favor while talking with Tony Blackstone, Pete Devita, Danny O'Brien, Ron Buffet, Rocky O'Rourke and Tim Gates.

"We should start our own meeting group," Tim said. "Guys With Guts."

"How about the 'I Can Spell Homicide Group,'" Danny said to laughs. "When two gay men killed each other, I told Jefferson and Coosimano it was a homo-cide. They believed me."

Rocky said, "I like the 'Real Men, Real Cops Group,'" and we raised our glasses.

They then asked, "Cal, do you have a name?"

"Name?" I asked.

"Name for the group?" Tony asked.

"No, can't match your choices fellas. Great year at 105, right?"

As the others talked about our sweeps, my mind drifted to a few years earlier.

Williams and I worked together late at night.

Seeing glass kicked in at O'Quinn's Restaurant, the owner made a call on a pay phone across the street to the 911 center. The dispatcher said, "Any car in the area? O'Quinn's Restaurant, Signal 4, Code 1 (in progress)."

I said, "150 going."

Williams said, "112 going."

A couple of other cops joined us – Jefferson and Coosimano.

Not one to wait for backup, I stood on the hood of my squad car where I saw a crook going into a closet. I went in and we exchanged shots. He missed me and I put a hole in O'Quinn's refrigerator.

The other guys surrounding the building heard two shots. They thought either me or the other guy got it. The crook came out first, about 20 feet from Williams. As he ran away, Williams pointed his shotgun in the air, then launched a round while standing still. Sometimes, the bad guy will stop but not this one.

While the cigar-smoking Jefferson got gassed while chasing, Coosimano got lost.

I chased the bad guy into the woods but while catching him, I got scuffed up and bled a bit but I was able to cuff him.

By the time I brought the scumbag out, Williams had left and returned to the station. He didn't chase, didn't follow, didn't know what happened, didn't care; but he later gave me an ass-ripping for going in alone.

I took good-natured shit from the guys the next couple of weeks as well as from the owner, who joked, "Callaghan me lad, what you gonna shoot next, me shepherd's pie?" He then gave me a big piece.

Now here we are, three years later. Williams is chief, Jefferson and Coosimano are detectives and I'm still hustling. For what?

The guys noticed I had zoned out.

"Cal?" they said.

I sucked it up, forced a smile and said, "Merry Christmas to my dear, loyal, fearless friends. Cheers."

We took a big drink of our beverages.

"Let's make that our group name," Blackstone said.

———

After causing mayhem and anguish in the Northeast and Midwest, Bart Gein received an assignment to travel West.

As he drove through Montana, Gein spotted a hitchhiker. He had just shaved, gotten a haircut and showered. Richard told him he looked handsome.

As the female climbed in, Gein reached out with his right hand to help her in. She looked young.

After she told him she was Kari Wolfgram, Gein asked where she wanted to go.

"Las Vegas," she said. That was 750 miles away.

"How old are you, darlin'?" he asked.

"Twenty-one," she replied.

Gein didn't believe her, but he didn't care.

"She's the marrying type," Richard said.

"If you're thirsty, I've got some soda in the cooler. There's also a glass."

As they continued to make small talk, Kari felt comfortable

enough to pour herself a glass of soda.

Big mistake.

He had laced the soda with a mickey (chloral hydrate), which puts people to sleep. She only needed a few sips before she passed out.

When Kari awoke, her left arm was tied a few feet from a cactus and her blue jeans, top and bra were off.

The only light was from a fire Gein had started. He held her right arm.

"What's happening?" she groggily shouted, shaking off the effects of being drugged.

"Darlin', we're in the middle of nowhere," Gein said. "If you yell, I'll gag you and if you keep making noise, I'll heat up my red hot poker and give you something to yell about. Understand?"

Kari nodded silently.

"Good girl," he said. "You are a girl, aren't you?"

Again, she nodded.

"Eighteen?"

She shook her head side to side.

"Seventeen?"

She again shook her head side to side.

"Sixteen."

She nodded, confirming her age. Tears started to well up and fall down her cheeks.

"Well now, I always wanted a child bride."

Gein brought out a Bible. "By the power vested in me, I pronounce us man and wife," he said. He then made her sign the Bible.

With the drugs in Kari's system now fully worn off, she gagged.

"Sorry I don't have a ring," he said. "But I have something else. Turn to the fire and take off your panties."

As Kari complied, he took out a Polaroid and took full-frontal nude photos. Then he consummated the "marriage" as they did in medieval times.

CHAPTER 10

Surviving By Faith

**In the failure of my plans and hopes;
in disappointments, troubles and
sorrows, Jesus, help me!**

**When my heart is cast down by failure,
at seeing no good come from my
efforts, Jesus, help me!**

**When others fail me, and Thy grace
alone can assist me, Jesus, help me!**

**Always, in weakness, falls and
shortcomings of every kind, Jesus,
help me and never forsake me.
Thank You, dear Lord Jesus.**

– The Help Me Jesus prayer

South of Reno, a clean-shaven Bart Gein and a drugged-up Kari Wolfgram heard sirens from a police car.

Gein had been weaving on the road because Wolfgram suddenly started hitting him. When he backhanded her, she came back and bit him.

When Gein pulled to the side of the road, Kari got out of the truck and started running away.

Almost in Lake Tahoe, it had gotten cold and Gein only had on a T-shirt.

"You stay here while I find the girl," the officer said.

Knowing escape made no sense, Gein realized his story had to be more convincing than the girl's tale. It would be a classic he said, she said, and Gein bet on himself to outfox the girl.

When the officer caught up to Kari, he asked for her name and address. She gave two different names and two different ages before saying her real name and address. When she started explaining what happened to her, the officer didn't know what to believe.

"Can I call your parents?" the officer asked.

"My mom is in prison and my dad's an alcoholic," she said, a story she also told Gein. "They live in California."

The officer told the girl to wait in the car. He then drew his weapon and told Gein to get out of the truck. Seeing someone having control over him, Gein quickly exited the truck, went to his knees and explained that he was returning the girl to her dad because they were friends. He had found her in a cult, as her father feared.

"She said he's an alcoholic," the officer said.

"It's not as bad as she says," Gein said, reasoning with the officer. "Wouldn't you take a couple of drinks if your wife was bat-shit crazy, in jail and likely heading to a mental institution?"

The officer was silent.

"Here, I've got his number," he said. While the officer had talked to Kari, Gein had reached a trucker friend in California by CB.

The officer called the distraught-sounding man who said

he couldn't bear to lose his daughter, even though she was showing the same neurotic signs as her mother.

"OK, Mr. Gein, get back in your truck."

While this conversation went on, Kari saw a black jack in the front of the police car. She grabbed it when it seemed Gein wasn't going to be arrested.

As the officer returned to his car, a relieved Gein went into his truck. Shaking and not thinking, he grabbed a glass and filled it with rum and Coke.

"Kari, you have a choice," the officer said. "I can take you back to the station where we'll likely have to put you in a foster home. Or you can have Mr. Gein take you home. You're a runaway, right?"

Nodding, Kari had heard horror stories from a friend about foster homes. They were worse than Gein. "OK, I'll get in the truck."

As she left the police car and took a few steps toward the truck, the officer got a dispatch that a bank was being robbed. He was 10 minutes away.

"Kari, sorry, I gotta run," he said. "Good luck."

As the officer sped away, Kari's heart rate also raced. As soon as she opened the truck and climbed up, if he lunged at her, she was going to lay a thumping on him.

Instead, Gein was passed out and snoring as he slipped himself a Mickey with his drugged soda. His wallet had fallen on the passenger seat.

Kari took out the money and ran down the interstate. She flagged down an elderly couple who took her to the bus station as she asked.

When the station manager asked her where she was headed, Kari said, "Anywhere but here."

As I woke up and prepared for my shift, I teared up again.

I tried to hide it from Jan and the kids, but on this morning, she caught me.

"Are you OK?," she said, quickly sitting up in bed.

"Yeah, yeah," I said quietly, turning away as I put on my shoes.

"You want some eggs with bacon and hash browns?" Jan asked hopefully.

"That's OK, hun," I replied. "I had a sandwich before I went to bed."

She came over to hug me and realized she could put her arms around me.

"You've lost a lot of weight Cal," she said.

"Need to," I said. "I was starting to become a lard ass."

I quickly departed before Jan said anything else.

————————

The stillness in Oldsmar at 6 a.m. was almost deafening.

Hardly a soul on the road. Even the birds hadn't started squawking. You could almost hear the morning dew fall off tree limbs or the sun rushing daybreak on this late April morning.

The eternal hope of spring was lost on me.

I had mentally struggled since the holidays. My New Year's Resolution? Try to survive the day.

Food tasted bland so I rarely ate. My weight had gone from 179 pounds to 149. I compensated by wearing my kevlar vest regularly but fellow cops noticed my sunken face.

I kept some weight on by eating junk food while I drank more. Lots of sugar in booze.

Since nothing went on in the first hour of my shift, I found a quiet spot to go to: Hope Cemetery, right next to St.

Michael's Church. I put my radar gun at 10 mph in case anyone came in to leave flowers on the gravesite of a loved one.

I drank my Double D coffee and reflected. Not good when you're depressed.

This is going to be a tough day. It's the seven-year anniversary of my start as a police officer. I vividly remember when Sgt. Jamison told me with pride that my interviews went well and that I was officially hired by the Oldsmar Police Department, pending I passed the police officer training academy.

I came across a story on the "Seven-Year Itch."

The article detailed how a lot of marriages end at this time because the honeymoon phase is over, the spark is lost in relationships and men, and some women, realize they're not cut out to be parents.

The phase police officers go through is similar.

Their excitement of going to work each day and making their cities a better place gives way to the reality that there is a lot of ugliness that goes on that the public doesn't see. And it's almost insurmountable to make a dent.

It's not just seeing abusive relationships or situations where some individuals control and use others; but it's the level prostitutes and crooks will go to just to put a few bucks in their pocket and in some cases, just survive. The scams run by people either fuel drug or drinking habits or create an illusion that if they make enough money, they can escape from the donkey chasing the carrot. However, the scammers realize they often have a different addiction – the excitement of manipulating and cheating others; and it can only be quenched by the next scheme. However, the law of averages usually catches up to those fools and they're either caught by the police – if they're lucky – or get the shit beat out of them by a trucker or someone frauded; or their life is ended and they wind up buried in a shallow grave or at the bottom of a lake.

Then there's the cops and the attorneys and the judges. Their own weaknesses are preyed upon by others. In many ways, they've become like prostitutes, whores to the dark side. They betray everything they swore to defend in their oath of office with their right arms raised and left hand placed on the Bible.

"I do solemnly swear that I will support and defend the Constitution of the United States against all enemies, foreign and domestic; that I will bear true faith and allegiance to the same; that I take this obligation freely, without any mental reservation or purpose of evasion; and that I will well and faithfully discharge the duties of the office on which I am about to enter. So help me God."

Then, there are guys like me who try to do justice to those words at the sacrifice of time with family and friends, even personal safety; and our efforts are not only downplayed but vilified by superior officers who are either jealous, not committed or not as brave.

Now I see why many cops don't make it to 25 years. Either the ugliness of the job, the internal politics or compromise of values does them in. They either find another job, fade away to bitterness, drink, do drugs – or they just end it.

On this day, I felt like death couldn't come soon enough. Maybe I'd eat a bullet. That's the way most cops do it.

As I sat next to all those gravestones, I thought about my own gravestone. What would it say? Callaghan Lee Raven, born 1959. He loved his job. He loved God. He loved his family.

I pulled out photos of Jan, Janet, Laura and Clayton as well as a family photo with Buster, our little cocker spaniel, who we only kept for a few years because he kept pissing on my polished black shoes. I still felt bad about giving him to a neighbor.

Along with their photos in my wallet, I kept prayer cards with me – Jesus Help Me, A Prayer of St. Francis Of Assisi, The Prayer In My Pocket and the Police Officer's Prayer to St. Michael:

Saint Michael,

Heaven's glorious commissioner of police, who once so neatly and successfully cleared God's premises of all its undesirables, look with kindly and professional eyes on your earthly force.

Give us cool heads, stout hearts, and uncanny flair for investigation and wise judgment. Make us the terror of burglars, the friend of children and law abiding citizens, kind to strangers, polite to bores, strict with law breakers and impervious to temptations.

You know, Saint Michael, from your own experiences with the devil, that the police officer's lot on earth is not always a happy one; but your sense of duty that so pleased God, your hard knocks that so surprised the devil, and your angelic self-control give us inspiration.

And when we lay down our night sticks, enroll us in your heavenly force, where we will be as proud to guard the throne of God as we have been to guard the city of all the people.

Amen

I could barely read the last few lines as the tears distorted my vision. I sniffled and my runny nose left droplets on the prayer card. I wiped it on my pressed shirt. Fuck the neatness, I said to myself, then stopped and gave the sign of the cross.

With it being a few minutes before 7 a.m., I went into St. Michael's. I needed help.

Dark when I went inside, I kneeled down and said my own prayer:

> *Dear Lord,*
> *Give me the courage to survive this day.*
> *I feel weak. Give me strength.*
> *I feel lost. Help me find the way.*
> *Help guide me and give me signs that I'm here for*
> *a purpose.*
> *I want my family to know I'm a good provider.*
> *Also, I'm not a quitter.*

As I rose and started to leave church, I heard a familiar voice:

"Callaghan?"

"Yes Father Hallahan." Whenever I wasn't working, I came to church with my family and greeted him after mass.

"Thanks for coming. I know you have to start your day but I wanted to thank you."

"For what Father?"

"I always feel safe when I know you're out on our streets."

Tears started to well up but Father Hallahan acted like he didn't notice.

"Callaghan, if you have a couple of moments, I'd like you to kneel at the altar."

When I went to my knees, Father Hallahan put his right hand on my forehead and read St. Michael's prayer. After he finished, he used his two fingers to give the sign of the cross on my forehead.

"Callaghan, are you familiar with this prayer?"

Reaching for my wallet, I pulled it out. "Father, you gave me this prayer card when I started as a cop seven years ago. I laminated it so it wouldn't wear out."

Now, Father Hallahan teared up. He came over, gave me a heartfelt hug and whispered:

"Callaghan, always know God and St. Michael are with you."

I felt like I was in a Hallmark moment. I just had to leave.

I broke away, gave a quick thanks and walked to the car. Once inside, I took my hanky, wiped my face and blew my nose.

Shortly after I left the cemetery, I received a call from dispatch.

"150, what's your 39?"

"South side."

"Need you to come to the station for a few minutes. JT Hamilton wants to speak with you."

When I reached the station, Hamilton was outside waiting.

"Can I get a lift?" he said smiling.

"Where to, boss?" I said.

"Take me to the 105 Truck Stop," he replied, looking me straight in the eye.

"You know, I'm not supposed to spend much time there."

"Cal, I'll handle the chief. Just get me to the truck stop."

As we rode, he complimented me on my work on the sweeps and my overall police work. He also gave me an off-the-record apology for not making detective.

"But maybe this will be a consolation prize," he said. "I've been thinking about your note about forming a regional or state task force. Your contributions to RISS and MAGLOCLEN have been outstanding. You've seen the newsletters. People are noticing your work. They're also noticing you're at the truck stop less instead of more. Are you still working there from 10 to 2?"

"Yes, but ..."

"But what?"

"The owners have had me working on the inside."

"Why?"

"Williams is up my ass about double dipping. I think I'm being spied on. Every time I'm over there, dispatch sends me elsewhere."

We arrived at the 105 Truck Stop.

"Pull over here," Hamilton said as he pointed to the first parking lot we reached on the complex that was empty of cars. "Let's get out."

When we got out of the car, he slammed his fists on the trunk.

"Fucking shithead, that jealous, cowardly son of a bitch."

He paused. "That's off the record, Raven."

I nodded.

"An eighth victim turned up last night. I got the report this morning. Letticia Coleman, 19. Fucking 19. Found in Indiana, about 50 miles from the Illinois border. Beside the beatings and choking, she had a scarf stuffed down her throat. Likely dumped from a reefer unit, which means she could've been dead for weeks."

"Sir, I'll check and see if she's been at the truck stop. The first seven victims have spent time here. Most of the deaths are similar."

"See, you're on top of it. Don't know how ..."

"Well, sir, I ..."

"Don't answer that Cal. I don't need to know. The last four murders as you know have been outside the state. Williams thinks that puts Oldsmar in the clear, but as you said, there's a goddamn good chance every victim has stepped foot in this truck stop. Right here. People are getting pissed at his inactivity and we can't afford this bullshit of having our best man not working the beat – on the clock or off. They've got you chasing your tail, rescuing cats in trees, investigating dented mailboxes and handing out parking tickets. You're not a fucking meter maid. The attorney general and governor have called me."

I nodded. He paused. "What I just told you ..."

"Yes sir, off the record."

"OK, from now on, spend about one-fourth of your day at the truck stop. Do we need to switch you back to your old hours?"

"No sir, the owners have moved my time there from 1:30 a.m. to 5:30 a.m."

"Nothing good after midnight."

"Right sir."

We had a short conversation with the 105 Truck Stop owners Jim Dail and Greg Shriver before returning to the police station.

On our drive back to the station, Hamilton didn't say much. He seemed to be plotting his next move.

Just before I dropped him off, he said, "Cal things are going to change. They are going to change with your beat. And they're going to change in the chief's office or Oldsmar will be looking for a new man. Not someone who is sitting on his ass and saying we have cloudless days when bodies are dropping from the sky. Stay in touch with me and report what you find to me. Call me from the 105 and the 105 only. Got it?"

"Yes sir."

While Frank Jamison and the guys took me to my anniversary lunch, because they all said in unison, "Gotta fatten you up, Cal," simultaneously Hamilton stormed into Williams' office and banged the door off the wall.

"Don't you knock?" Williams uttered in a perturbed tone.

Hamilton took the door and slammed it shut.

"Do I have your attention now?" he shouted.

Realizing that Hamilton had clout around the state as regional director and could say anything to him without repercussions, Williams went quiet.

"I've heard from the governor. I've heard from the attorney general. And I've heard from county sheriffs. Those aren't pleasant conversations, Conrad. People are wondering why you're playing with your balls and keeping your best men off the investigation."

"The last three murders have been out of state. What concern is that of ours?"

"Conrad, you pompous ass, all of those women have spent time at the 105 Truck Stop."

"You deal with your people and I have to deal with mine. They don't want me spending resources on finding out who's killing whores. By the way, what best men?"

"Blackstone, O'Brien, Raven ..."

"Raven, he's a headline hunter. He's double dipping. He's ..."

"I don't fucking care. He talks to prostitutes, he talks to truckers, he gets results. Have you seen his contributions to the MAGLOCLEN newsletter?"

"So what's your point? Anybody could've done that."

"No, no, no. Anybody had the opportunity to contribute. He did. Only he did what I and Jamison asked him to. And you're handcuffing him. Why didn't you make him a detective?"

"He's overzealous. He endangers the men. He ..."

"Endangers the men? You know, someone mailed me a report a few years ago. It wasn't Raven. Seems like a man who broke into a restaurant. You were there. You wrote about Raven being too aggressive, going into the restaurant, chasing the man down in the woods. And you not only didn't follow him but you left before he came back."

"JT, you read that report wrong. I ..."

"You left before knowing your men were safe. I didn't read that in the report. I talked to a couple of cops who were there. You left a man behind. And you're doing the same thing now. I think part of you is jealous because you don't have the balls he does."

"Not true, goddamnit!"

"Conrad, you've played it safe your whole career, played the angles, made a few bucks on the side and you've become soft, a pussy."

"Fuck you, get out of my office."

"One last thing. We found an eighth death last night in Indiana. Type of death is similar to the others. Good chance she spent time at the 105. Two more and the FBI is coming in. For once in your goddamn life, become a man, become a leader. People want results."

With that, Hamilton left, and he slammed the door behind him on the way out for good measure.

———————

Having such a good day, I thought I'd give Dorothy Douglas a call.

My respect for her had grown and grown; and on this day, she showed me how smart she was.

After offering me some banana bread with a latte, she shocked me with some news.

"Cal, my son Thomas worked for the Oldsmar Police Department for 15 years," she said.

"I'm sorry, I didn't know that," I said. "Why did he leave?"

"Too much stress. Not so much the job. The cops had groups. If you were in one group, that helped your chance for promotions. My Tommy, he didn't like that group."

"Why?"

"They played games, cut corners, maybe even took handouts for looking the other way. Minimal thinking, minimal arrests, minimal paperwork, he said. You don't rock the boat, your bosses don't work too much and you can skip through your day."

"That's how crimes go unsolved."

"Tommy said that. He challenged people to do better. They didn't like it. They made life tough on him. His superiors didn't back him. Tommy got so stressed, he had ulcers. His wife Gail said 'No more.' So he left. Took a buyout."

As I left, I again realized I'm dealing with a toxic culture.

Tommy Douglas was another victim of Intentional Infliction of Emotional Distress. Or bullying to put it plainly. We were kindred spirits. And it helped to know there were others before me. That I wasn't the only one that's dealt with this shit. It felt like a sign to get this revelation from Dorothy.

————

As I finished my light paperwork in the squad room, ending my day, Williams came by where I sat.

"Raven, until we catch the ser... truck stop guy, I want you spending more time at the 105."

I nodded.

"Spend about two hours of your day there. Are you still working there at night?"

"Only inside."

"Don't worry about double dipping. Just use your judgment."

With that, Williams left.

I put my hands together, looked up and did a quick, "Thank you God."

His dig insinuating that I was on the pad really pissed me off, but even that couldn't erase my smile. I was thrilled to be back on the case.

———

Jan and I had a wonderful meal together with the kids at Costello's Restaurant.

I ordered surf and turf with a side of pasta, much to the delight of my family.

I ordered a pitcher of root beer, filled everyone's glass and raised a toast.

"To the best family a man could have," I said, tearing up as I finished my thought, but I didn't care. "You mean the world to me."

The kids looked at mom who had tears running down her face. Clayton broke the awkward silence as he asked, "Dad, can I have one of your shrimp?"

I laughed and called the waiter. "A side order of fried shrimp," I said.

———

At night, Jan and I kissed, cuddled and made love. A great ending to a great day. I fell right asleep while we held each other.

A few hours later, Jan awakened me.

"Cal, Cal," she yelled. I was on the floor. I felt something coming down my nose. I touched it with my fingers and I was bleeding.

I looked around. I had taken a piece of the nightstand out.

"You were kicking and moving and talking in your sleep again," she said.

Jan turned on the light. There was a big cut on my head.

"We're going to the hospital," she said.

I protested but she gave me a look that said I had no choice.

She wrapped a towel around my head, called my folks to babysit the kids and she drove me to Mercy Hospital.

Then Jan said, "Cal, when you get stitched up, we need to talk."

CHAPTER 11

Getting Help

**Her perception changed
once she realized the
culture started at the top.**

– Cindy Esposito's revelation

As the doctor and nurse stitched me up, the pain I felt would be nothing like what I'd feel once they left the room.

"Mr. Raven, you needed 12 staples," Dr. Marcus Kiley said. "That must be one hard nightstand you lost to. You're going to look like Frankenstein until we take them out. You're going to have a big bump on your head for a few days and your eyes are dilated so you have concussion symptoms. You're lucky. Any questions?"

Jan quickly interjected the question at the top of her mind, "How many days would you suggest he take off from work?"

"What kind of job?"

"I'm a cop," I proudly announced before Jan could answer.

The doctor paused, then offered some guidance. "I'm new here," he said. "Our main physician should answer that question but first my instinct tells me at least a week."

"Doc, I haven't missed five days of work in my career," I pleaded as my frustration simmered.

"Mr. Raven, you may not have a career if you get banged on the head like that again. I can guarantee a concussion if you hit your head in the next week. Cranial bleeding also is possible. If this wound was two or three inches lower, you could've lost your right eye!"

Jan spoke up, before Cal could, and asked authoritatively, "Doctor, please see if your boss can make it 10 days?"

I raised my arms in protest, but I took one look at Jan and I quickly brought them down.

As the doctor and nurse left, I looked at my scared wife.

"You know I had a great day yesterday." I said. "Spent a few moments in prayer at St. Mike's. Father Hallahan blessed me. Hamilton came by and said he wants me to be part of a task force. The guys took me to lunch. Dorothy and I had a good talk. Even Williams said I could spend more time at the 105 Truck Stop."

"Oh great," Jan said sarcastically.

"But the best part was at night. The meal, us." I looked at her and moved my eyelids up and down, which hurt like hell and made me dizzy.

"Overdoing it already," Jan said with a smile.

I looked at her and shrugged.

"Here's the thing Mr. Raven," she said. "If you had such a great day, then why did you have nightmares? Why did you flail around again? Why did you fall off the bed? You didn't even drink."

"I don't know."

"Neither do I. That's why we need to see somebody."

It dawned on me that I told God in my prayers the previous morning that I needed help and I asked Him to "help guide me and give me signs that I'm here for a purpose."

I guess a thick-headed Irishman like me needed to get KO'ed by a 3-foot nightstand to get it in my noggin that I should see somebody.

"OK," I said. "We can use the time off to see a shrink of some sort."

"Maybe he can start by shrinking the size of that melon," Jan said with a straight face.

I cracked up and shot back, "Has Tony been giving you ball-busting lessons?"

————

When we got home, the main doctor, Dr. Chad Shepherd, called and said 10 days is good and added, "That's about the time we'll take the staples out."

Jan reached out to 1-800-COPLINE to see what therapy I could receive. I insisted on an out-of-town shrink.

"Jan, if the department finds out I'm seeing a therapist, I'll be pushing a pencil at a desk and carrying a rubber gun."

"Hun, at least you won't hurt yourself."

"Smart ass. When will this end?"

"When you're in the office of Dr. I-Can-Help-You."

Point made.

Response to Jan's call came within a couple of hours. A sweet voice on the other end said, "Is this Jan and Cal Raven?"

When we said yes, the voice said, "Did we understand, your husband needed stitches?"

"Yes, he banged his head on our nightstand."

"Oh. Sorry to hear that. No need to explain. None of my business. Can you meet with the psychologist at 4 p.m. today and the psychiatrist on Friday at 1:30 p.m.?"

"Why yes. That's quick."

"Well, we don't want unseen patients having to wait through the weekend."

While we waited for 4 p.m. to come, I received calls from the guys, the 105 owners and Hamilton.

"Take care, heal up and if you're up to it, think of a plan of attack for when you return," Hamilton said.

Williams called and was more direct.

"How's the head?" he asked.

"Better," I replied.

"Good. Next week, O'Brien will bring some files over. Take a peak with fresh eyes, maybe make a couple of calls and see if there's anything new you can uncover. Can you do that?"

He barely waited to hear a yes before he said, "Good. Gotta go."

———

On our way to Lowell Psychology, we passed by two Oldsmar Police Cars. My anxiety level went up.

"Is this a good idea?" I said.

Jan glared at me.

Upon entering the office, I saw a former classmate, Elvis Jones, walking into another room close to the exit. Not wanting to exchange pleasantries, I turned my back, looked at Jan and softly uttered, "Fuckkkk."

"I see him," she said. "He just looked back. Don't turn around."

Jan then hid behind me. I lifted my fingers up as if to say 1-2-3-4-5, and then we turned around. We could see from a window that Elvis had left the building.

"Feel my heart," I said.

"It sounds like it wants to explode."

I glared at her.

"Need a stick of gum? It's good for halitosis," she said, trying to distract me.

When I met with psychologist Ben Lowell, he asked about my history going back to a teen.

When I explained in detail my experiences working with truckers, working in an ambulance/hearse, working in the funeral home and being a cop, Dr. Lowell leaned back in his chair, put his hands above his head and uttered, "Wow, wow, wow."

He inhaled, exhaled heavily, looked at us and said, "Have you heard of PTSD or PTSS?"

We shook our heads no.

"Post Traumatic Stress Disorder or Post Traumatic Stress Syndrome. It came out about 10 years ago when researchers studied those who fought in Vietnam or who were victims of rape or incest. They found out our soldiers and victims had repercussions anywhere from five to 15 years later. It led to anxiety, depression, weight loss, mental exhaustion and sometimes even death. Studies have shown these symptoms have sadly led to suicides."

Dr. Lowell continued, turning his focus back to me, "I think the people who have PTSD or PTSS goes beyond soldiers or rape victims. I think you're an example of that. What you've seen. My God, I think I'd be in an asylum. So actually, Cal, I think you're doing better than most."

Jan stepped in, reading from the long list of questions in her head, "How about the nightmares?"

"Typical, you're probably reliving experiences from the past. It's like rewatching a real-life murder film. And if you're drinking alcohol or taking drugs, it may be adding to your condition."

I looked down.

"Cal, I'm not here to judge. I'm here to help. I'm going to do two things. I'm going to make notes for Dr. Robert Farnsworth, a psychiatrist, so you don't have to retell your stories. The other is I'm going to prescribe you some Effexor (Venlafaxine), which is an anti-depressant."

The last thing I wanted was the crutch of medication, but I bit my tongue.

Being a cop is important to me, but my wife and family trumped that.

"If you have side effects, we'll put you on something else," Dr. Lowell continued. "You don't need to suffer any more. We'll keep working on this until you feel better. As a side note, I'd be careful mixing this with alcohol. If you want a beverage, give it at least four hours after taking the pill."

Two days later, we met Dr. Farnsworth. More stress.

Upon checking in, I saw a woman in the back office I knew. A friend of Tony Blackstone's who I met at a party. She glanced at me, then glanced at a chart, then glanced at me, then looked down, then looked at me, gave a quick wave, then put her thumb and finger over her mouth as if to say, "My lips are sealed."

I gave her a thumbs up.

Jan bowed to her.

Dr. Farnsworth listened to me for an hour. He asked a lot of questions, nodded occasionally and showed a lot of empathy. The doc also made a few jokes and occasionally gave me a pat on the leg. We got along great from the start.

"I have a brother in another state who is a police officer," he said. "We talk a lot. He has experienced some of what you have. Cal, you've been through a lot. Dr. Lowell told you about PTSD and PTSS?"

I nodded.

"Thank goodness, you like to talk things out. My experience has been that silence eats people up. Let's schedule a time to talk once a month."

"For how long?"

"Maybe the rest of your life. But that's normal. If you want to come in earlier, call us and we'll get you in. Here's my card. If it gets really bad, call my personal number. I don't want your challenges to linger. You gotta get this stuff out. It's like poison."

He shook hands with me and Jan.

"Please, stay in touch."

We walked to the car. Once inside, Jan and I embraced and hugged and cried.

"I did the right thing," I admitted.

"Yeah," Jan replied. "On the next visit, maybe we'll see our next-door neighbors."

———

After his debacle near Lake Tahoe, Bart Gein gladly took an assignment to head East.

He drove down toll road 68 to his destination of Bangor, Maine. In the back of his reefer unit were beef, chicken, pork, flash-frozen vegetables – and a body he killed 15 days earlier.

The red-haired woman wanted to give him sex and earn a few bucks.

He wanted to kill a fourth redhead.

The time approached 3 a.m. Hardly anybody out at this time. Gein got off at a rest stop, drove to the farthest corner and stopped.

He took the woman's body, put it over his shoulder and walked into the tall grass where he tossed her like a bag of trash.

Saturday, Dec. 11 was the department's Christmas party but Chief Conrad Williams and a few of his guys thought they'd get an early start.

Having cracked open a third round of beers and after cracking a few off-color jokes, they were interrupted by a knock on the door.

"Chief, can we talk for a second?"

Cindy Esposito, Oldsmar's fourth female trying to become a police officer on the force. The previous three didn't last long. Cindy just went through a divorce and needed a job. She graduated from the academy with honors. She also knew how the game was played.

As Esposito walked toward the chief's desk, Lieutenant Matthew France pretended to sneeze, but the word "bitch" could clearly be heard. Chuckles from the other guys followed.

"Sweetie, can't you see we're busy?" Williams said smiling, completely ignoring Lt. France's comment.

Sweetie, cutie, honey, Cindy Lou, Esposito could handle those names. If there was anything she learned from her ex-husband cop, it's that you gotta have thick skin.

But bitch, that was crossing the line. So were cunt and whore.

But she had been taking notes.

Esposito composed herself, looked Williams squarely in the eye and said, "Chief, there's a job I'm interested in applying for."

"What's that?" Williams said, winking at the guys.

"Chief, I'd like to work with the canine unit. I grew up with dogs and they respond well to me."

Williams, his tongue loosened by a few beers, responded like he and the others were a foursome on the golf course.

"Sure, sweetie," Williams said, barely containing a laugh. "Just one thing."

"What's that chief?"

"Well, to really make you feel at home with the canines, you'll have to wear a collar, too."

Spitting out beer, some of it spraying Esposito, the three other guys bent over laughing.

Esposito stormed out. She now knew why Williams' men kept harassing her. Their boss not only didn't stop their actions but he encouraged them. Her perception changed once she realized the culture started at the top.

She thought about slamming the door, but had the presence of mind to keep it open. She acted as if she disappeared around the corner only to quietly back track and listen to what else they had to say. She pulled a cassette recorder out of her purse and hit record.

"Chief, that's funny. Put a collar around that whore Esposito."

"A bitch running the male dogs."

"Maybe Esposito can get lucky with those canines. She sure can't make it with humans."

"Maybe she just needs a real man – giving it to her ... doggy style."

The howls drowned out clicks made when Esposito turned off the recorder and walked away quickly.

No tears, no hurt feelings, Esposito just felt rage. And revenge.

To herself, she said, "You boys are going to get it from behind real soon."

CHAPTER 12

Chief In The Crosshairs

"Chief, your nose is growing."

– Dorothy Douglas to embattled
Chief Conrad Williams

In early January, Cindy Esposito did some late-night work from a near-empty Oldsmar Police Department when she heard laughing by the bulletin board.

She quietly walked behind a wall and took a peek.

Chief Conrad Williams and Lt. Matthew France snickered as they tacked a cut-up newspaper clipping of her story on being hired as a canine officer to the center of the board.

Little did the two know but they were about to hand wrap Cindy a belated Christmas gift.

Williams and France thought they'd give it their own headline.

She waited until they left. When she approached the bulletin board, the clipping had been glued to a white piece of paper. It read: Queen Bitch.

Again, Esposito didn't get mad. She put on a pair of rubber gloves, she put powder on the edges of the paper, brushed the paper, taped the prints, then took photos. She then put the paper in a sterile manilla envelope.

Just before Christmas, she had reached out to a young attorney, Stu Levin, recommended by her divorce attorney. Levin had tried a few sexual harassment cases and won.

Hell hath no fury like a woman scorned; and then humiliated.

"We have a lot of good evidence here," Levin said. "We have enough to go forward with a lawsuit. You could maybe settle for $75,000. That doesn't go far. I think you need a smoking gun, pardon the pun. Let's give them some more time to shoot themselves in the foot."

While not a fan of Levin's quips, Esposito agreed. Now she had a key piece of testimony right in her hands and would let these clowns strengthen her case.

Bart Gein found when he hadn't killed a prostitute in a few months, his hunger went beyond food. Richard said, "I want action."

Gein found three full plates at the truck stop's buffet didn't satiate him. Nibbling on snacks as he logged miles didn't help, either.

"Feed me women," Richard said.

The urges consumed Gein.

While listening to the call of the wild on the CB – Channel 19 – he got a haircut, drove to the truck stop, cleaned himself up and waited.

When a Lot Lizard tapped a quarter on his window, Gein pretended to be asleep.

"Yeah?" he said, sounding groggy.

"Hey honey, can I warm up?" the woman's voice said.

"OK, what time is it?"

"It's not too late, honey."

"For what?"

"For a little lovin, honey. What would you like?"

"How about from behind, darlin'?"

"That'll be extra, $75, honey."

Richard told him to give the woman eight 10s. "You'll get the money back," he said.

As the woman turned away from him and counted the money, Gein pulled out his black nylon rope, put it around her neck and then looped again.

The woman fought valiantly, kicking and trying to scratch Gein; but she couldn't speak because her vocal cords, windpipe and esophagus were getting crushed.

In three and a half minutes, the woman lost consciousness, then her life.

After this kill, Gein had no appetite for days. He resembled a predator, like a gator who can go a month without eating after a kill, or a python, who can go for almost a year.

In the meantime, his victim got a ride in his reefer unit for a couple of weeks.

———————

Williams turned serious when he learned in early February that another Jane Doe and Tanya Maria Crookston became the ninth and tenth victims killed, three weeks apart.

The time of death was hard to tell for each victim.

But here's the bizarre part. Jane Doe No. 2's location of death – at least the location she was discovered – came within 15 miles of Jane Doe No. 1, in Lawson County.

After Victims 5, 6, 7 and 8 were found out of state, bodies

started literally being dumped in Illinois again.

However, the common denominator remained: They all spent time at the 105 Truck Stop.

And the death of the second Jane Doe (Victim No. 9) fit the profile – blunt-force trauma and strangulation. The M.O. was consistent and it was becoming clearer these were not random homicides.

Tanya, found 15 miles from my house, was killed differently. Eviscerated, her intestines hung out when sheriff's deputies found her. I didn't think this was the work of our serial killer but it's hard to stop a boulder when it's going downhill. People felt that any woman who spent time at the truck stop and later was murdered had to be a victim of the same serial killer.

Because four victims in a row had been killed out of state, Williams thought the killer had moved away. But the dead bodies had returned on the chief's doorstep, putting him in the crosshairs of state law enforcement officials, media and the public.

————

In late February, Johnson County Sheriff Bill Jarrold called an emergency meeting in Schaumberg.

When county sheriffs and police chiefs arrived, they were greeted by an intimidating presence – attorney general Ed Price.

Williams' seat warmed up real fast.

"Gentlemen, thanks for coming," Price said. "This week, I will be announcing The Highway Task Force Initiative. I will be working with the state of Illinois law enforcement. I expect full cooperation. Any questions?"

All eyes turned to Conrad Williams.

"Whatever you need Mr. Price, let us know."

Papers shuffled. Eyes turned toward Price.

"Bill?" he said, prompting the sheriff while not responding to Williams.

Jarrold made a few comments, then adjourned the meeting. Williams bolted for the door, but Jarrold blocked him."

"Conrad, a few words," Jarrold said.

Williams nodded quickly and the two went into a hallway.

"You sat on this too long and now it's blowing your ass up. The AG is pissed. In the coming weeks, I'm told you'll be getting a call from FBI officials telling you they'll also get involved in the investigation. Just as I thought. You know when it's five, six or seven dead, the Federal Bureau of Investigation isn't interested. When it gets to double figures, and there's more coverage, they get interested. Real interested."

"Bill, I'm telling you, these are isolated cases," Williams responded, still trying to defend his actions – or inactions. "In four states, bodies have been found hundreds of miles from us."

"Conrad, shut the fuck up," Jarrold snapped. "Six of the 10 have been found in this state. All 10 have spent time at the 105 Truck Stop. Your theory isn't worth a shit. Wake the hell up."

A series of events followed over the coming weeks:

In sweeps on back-to-back-to-back nights that I coordinated as security manager at the 105 Truck Stop, 20 women were arrested for either trespassing or solicitation, fined $100 and put in jail for five days. Most pleaded no contest. We told the women that, "During this time, it would be wise to reflect and seriously consider a career change." We then showed photos of the murdered women with their badly beaten faces and heads as well as marks around their necks caused by being strangled from ropes or the killer's hands. While the women cried and shook after seeing the photos, job counselors came in and spoke with them about free educational opportunities, work options and temp positions available.

Williams didn't compliment my work but 105 Truck Stop owners Jim Dail and Greg Shriver did. They also praised the joint venture between their company and police during a press conference. After making comments to the media, Dail and Shriver gave them a tour of the facilities, which included a $400,000 fence that surrounded most of the facility and blocked the entrance by the trolls at the 44 Magnum Lounge. In addition, there was controlled parking with lot alterations, security gates with guards and parking attendants on site.

Dail and Shriver, who noted that only 2 percent of their business came from the community, announced in the media they'll have an open house with free food and drinks, plus games for the kids. Joining them would be members of their Fellowship Church and a band that played gospel music.

After word got out of the arrests, a TV reporter came out with her cameraman and they did a ride-along with us. During the ride-along, they saw how successful we were at totally cleaning up the truck lots with the enhanced security lighting, fencing, signage and security officers monitoring activity.

These events were all geared towards dissuading the predator and protecting the women from themselves – and their Johns.

A safer 105 Truck Stop was a good first step in stopping the killings or forcing the killer to change his or her patterns. That deviation is usually where mistakes happen and more clues are left behind.

What really spiked Williams' blood pressure was an unexpected visit from Karl Raymond with the Chicago Tribune. It was late March and Raymond had been working for a month on a story of the murders connected to the 105 Truck Stop. By collaborating with reporters around the country who also had written about interstate killings, the press realized prostitute killings had turned into an epidemic.

"Chief, I wanted to talk in person," Raymond said.

"Why didn't you call before coming?" Williams replied.

"I did, but I never heard back from you."

"My assistants. Good help is hard to find. We'll have to make this short."

Raymond raised his eyebrows briefly.

"What can you tell me about a potential serial killer who has murdered 10 women?"

"We don't believe it's a serial killer. Dead women being found in Ohio, Indiana and New York State don't have a connection to us."

"But six women have been found in this state."

"Most were found hours away from here, Karl."

"Sources have told us the prostitutes spent time at the 105 Truck Stop. What do you know about this? What are you doing about it?"

"Who are your sources? First of all, we don't have definitive proof that any women killed have been at the 105 Truck Stop?"

"Any women? That's your response?"

"Yes. To answer your second question, we have our men working on this. Our top men. It's an ongoing investigation so I'm limited in what I can say."

"Do you have any information on the latest victims?"

"No."

"What can you say about this murder epidemic?"

"Strong word, Karl. Very little. We don't want anyone – including the killer, killers – to know what we know. We are working with authorities all over the country. We also take these deaths seriously. Very seriously."

"If you're working with authorities all over the country, then ..."

"That's all I want to say now," Williams sternly responded, cutting off the question.

"Chief, one last thing," Raymond quickly followed up. "Have you attended secret meetings with Bill Jarrold and county sheriffs?

"What secret meetings?

"Two secret meetings. One included the attorney general."

"Who told you? There's a reason they were secret meetings."

"The attorney general. I guess the secret's out."

"Yes, I attended those meetings, Karl. Very productive but that's all I'll say."

As he left the police station, Raymond saw a poster with Tanya Maria Crookston's photo and a reward being offered. The poster read: LAST SEEN AT THE 105 TRUCK STOP.

One of the biggest mistakes a public official, or anybody for that matter, can make is to lie or deceive the media, especially one of the best investigative reporters in the Midwest.

I learned this from cops I knew in Chicago. I called them because Raymond called me.

When I asked about him as a person, they all said, "He's on the up-and-up."

I wanted to talk to Raymond, even though my gut started flipping like Mary Lou Retton. Dail and Shriver said I could park in one of their garages and meet him in a private area to talk.

When we met, I told Raymond I trusted him but if Williams found out, my career would be over.

"And I have a wife and three kids," I said.

"Cal, any information you give me now will be deep background," Raymond said. "The public needs to know Williams has been covering this up."

The deep background information I shared with Raymond was that:

All 10 of the prostitutes killed spent time at the 105 Truck Stop. We have Field Interview cards with seven of them. The prostitutes confirmed the others.

The majority of the police force didn't care because Williams didn't care.

While there was a pattern in many of the killings – beatings, stranglings, gaggings, clothes removed and jewelry taken – seven were similar while three varied in the way the victims were killed and then positioned. "Three weren't dumped," I said.

The problems at the 44 Magnum Lounge – pornography, glory holes, drugs, gay meet-up sites, prostitution, increased pimp presence, larceny – had started to seep into the community and attracted unseemly characters. Derelicts. Perverts. Stalkers.

"The fast-food joints over there are getting robbed repeatedly," I told him. "Guns are being pulled on teenagers working there. It's like a cancer. The tentacles are spreading."

Raymond then told me a couple of things, which elevated my blood pressure.

"Cal, the chief flat out lied to me," he said, explaining the poster story. "I also have a couple of people on the record, among them Dail and Shriver. They praised you but not the chief."

He paused, then continued, "As to Magnum 44, a source told me the FBI is bugging a restaurant. They want to nail a mob family."

If it was the Downstairs Retreat, I had a few drinks there and talked shit about Williams. Gotta keep my big mouth shut.

As he was leaving, Raymond turned around and asked, "Do you know a Dorothy Douglas?"

"Yeahhh," I said cautiously.

"She also praised you. She also said, and I'm looking at my notes, 'I'd like to talk to Williams and have a come-to-Jesus meeting.'"

"How did you know to contact her?" I asked.

"She called our publisher," he said. "Her late husband did the taxes for our newspaper."

I shook my head.

————

In May, internal affairs officers temporarily delayed Williams with an impromptu meeting as he headed to the golf course.

"We're hearing things, Conrad," one of them said.

"What kind of things?" he asked while reading a golf magazine and walking to his car.

"Saying things about women," the other said. "Have you said anything that would be considered insulting?"

"Nothing other than the usual," he said.

"What would be considered usual?"

Williams stopped and looked at the officers.

"We kid women all the time but it's all in good fun."

"All right. Nothing that could come back to bite us in the ass?"

"No. Gentlemen, now, I have a 3 p.m. tee time. Would you excuse me?"

As he left and quickly brushed past them, one officer said under his breath to the other, "I think he's hiding something."

———

After more than six months of investigative reporting, Chicago Tribune reporter Karl Raymond published a four-part series on the dead prostitutes just before Independence Day. The stories centered around the 105 Truck Stop, the Oldsmar Police Department, Chief Conrad Williams and the number of prostitutes being killed at truck stops all over the country.

While fellow cops told me they heard Williams kicking garbage cans, throwing pens and ripping off every piece of paper thumb tacked to the bulletin board after reading the story, a couple of trustees – Wayne Keller and Dennis Dahl – came in and chewed Williams a new ass for his unprofessional behavior. Then they told him of the need to hold a press conference or town hall to talk about the story and calm residents' fears.

The points Raymond made in his story included:

A serial killer murdered most of the women; and there may be copycat killers.

There have been serial killers operating along other interstates around the country. They cover the Northeast, South, Midwest, Southwest and West.

Illinois law enforcement agencies didn't communicate well, which left them searching for answers on the killings.

The attorney general and local county sheriffs criticized the Oldsmar Police Department in general and Chief Williams in particular for not being more proactive on the investigation and letting other local and state agencies take leadership. The message Oldsmar PD sent: Williams and most staff members didn't care about the murders because the women were known or suspected prostitutes.

Williams withheld information from the public for more than three years. Without using the word lie, Raymond also gave a strong impression Williams wasn't forthcoming.

In the story, my quote of "I'd love to talk but those conversations aren't authorized" was used. Conrad Williams seethed.

After reading the full four-part series, TV station WILL offered me a side job as a field consultant. When I heard scanner calls at home, I'd reach out to WILL's reporters. I think they hoped I'd eventually be a source.

———

Williams tried to soothe things over with a town hall meeting, as suggested by trustee members Keller, Dahl and Jim Hole.

"Get in front of it," Hole encouraged.

"Now's the time to show leadership," Dahl added.

Secretly, they thought Williams would fail; and he did.

"Oldsmar never has been safer," he told the assembly.

"Then why do we have a serial killer on the loose, higher rates of crime, increased numbers of youths being treated for drugs and more DUIs than in the last five previous years?" *Oldsmar Independent* reporter Barb Hahn said.

"That information you have is incorrect," Williams said.

"Chief, this comes from the daily police reports from your office," she responded.

"You interpreted them wrong," he said to groans in the crowd.

Dorothy Douglas then stood up, glared at Williams and said, "Chief, your nose is growing."

Howls filled the room.

Williams turned red, then actually rubbed his nose with his fingers.

"Hitchhikers have been reduced greatly," he said. "Drifters, mystery people who caused all sorts of havoc, have almost disappeared."

"What person in their right mind would be hitchhiking with serial killers loose?" somebody shouted.

"There's no serial killer," Williams responded. "Isolated incidents."

He turned to 105 Truck Stop owners Jim Dail and Greg Shriver.

"Prostitution activity has decreased at your truck stops, correct?"

"First of all, chief, it's truck stop, singular," Dail said. "Magnum 44 Lounge and the adjacent massage bath house continue to put a stain on our truck stop and the community and you've done nothing about this for years. Second, only through a change of leadership from 10 p.m. to 2 a.m. did we see a reduction in prostitution activity."

Shriver added, "Before that, men you approved through seniority basically circled around the complex, drank coffee, ate donuts and who knows what else they did."

Someone said, "Maybe they got free BJs."

The crowd laughed some more while other citizens shook their heads.

"That concludes our press conference," Williams said. "Have a great day."

As he stormed through the office, he looked at trustee Jim Hole.

"Great idea," he snapped.

Williams then eyed me and sneered.

"Pretty boy, your day is coming," he said. "Stay the hell away from that truck stop while you're on duty."

———————

When I arrived at the Archway Hotel in St. Louis for a MAGLOCLEN conference in mid August, fellow officers greeted me by giving me Chicago Tribunes.

"Your chief got lit up like a Christmas tree," one said.

"When does he get the boot?" another asked.

"Don't know," I said. "Before he goes down, he may take me out with him."

"Why?"

"He hates me."

John Powers, police chief in Las Cruces, N.M., then introduced himself to me.

"Callaghan, I don't know if you remember me but we competed in the 800 meters in high school at the conference meet," he said.

"Yeah, you beat me by half a second," I said.

"You stayed with me until the end. You're a great competitor. How are things going?"

I showed him the paper. He glanced at the article.

"My wife's mother sent me this," he said. "You're quoted. Why are you speaking to the media instead of the chief?"

"Because the chief would rather throw me out there than do it himself."

"Fending off the wolves?"

"Something like that."

"Keep fighting. Good to see you. Call me if you need anything."

He then gave me his business card. I looked at him.

"I mean it," he said.

After listening to various topics – including one on state communication among police agencies – I lowered in my chair as the moderator and panelists talked about the Oldsmar situation.

One panelist said, "This had to be embarrassing for that department, but there by the Grace of God go we. If local, county, regional and state agencies do not communicate better and share information, more problems like serial killings will go on longer and families will suffer more."

After the topics ended, I sat down with a few guys I had gotten to know from previous conferences and we knocked down a few brown bottles. Soon, we were joined by the panelists who spoke about my police department.

After making introductions, they turned to me and said, "And you are?"

"Cal Raven."

"From Oldsmar Police Department," my buddies said in unison.

I lowered my head and a panelist said, "There by the Grace of God ..."

Another said, "Cal, I've seen you at other events. When you bring back information from other conferences, do you share it with the force?"

"I used to," I admitted. "But when I brought back binders from a conference in Rochester on reviewing solvability factors, case processing as well as a crime-scene checklist, cops tore up the checklists and put the binders in a corner of a seldom-used office, and now they collect dust."

"Cognitive dissonance," one said.

"Cognitive what?" asked another.

"Cognitive dissonance. It's seeing a problem in front of you, having a possible solution but completely ignoring it. Bad leadership."

"Cal," another said. "Join the party." He raised his bottle and we all raised ours and took a drink.

"To SNAFU," another said referring to the term meaning Situation Normal, All Fucked Up.

We raised our glasses and took another swig.

"To FUBAR," another said, referring to the term Fucked Up Beyond All Repair.

We repeated the exercise and everyone relaxed and cut loose.

As we spoke, one of the main issues we talked about was that when early laws were made by law enforcement, they did so to avoid a monopoly by any particular law enforcement unit. That led to different departments, like FBI, state troopers, county sheriffs, deputies and local police.

However, problems popped up from this fragmentation, like:

There wasn't an effective way for these organizations to share resources, hence the need for MAGLOCLEN.

Officers didn't do a good job of sharing their information because they were overwhelmed or just lazy.

Different levels of law enforcement didn't respect the other. Turf battles became regular among the agencies.

Most cops highly dislike state troopers.

"They're pussies," one said. "Do you see any of them at this conference? All they do is arrest guys going 90 mph, escort governors, take college football coaches off the field after games and train new officers from not shooting their feet off."

The guys around the table laughed.

"They would never arrest truckers with stolen cargo, prostitutes who lifted wallets or pimps who had pornography on them," another said.

"They can't," another added. "They literally can't."

"Even if they could, they'd be like, 'Oh, no, that's beneath us,'" one said mockingly. "They prefer to delegate and pass that information along. But they can give expert and technological and scientific advice."

"Yes, like this is a rubber balloon," said a guy holding a condom he brought for one of the training sessions. "And if it's dripping, that's because there's a foreign substance."

Guys pounded the table, and laughed deep belly laughs.

"Meanwhile, nobody has to report anything to the FBI," I said.

"Those pricks," another said. "Why would we give them anything? They love to come in and take the credit. The Federal Bureau of Image. Ever since *The Untouchables* came out, they think they're untouchable. They love to remind people how they got rid of the public enemies."

"And J. Edgar Hoover. Rumor has it he liked to dress like a woman."

"And play around with the boys, if you know what I mean?"

As we broke up for the night, one of the guys shared some foresight.

"Speaking of the FBI," he said. "They're coming to your neighborhood soon. Ten killings. That's the kind of number that draws publicity."

CHAPTER 13

Amateur Hour

**"Those who forget history are
condemned to repeat it."**

– Sal Hershkowitz, Oldsmar lawyer
quoting philosopher George Santayana

I returned from the St. Louis conference with mixed feelings. I liked what reporter Karl Raymond wrote. The public needed to know.

I didn't like some of my fellow officers from around the country thinking our department was a joke.

I liked Chief Conrad Williams being held accountable.

I didn't like that Williams turned on me for something he should have done.

It was the middle of September and I needed to clear my head so I set up an appointment with Dr. Robert Farnsworth.

"How do you feel about Chief Williams?" Dr. Farnsworth asked.

"I always have a knot in my stomach around him," I responded. "He calls me a control problem. I knew a lot of the guys in the department before I got the job but I never heard of him until he broke my balls. He jams me up – a lot. I'm surprised he became chief. I know his job is hard. There's a lot of inter-office politics. You have to please some people and lay down the law with others. But when there's a problem circling around you and you don't address it, the problem gets worse."

"Do you think you could do a better job?"

"Maybe. I'm not even 30 so I'd make some mistakes. But I'd be a lot more proactive. I definitely would implement some ideas."

"Like what?"

As I shared those, Dr. Farnsworth paused for a few seconds, looked at me and smiled.

"Here's an idea," he said.

"Shoot," I said.

"Cal, maybe a better word?"

"Right, right, go ahead."

"Cal, why don't you write a recommendation or proposal for the chief? Be positive, tactful, don't judge, share that you appreciate the strain he's under. Maybe even share that it can be his idea."

"That happened before. I made a bust on a guy in a Cadillac. He sold drugs. The police department impounded the vehicle, then we're able to keep it through a forfeiture. Williams then has a photo taken of him next to the car with the county prosecutor and my lieutenant. Williams then kept the car. It didn't sit well with me. Chief likes to take credit for things he's had nothing to do with. And he likes to take gifts, too!"

"Cal, point taken. But here's the thing. It's important. Don't expect he'll implement your ideas. In fact, prepare yourself that he will reject your suggestions. How you respond to this interaction will give us an idea of how you're progressing on your journey."

"You mean if I don't go on a binge, if I don't cry, if I don't vent with Jan and my co-workers?"

"Something like that. Keep me informed."

———

I took his advice and in my letter to Chief Williams, I made the following points:

a) The Oldsmar PD hasn't evolved in its policing the past five decades. "We've been marginally effective," I wrote.

b) We have to be more innovative and consider concepts I learned from other departments while attending various conferences.

c) His job is difficult and I understand that.
d) With fiscal constraints, "We have to do more with less."

e) I wanted to be considered to spearhead a Criminal Management System, based on what other departments did around the country.

f) I wanted my memorandum to be confidential until he and I talked.

After making me wait for three weeks, Williams proceeded to write me a letter, which he copied to 10 other cops.

He wrote that my ideas were "pie in the sky." And he continued with more excuses, writing that, "We aren't Los Angeles PD, New York PD, Chicago PD or even Champaign

PD. You aren't Hollywood and this isn't the movies. We're also under a lot of media heat, thanks to your big mouth. Come up with a better, more realistic plan or I'll put you on desk duty."

I shook as I read the response. I wanted to reach for the booze but held off. I took it personally that he not only totally rejected my ideas but he distributed them among his buddies who would back him. My hand kept shaking and I started hyperventilating and sweating.

I called Dr. Farnsworth. Fortunately, he had no patients.

"Doc, I'm having a panic attack," I said.

"Williams turned down your suggestion?" he asked.

"Not only that, he copied 10 co-workers. I wanted this to be confidential. What am I going to do?"

"Cal, breathe in. Hold it. Breathe out."

I did it about 10 times but the shaking wouldn't go away.

"Cal, I'm not supposed to tell you this," Dr. Farnsworth said. "But word on the street is that Williams is in big trouble if he isn't directly involved in catching the serial killer."

"Really?"

"Really."

My shaking and anxiety stopped.

"Doc, I'm feeling better," I said.

Suddenly, the doctor started sweating.

"Remember, this is our secret," he said. "Cal, is there anybody you can send your memo to that you trust?"

"Yeah, I think so," I said. "There's a lot of people who respect my work."

I started using email, which had just rolled out at the station, and liked the idea of sending my work to Jim Dail and Greg Shriver, JT Hamilton, Cindy Esposito, Tony Blackstone and Frank Jamison.

I then called to let them know what I sent.

Within 30 minutes, the responses came in.

"This is outstanding," replied Tony.

"Keep carrying the big stick. I'll send this to county sheriffs," advised Frank.

"This will complement the state task force. Will run it by MAGLOCLEN, state people," added JT.

"Terrific, terrific. Let's update the department. Thanks for including me Cal. You have my support," Cindy wrote back.

Dail and Shriver said in a group email: "More insightful thinking. Outside the box thinking. Can we send this to Trucks Stops America corporate?"

I felt validated.

I also realized something else – Conrad Williams made me feel physically ill.

———

As a courtesy to Cindy Esposito, I met with her and attorney Stu Levin for beers at Costello's around the end of October.

"Cal, this is just an informal conversation," Levin said. "We don't want to use you as a witness, we just want to get some information on Williams – unless you want to?"

"Not really," I said. "You want deep background."

Levin looked at me surprised and enthusiastically replied, "Yeah, yeah, that's a good way to put it."

Esposito trusted me because she liked my honesty. I liked her because she did her job, didn't try to be in Williams' club and wanted to make a difference.

Esposito told me the disparaging comments the chief and his buddies made.

"Cal, has Williams verbally harassed you?" Esposito asked.

"Not the way he has with you," I said.

"Of course not. Other ways?"

I inhaled and exhaled deeply.

"Yes. I've tried to give him different ideas on how to handle this serial killer case and he not only has ignored me but has been highly critical."

"Do you think he views you as a threat?"

"It's possible. His criticism often is personal. I reached out to an attorney and I talked about doing what you're thinking. Have you heard about intentional infliction of emotional distress?"

"I have," Levin said. "Illinois case a few years ago. Cal, this is helpful. Let me ask you, are his guys better or worse than him?"

"Get them together and it's gas on a fire. They feed off of each other. And they've covered shit up."

"Such as?"

"Well, a couple of years ago, Lt. Matthew France beat the shit out of Enzo Corporelli."

"Enrico Corporelli's kid?"

"Yeah. Really messed him up. Caught him with a stereo system and some drugs. Enzo talked about his rights and his old man, they cuffed him, then France went to town."

"You were there?"

"Yeah."

"Cal, that's a tough spot to be in," Esposito said. "I've heard stories of other things those guys do to keep the lid on the can."

"Cal, you need a refill?" Levin offered.

"No," I said. "I think I've said enough."

Esposito grabbed my arm as I left, and said, "Cal this means a lot. I'm young, but I'll be in your corner."

Levin turned to Esposito.

"Cindy, my old man got Enrico Corporelli off on a racketeering charge."

"Yeah?"

"I have an idea."

____

Lt. Matthew France was watching the Chicago Bears game against the Detroit Lions the day before Halloween when his phone rang.

"Who's this?" he answered with an attitude.

"Attorney Stu Levin," he said, overhearing the announcers. "Sorry to bother your game. Are the Bears going to win?"

"How the hell do I know?" France said. "But it's the fourth quarter and I need …"

"This won't take long. I need to meet with you, Monday."

"About what?"

"Enzo Corporelli."

"Talk to our police lawyer."

"And maybe I'll talk to his dad Enrico. He knows our family well."

"What time?"

"7 a.m. I know you don't want to miss any work."

____

France came alone on a cool, fall Halloween's Day. As soon as he arrived, Levin invited him into his office. Assistant Jim Brewer also sat in on the meeting.

"Your bodyguard?" France said.

"If he needs to be," Levin said, looking him in the eye. "I have a tape to play for you."

As France heard Williams, himself and co-workers insulting Cindy Esposito behind her back, his facial expression turned from anger to vulnerability.

"Where did you, you, you get that?" he stammered.

"Oh, there's more," Levin said. "We have your fingerprints on a nasty note you put on a newspaper clipping on the police department bulletin board."

"Esposito, that, that, that," France said.

"Watch it," Brewer said.

"Here's the deal," Levin said. "Agree to testify against Williams. To be honest, if he and his legal team are wise, they'll settle out of court. We have so much shit on him, and you and the department that he'll be lucky to be a crossing guard if this goes public."

"What if I don't sign your agreement?" France said indignantly.

"Then I make that call to Enrico Corporelli. See, here's the thing. You beat Enzo so badly, he suffered memory loss. He had a hard time remembering who beat him. His father had such high hopes for him; but the two hardly have talked since that night. His father, see, cries when he visits him. But Enzo's memory is getting better. He's been in therapy and I've been told he remembers a cop beating him. All I have to do is point him in the right direction. Capiche?"

France got up quickly. "You prick. You son of a …"

He took a step toward Levin but Brewer caught him with a right to the midsection then belted him in his neck and lip for good measure.

"Sign the paper Matthew," Levin said. "Or Jim here calls a couple of friends and takes you uptown."

Spitting blood, France whispers, "Give me the paper."

I've had many memorable Halloweens at the funeral home, but after hearing what took place, this fancy lawyering shot to the top of the list of favorite Halloween tales.

———————

Stu Levin met with Sal Hershkowitz, Oldsmar's legal counsel, for lunch the following January. Hershkowitz is considered one of the Midwest's top attorneys. His connections are vast. He kept the mob at arm's length yet he seemed to know everything going on around town.

"Sal, lunch is on me," Levin said. "That New Year's Eve party was so good. Edith and I loved it. Thank you so much for inviting us again."

"Glad you enjoyed it," Sal said. "However, I'm sure there's another reason you wanted to have lunch."

Levin paused. "My dad respects you highly and so do I," he said. "You and Dad are the best mentors I could have. I can't tell you ..."

"Spit it out Stuart."

"I'm representing a client who wants to sue the police department."

"Cindy Esposito. I thought we'd have a conversation about this soon."

A bit shocked his mentor knew of this situation, Levin continued, "Yes, we have a taped conversation of police officers mocking her."

"Which is inadmissible in the state of Illinois. Two-party recordings must be approved of by both parties. I can assume Conrad Williams didn't approve the recording."

"You're right. But, there's more."

"I'm sure there is."

Levin paused.

"What else do you have, Stuart?"

"Respectfully, I'd rather save that for a meeting."

"A meeting?"

"Me, my client and my staff; and you, Mr. Williams and your staff."

"Leave Jim Brewer at home. Bad look."

"All right. When would you like …"

Hershkowitz waved down a waiter with his hand, stopping Levin mid-question.

The waiter brought over a phone and the attorney plugged the phone's cord into a jack.

"That's why I always have this table," he told Levin.

Hershkowitz dialed a number and asked for Williams.

"Conrad, Sal here. Do you have five minutes right now?"

"What's this about?"

"There's a lawsuit coming your way. Looks serious. Got you sexually harassing a woman. Cindy Esposito and her attorney want to meet with you in two days."

"Can't you stall them?"

"No. If we don't meet with them in two days, they'll go to the media. They believe they have a strong case."

"Sexual harassment. They can't win that."

"Oh, I beg to differ Conrad. Remember Anita Hill and Clarence Thomas?"

Silence.

"Three years ago, Hill was a law professor who claimed Thomas, a supreme court nominee, sexually harassed her. Thomas was nominated to the court but since then, sexual harassment cases have more than doubled. Most plaintiffs win these cases."

More silence.

"Will 2 p.m. work, Conrad? You can only golf at an indoor range at this time of the year."

"Yes."

"All right, Conrad, when are you free to chat?"

While Hershkowitz went over the details with his client,

Levin realized his mentor had made things easy for him, almost too easy.

"Sal, I don't know what to ..."

"Son, listen to me closely," Sal interrupted him again. "You didn't come in here with guns blazing. You were respectful, I appreciate that. In return, I saved you the unpleasantness of threats and legal maneuvering. Lawyering doesn't have to be in the gutter. But two days from now, you better come into our meeting strong and with admissible evidence or I will tear your argument apart. You understand, that if this goes to court or the Oldsmar Police Department has to reach a settlement, Conrad Williams likely will lose his job?"

"Yes, I do, sir."

Levin paid the bill and gave a generous tip. As they walked out of the restaurant, he asked his mentor, "Can I be frank?"

Hershkowitz looked at him and nodded slightly.

"I don't sense you respect Williams."

Hershkowitz looked away.

"Those who forget history are condemned to repeat it."

———————

Two days later, an angry Cindy Esposito arrived at the back door of the Oldsmar Police Department with Stu Levin and two members of his staff where they walked upstairs to a seldom used meeting room.

Sal Hershkowitz, Conrad Williams and internal affairs officials were seated and impatiently waiting.

Internal Affairs Officer Edward Nettles cut to the chase.

"Why are you here?" he asked.

"First of all, thanks for agreeing to meet with us," Levin said. "We're here to address Miss Esposito's serious charges against the Oldsmar Police Department."

Esposito's stare matched Williams' and he looked away.

"I would like to play a tape," Levin said.

Williams shifted in his chair slightly.

Internal affairs officials looked at him briefly as if to say, "You lied to us."

"Dramatic but inadmissible," Hershkowitz said sternly as soon as the recording stopped.

"That is true," Levin said. "But one of the persons who was there has signed a confession that these words were said and that he'll take the witness stand to say as much."

"Bullshit," Williams said. Hershkowitz then immediately put his left arm on Williams' right shoulder to silently muzzle his client.

Ignoring him, Levin said, "I've also subpoenaed other witnesses. You've said some interesting things over the years. We've collected some memos you've written. You don't treat your employees well."

"Goddamn Raven," Williams said.

Esposito interjected, "No, he's not on the list. But I sure as hell wish he was, based on your response."

"And there's one other thing. This," said Levin as he slid a photo to Hershkowitz, which showed the newspaper clipping glued to the piece of paper and "Queen Bitch" written.

"I didn't write that," Williams said.

"Your fingerprints are on it. We have had them analyzed by the Illinois' FBI. Those are your prints. Yours and ..."

"That's enough," Williams said defiantly. "You cocksucker. Fucking son of a bitch."

Hershkowitz matter of factly stated, "We're through here, everyone."

Esposito, Levin and team left with her staring at Williams until they broke eye contact as she cleared the doorway.

"You fucking lied to us!" Nettles yelled after he closed the door. "You fucking lied to our faces!"

Hershkowitz waved both hands up and down, trying to get Nettles to lower his voice.

"I tried to get the city to sound proof this room," he said. "My guess is, they all heard what you said, Edward."

Terry McClure of internal affairs added, "Conrad you didn't even lie to our faces. You had your head buried in your golf magazine. How's that handicap looking now?"

"Fuck you!" Williams shot back. "And fuck you counselor. That was a goddamn ambush."

Hershkowitz slammed his fist on the table.

"There's one person in here who messed up and that's you, Conrad," he said. "You're the one who calls the women cutie and sweetie. Not good. You're the one who sexually harassed a young woman who wanted to work for the force. Not good. You're the one who put his hands on a piece of paper and gave them evidence to prosecute. Idiot. You're the one who refused to talk with internal affairs, who could've helped you out of this mess. And now that witnesses have been subpoenaed, these fine men can't talk with them because that would be tampering with an investigation. In other words, you're fucked. You might as well open your asshole and insert your mouth."

The room went silent, partly to ponder the visual.

"You have two options, Conrad," Hershkowitz said as he authoritatively walked his client through what's next. "Option A. Fight this thing, air all the department's dirty laundry and then we'll see what else Levin's investigators come up with. And Levin's dad's investigators. They're pretty good, too. And don't forget, that tape is inadmissible in court but can be used by newspapers. They play by different rules. TV can play that tape three times a day for weeks. Wanna lose in the court of public opinion?"

Hershkowitz stopped to see if Williams listened and comprehended what he just said.

He then continued, "And by the time this plays out, maybe Raven decides to take the stand himself. And chances are, Levin's informant either beat someone up, stole something or broke some kind of law that makes him real vulnerable. You want that public? Moles in your department? Loyal men? You might as well pack your bags, Conrad."

"All of this because I made a few jokes," snapped Williams, still trying to defend his position. "It was just locker room humor. Or police shenanigans. Whatever you want to call it."

"I'm not finished, Conrad," Hershkowitz snapped back.

He paused, shook his head in disgust, took a deep breath and explained Option B.

"The other option is to settle," Hershkowitz explained. "The going rate for these things is $500,000. Maybe we get them to agree to half. Get them to sign a non-disclosure agreement. She can't speak with the media, she can't play the tape, she can't even talk to her parents about this."

Hershkowitz thanked the internal affairs officers and asked them to leave.

He then walked around the room to see if Williams would speak up and offer anything of value. He didn't.

"Conrad, I don't think you have a choice," Hershkowitz said, lowering his tone.

"Fuck!!!!" Williams shouted.

"Here's one other thing to keep in mind. If you go to court and win, you still lose your department, especially those who go on the stand. If you go to court and lose, you probably will not only get fired but lose your pension. But if you settle, maybe this is kept quiet. If you resign, you can get a nice severance."

Williams said quietly, "Sounds like a lose, lose, lose."

"Could be worse," Hershkowitz said. "You could have a contract out on you because you beat up a mob guy's kid."

CHAPTER 14

The Forensic Body Institute

**"You wouldn't believe how
many times we've heard that one."**

– An anthropologist replying to Cal Raven
when he said people are dying to get
into The Forensic Body Institute.

A couple of years earlier, while attending a conference in Rochester, N.Y., I met Terry Shannon, a detective in Knoxville, Tenn.

He invited me numerous times to visit, telling me how great the Smoky Mountains are. Then he mentioned The Forensic Body Institute.

Jan wanted to see the Smoky Mountains. I wanted to see The Forensic Body Institute. Shannon took us to both places.

Also called The Forensic Anthropology Center, The Forensic Body Institute is a closed research facility at Cambridge University in Ollieville, Tennessee. If you don't work there, you need an invitation. It's located on a two-and-a-half acre wooded plot but visitors, like myself, aren't authorized to walk in many of the areas. Despite the dead bodies, they want to keep the grounds as sterile as possible.

It has earned an international reputation for research on human decomposition. More than 2,000 people have donated themselves – when dead, of course – to the school's Donated Skeletal Collection. There are more than 4,000 registered future donors. God bless 'em.

When I joked that people are dying to get in here, they rolled their eyes a bit while chuckling half-heartedly. "You wouldn't believe how many times we've heard that one," one anthropologist said.

At The Forensic Body Institute, human remains are left outside where they're exposed to rain, sun, cold, wind and nature. Some bodies are covered with plastic or clothing, some are naked, some are buried, some hang from scaffolds or are in the trunks of cars.

The bodies are studied as they putrefy or decay. We also talked about the four stages of death – pallor mortis, algor mortis, rigor mortis and livor mortis:

Pallor mortis: The first change in a body that occurs in a dead body is increased paleness in the face and other body parts. That's because blood no longer is circulating.

Algor mortis: Within seconds of death, brain cells also die, and the heart stops pumping blood. Without the brain and the blood distributing heat, the corpse eventually starts to match the temperature of its surrounding environment.

Rigor mortis: The most commonly known of the four, a corpse will go floppy. All the muscles will become relaxed and limp, but the whole body will stiffen after a few hours.

Livor mortis: The final stage of death, when the heart stops beating. Blood submits to gravity. If the body is on the ground, blood collects in the parts that are touching the ground.

As I walked with Shannon and University of Cambridge professors and students, I noticed roped off areas around the bodies so they wouldn't be contaminated. They explained how to correctly map and recover remains from a surface and a burial site while they slightly moved bodies to see what bugs they may have killed or what larva had started to develop under and on them.

"That helps show us how long the body has been here," a student explained.

The institute also has a state-of-the-art scientific research facility, which includes forensic odontology — applying dental science to the identification of remains — and how to best manage the recovery of remains from fire scenes.

They invited me to return in June when they welcome law enforcement officials from around the country to take part in summer training.

I took detailed notes and asked a lot of questions. My instincts kicked in again and told me I just may have to put these skills to use.

———

Conrad Williams brought coffee and egg, ham and cheese sandwiches to Travis Simoneau at his insurance office before he opened.

Their friendship went back to grade school where they played sports together.

Shortly after Williams joined the force, he protected his buddy from getting speeding tickets – as well as the time Simoueau accidentally hit and killed an elderly farmer on a back road.

In return, Simoneau secured a spot on the board of trustees. He helped get a friend the second of the three spots on the board; and they did work behind the scenes to get Williams the chief's job. It meant an extra $25,000 a year in pay.

When Simoneau and his friend saw their terms end, that left Williams vulnerable.

"Doesn't look good, CW," Simoneau said. "Citizens and the new board aren't happy, local county sheriffs aren't happy, hell even the attorney general isn't happy."

Williams sat quietly. "What should I do?" he said.

"You said the FBI is coming in soon? The AG has asked for their help. Plus, they can tie in a couple of those out-of-state deaths and make it a federal issue.

"Buddy, when the FBI comes in, offer your full support. Show them everything you have."

"Everything? All we have is what Raven has; and some of that we don't have access to because the truck stop owners have them."

"That's fine, get what you can. In the meantime, start doing your own investigating with your guys. Don't let the FBI or anyone else on your staff know what you're doing. There will be another murder, it's inevitable. When that happens, be on top of it. Follow every lead. Catch the killer. Plant evidence on him, do whatever you need to in order to nail a guy. Get the glory and keep your job."

"So you think I should break the law?"

"Drastic times, drastic measures," Simoneau replied. "This isn't your first rodeo with tilting the scales of justice.

"And I tell you what. You make that collar, we can do TV ads. The man who caught the serial killer has home improvement tips to stay safe."

Meanwhile, Bart Gein just disposed of his latest victim, at Richard's request. He had wiped off the tire buddy after hitting his victim repeatedly before dumping her at a rest stop.

Gein took his T-shirt off, used it to wipe his face and threw it in his laundry bag. He noticed that strangling victims first in the truck left a mess so he killed them outside the truck. He also didn't want them kicking out a window. He also placed his rope in his laundry bag.

On this night, luck was with him. A state trooper pulled him over.

Gein didn't panic. Part of him believed the state trooper would find nothing on him; but part of him felt like if he was caught, God was telling him the gig was up.

"Sir, did you know your back tail light is out?" the trooper asked.

"No I didn't, officer," Gein said. "I can stop at the next exit and get it taken care of."

"Sir, would you mind opening the back of your reefer unit?"

Gein hesitated for just a second. "Sure officer," he said. "Any reason why?"

"If your light is out, maybe your reefer unit isn't working."

Gein knew the trooper made that up, but he didn't get in an argument.

After he opened the back, the trooper – working outside his lane – asked if he could look around. Gein agreed.

The trooper turned on his flashlight and looked in every corner, around every carton. Then he jumped off the rig.

"I caught a killer a few months back doing this," he said. "My boss said if the spirit moved me, I should keep checking. Never know."

"Thanks for keeping us safe, trooper."

Gein started his truck. While driving down the road, he rubbed his shaggy hair and a piece of flesh, dislodged from his victim's body, fell out and landed on his jeans. He was really lucky.

The sequence of events had Gein thinking he should avoid keeping bodies in his reefer unit any more than a few hours.

———————

Jan and I broke up the trip coming back, covering the first 400 miles before stopping at a hotel, then getting up early the next morning to finish the trip.

Early risers, we got on the road about 5:30 in the morning after breakfast. Thank goodness for The Pancake Hut. After we passed the Richland County line, I stopped at a rest area exit for a bathroom break.

As I walked out of the bathroom, I saw a county coroner's car parked in a far corner of the lot. The sun started to spread its wings and bathe the area in light. It was just a little bit before 8 a.m. Jan and I drove over where we met Jeff Bingham, the county coroner. I asked Jan to stay in the car.

"Jeff, you need any help?" I asked.

Bingham had just roped off the area.

"Cal, good seeing you," Bingham answered. "We have our next victim. I came in to work early and took the call myself. I haven't called it in yet."

"Why's that?"

"First, I wanted to see if there's a body. Second, I didn't want cops trampling over the crime scene. Third, I heard the FBI is entering the picture and I wanted to give them a clean report."

He paused.

"Cal, can you take some photos, first outside the tape, then inside? The camera is in the car."

With there being a light rain the night before and a muddy track on the grass, I took photos of those as well.

The problem? There was more than one truck track.

The body of a female, nude from the waist down except for the high-heeled shoes, was dropped recklessly on the edge of the cement parking lot like someone would discard a barstool. The body just rolled down a bit before landing sideways with her back to a medium-sized tree.

While I took photos, Bingham did a body temperature check via rectal thermometry, which is taking a thermometer and inserting it in a person's anus. This is the most accurate way to find the body temperature and also get an idea of how long the body has been dead.

"Cal, I have 86.5 degrees," Bingham reported. "This body hasn't been here long."

With the body having a normal temperature of 98.6 degrees, this is a 12-degree drop.

"A dead body drops in temperature about one-and-a-half degrees an hour," Bingham said. "That means …"

"About 8 hours," I said.

"Yeah, that sounds right," Bingham confirmed.

As Bingham looked around the area for evidence, I treaded lightly while taking photos from different angles. When I focused on the eyes, I saw something that looked like gelatin. My training in Tennessee taught me that some insects would lay larva on bodies minutes after they died.

"Jeff, do you see something around the victim's eyes? Something gelatinous?"

"Yes, that looks like a fly larva. How did you notice that?"

"I just came back from The Body Institute."

"The what?"

"It's a forensic anthropology center. In Tennessee. They use a fly's larva to help determine cause of death. Its full name is The Forensic Body Institute. You'd find it fascinating, Jeff."

"Usually, most people visit Tennessee to see the Smoky Mountains. Cal, you notice pallor mortis and rigor mortis have set in?"

"How about livor mortis?"

"Yeah, looks like the blood has started to settle in her right hand, right side of her face and right ankle."

Bingham then called it in. That gave me time to leave before being sighted. Didn't want to be accused of interfering with an investigation.

"I won't say anything," Bingham said.

As I drove away with Jan and headed home, I could see and hear two Oldsmar squad cars on the other side of the highway racing toward what I assumed to be the rest stop.

———

It took a week for police to identify the victim – Pamela Amy Connors.

It took another week for word to leak out that the FBI was getting involved.

During that time, Chief Conrad Williams and his guys started acting like cops, best they knew how. But this isn't a profession you can turn on and off like water, a light bulb or your car.

You have to have investigative skills, you have to have informants, you have to know how to communicate, you have to have instincts and you have to stay current with the technology.

When some of Williams' men joined Bingham at the crime scene, they trampled inside and outside the ropes, completely missed the truck wheel marks, dropped the body, then refused to sign papers saying they participated. That pissed Bingham off.

They then went to the 105 Truck Stop – during the day – and badgered hard-working truckers with threats of putting them in jail if they didn't provide information.

After calling their owners, the owners' lawyers called the Oldsmar Police Department. The pissed-off truckers then got on their CBs and warned of smokies (police cars) and polar bears (white, unmarked police cars) that they'd likely patrol the truck stop the next few nights. Boogers, coin-operated beavers, commercial company, lot lizards and sleeper leapers also were warned.

As a result, Williams and his crew arrived at a near-empty truck stop for the next few nights. Even the 44 Magnum Lounge had closed signs.

The furious owners got so upset they charged the cops for coffee and donuts.

"You scared all our good truckers away," Jim Dail said.

When three of Williams' officers came up – guns drawn – on a trucker dozing in his sleeper, he awoke, then begged them not to shoot.

"I'm a suicide jockey," he said.

"What's that?" they said, not having read the CB manual I gave them.

"Explosives, man," he said. "You'll get us all fried."

This time, the cops nearly shit in their pants.

Meanwhile, I reached out to my friends in Tennessee while quietly working with Bingham.

I sent them photos of the crime scene along with the report Bingham wrote.

"Cal, the larva in the eyes are from a blowfly," said Gerald Wichlasz, a forensic entomologist. "The fact that there are no eggs on the body, along with the 86.5 degree temperature when found, leads me to believe that the body was dropped between 12 a.m. and 12:30 a.m."

After Bingham added the notes to his report, he made copies and put them in an envelope.

"I'll give a copy to the FBI first," Bingham said. "Williams' guys fucked up my crime scene."

———

Jan, the kids and I had just sat down to eat when I received a call.

"Mr. Callaghan Raven?" the voice on the other end said.

"Yes, who am I speaking to?"

"Mr. Raven, this is Jeff Coffey with the FBI. Can we talk?"

"Yes," I said.

A second later, the doorbell rang. When I opened the door, Jeff Coffey held a cell phone. The FBI always had the most new-fangled gadgets.

"Sorry to disturb," Coffey said. "Can we come in?"

His partner Kent Hubred joined us and they apologized for interrupting our dinner.

"We're having a press conference at the Oldsmar Police Department tomorrow and we've been told you would be the best person to speak with," Coffey said.

After I gave them an overview of what I learned, Hubred said, "Agent Coffey and I believe there's a serial killer. The FBI believes there's a serial killer. I think Conrad Williams finally believes it, too."

"His ass is on the griddle," Coffey said. "How aware is he of what you know?"

"If he asked ..."

"Don't need to say anything more. Any new developments?"

"Well, Jeff Bingham, the county coroner, has information on the last victim."

"How do you know that?"

"I was with him when we received some information from The Forensic Anthropology Center in Ollieville."

"The Body Institute," Coffey confirmed.

I nodded.

"We work with them all the time. Outstanding."

Hubred added, "Any other thoughts?"

"I think you men should go out and talk to the prostitutes."

Silence.

"Guys, if you want to find out what's happening, you have to go to the sources. I've spoken with them and they're starting to open up."

Coffey and Hubred looked at each other. As if a light bulb went off in their heads, they turned to me and asked, "Can you take us out there?"

"Yeah," I said. "But we'll have to go to the truck stop in Indiana."

"Why?"

"I was told Williams and his guys scared them away from the 105 Truck Stop."

Coffey and Hubred shook their heads.

"FUBAR," they said in unison. "Can we meet you there at midnight?"

———

Outside of the fencing and the 44 Magnum Lounge, the Hoosier Truck Stop looked almost exactly like the 105. Talk about cookie cutter designs.

I told the FBI guys to meet me in the back parking lot by the restaurant. Dressed in their suits and ties, I quickly said, "Guys, c'mon. First of all, lose the ties."

Then I mussed up their hair, took off their ties, unbuttoned the first button on their shirts and crinkled them. "That's better," I said. "Otherwise, you'll scare them away. Have any boots?"

When they nodded, I said, "Put them on."

As we approached the trucks, I noticed some familiar faces. I raised my hands and said, "Ladies, we come in peace. These guys are from the FBI. They're going to get involved in the murders around here."

"Where's the ties?" one asked.

"We kept them in the car," Coffey said.

"Good, you'll scare the other ladies away."

As the ladies spoke, a man I hadn't heard of before kept being mentioned.

No name. But the more they spoke, the bigger he got.

"He must have been 250 pounds," one said.

"I'd guess 280 pounds," another said.

"Three bills, at least," guessed another.

"He's gotta be 325, maybe 350," the last girl said.

They never serviced him. He came around every few months, then seemed to disappear, as if a man that big could disappear.

The problem was, they couldn't give a good description because some mentioned a clean-cut man and others mentioned a disheveled man. Both times he wore a hoodie; and when we spoke to the owners and employees, nobody recognized him.

Same with Dail, Shriver and their staff.

"Maybe it's nothing," they said.

"Maybe," I said. "I've never heard of a man with that description before."

———————

Chief Williams and his guys zeroed in on a suspect in the killing of Tanya Maria Crookston, victim No. 10.

They scanned lists of state-wide truckers with criminal histories. Their search zoned in on a man – Anthony Volpiano, 6-foot-3, 255 pounds. Former high school and college football player.

They prepared their own profile. Divorced. Assault charge. Breaking and entering charge. Handgun owner. Truck driver for 15 years. One of the chiefs' guys obtained records of Volpiano's trucking history through a friend of his who worked for the man's company, 18-Wheel Trucking. The list included a lot of overnight stays for his truck at the 105.

"Sounds like a violent guy," Williams said.

"Oh yeah," Lt. Matthew France said. "I remember him in high school football, he used to get penalized all of the time. Went to Livingston State but rarely got off the bench. Married a knockout but they split up. Likes to go to the gun range. Dad died. Brother is a grease monkey."

"Normal redneck," Williams said.

"I saved the best for last," France said. "He was arrested for solicitation."

"Bingo," Williams said.

"He'll be coming through tomorrow night," Lt. Jordan Kelly said.

———

In their press conference to the media, FBI officials extolled their virtues, talked about leads they already developed and gave citizens numbers to contact if they had information.

Chief Williams and his guys stood to the right of the podium, nodding their heads regularly. Other FBI agents, including Coffey and Hubred, stood to the left.

I stood with other cops, media and concerned citizens in the audience.

When Chief Williams came to the podium, he spoke briefly.

"We are honored to work with the FBI in whatever capacity they need," Williams said. "Our collaboration will lead to results. Thank you."

He and his guys then smiled widely, shook hands with FBI agents and tried to initiate a conversation. The agents looked as if they wanted to escape. Coffey and Hubred followed me as I left the press conference.

"Cal, thanks for your help," Coffey said. "The information from Bingham and your introduction to the prostitutes and background information are more than the chief and his men have given us."

"Williams doesn't know your role in this," Hubred said. "But the bureau in D.C. does. Based on what you said, we thought that would be better."

I nodded.

I started to get that feeling in my gut of me having to tip toe around my chief.

Time for a call to Dr. Farnsworth.

CHAPTER 15

Out Of Their Depth

**"A few more minutes and
he might have confessed to
the Kennedy Assassination."**

– FBI Agent Kent Hubred
to partner Jeff Coffey

Anthony Volpiano arrived at the 105 Truck Stop around 6 p.m. on a warm Saturday night in mid May. Summer had arrived.

He greeted his mother Theresa – in a wheelchair after a minor stroke – and brother Tommy for an evening meal. All you can eat, $7.99.

Theresa showed a big smile when her son told her he'd spend more time with her and use his education degree to teach high school history while he'd continue to assist the football team, now full time. Tommy had fixed up a 1986 Chevy Suburban, which he bought in a car auction.

Oldsmar police officers, with Conrad Williams behind at a safe distance, interrupted the conversation to tell Anthony Volpiano he was under arrest for the death of Tonya Maria Crookston.

With hands on their revolvers, they shocked Theresa Volpiano who collapsed in her chair. When her son rose to attend to her, officers tackled him, handcuffed him behind his back and took his truck keys.

As officers read him his rights, Volpiano turned to his brother and said, "Call Stu Levin."

Williams then moved in and said, "We're taking your sorry ass to the Richland County Jail."

"Guys, you're making a terrible mistake," Volpiano said. "I just got …"

"Don't want to hear it," Williams interrupted in a loud voice, drowning him out. "Get him up and out of here."

As they left the diner, TV and newspaper reporters – tipped off by Williams' men – greeted them as they made the perp walk. Williams, front and center, held Volpiano's arm and put him in a squad car. Meanwhile, his lieutenants went to Volpiano's truck. They opened the back and threw in soiled women's underwear and ripped bras while putting the victim's blood on a tire thumper.

"We received a tip that led us to an arrest tonight of Anthony Volpiano," Williams said, stepping into the bright camera lights to address the assembled media. "A word of thanks to our fine officers who followed those leads and discovered that Mr. Volpiano had just arrived at this diner."

Williams didn't mention a word about the FBI's cooperation.

"Chief, is this man a person of interest?" TV reporter Jamie Conom asked.

"He's more than that," Williams said. "He may be linked to a number of deaths."

"Chief, do you realize Volpiano is highly respected in the community and one of his players said he was the best coach he's ever had?"

"And what player said that?" Williams snapped.

"Your son David," the reporter said.

As a couple of people gasped, Williams gave the reporter a cold stare. He and his son had been estranged after Williams had divorced his wife.

"A clever ploy. That's all," Williams fired back, keeping his composure as he fended off "planted" questions.

FBI officers Coffey and Hubred, tipped by the cops as well, arrived in plain clothes and watched with a high level of skepticism. They also kept an eye on Williams' men.

"This looks staged," Coffey said. "Let's call Raven."

———

Two days after Volpiano's arrest, I met with Dr. Farnsworth in his office. I had been doing well, keeping busy, traveling to Tennessee, working with the FBI and keeping my distance from Williams. But when Coffey and Hubred said they told their bosses of the work I did rather than Williams, it really bothered me. I shouldn't have to be working behind the chief's back; and we should all be working together.

"Doc, I just really have a tough time working with Williams," I said. "He's hurting my chance at advancement. He's hurting my chance to excel personally while helping the force and community. He's also taking money out of my family's pocket."

Dr. Farnsworth asked quite a few questions, some of which I didn't understand why he asked. It almost seemed like he had something on his mind.

Finally, he looked around, which seemed strange, then moved over and sat on a chair close to me, like the room was bugged.

"I'm going to tell you a couple of things but you can never ask me why," instructed Farnsworth, almost asking for permission for what he was going to say. "If you do, I will no longer be able to have you as a patient. Understand?"

I nodded and shook his hand.

"OK. I have been doing this for 27 years. I know a lot of people. I know a lot of cops. And I know how the human mind works. About the time you started as an officer, Williams' chief demoted him. Caught him working handyman jobs during work hours."

He paused, then continued, "But an insurance guy – who Williams has known since they were kids – became a trustee and he brought on a banker who became the second trustee. The insurance guy and banker worked on home loans and home improvement deals together. They also worked behind the scenes with Williams' father to help him advance in his career."

Dr. Farnsworth stopped as he saw my face turning red and getting angry. Inside, I was boiling over like a pot left on the stove too long. But I was trying to remain calm.

"Should I stop?"

"No," I quickly said. "Tell me there's a happy ending."

"There is, I think. The arrest of Volpiano isn't going to stick. Planted evidence. The kid's also had a tough run. He's actually a good man – and a helluva football coach and leader of young men."

Now I leaned in toward Dr. Farnsworth.

"This between us?" I asked.

He hesitated but nodded in agreement.

"Yesterday, the FBI called," I informed him. "Said the arrest is sketchy. Saw a couple of Williams' guys coming back from Volpiano's truck. I told them the victim was dumped almost immediately after being killed. Rigor mortis hadn't set in. Based on her body temperature when found, she was killed around midnight. Volpiano was two states away at that time."

"How do you know?"

"You said no questions."

"Right, right. This is going to be embarrassing for the chief. He can't survive this. He has no support from law enforcement, no support from the community and there are new trustees. Cal, I think your days with Williams will be over soon."

The upset stomach I came in with disappeared.

"Doc, you got anything to drink?"

"Water, tea and soda Cal."

———

After talking to me and observing Williams' men, Coffey and Hubred told their bosses they'd be doing a joint federal investigation with state officials on the 10th victim. When Williams objected, Coffey said, "The moment you arrested Volpiano coming from another state, it also became our business."

Williams rounded up the men and told them, "Tell them you're not talking."

Lt. Matthew France added, "Say you're taking the fifth."

———

When Coffey and Hubred asked me which of Williams' men seemed most vulnerable to talk, you bet, I didn't hesitate.

"Dom Coosimano," I said. "They call him Dum. Because he's, you know."

"Got it," Hubred said.

Coffey called Coosimano and asked him to meet them at 2411 Champagne Lane. When he arrived at the Oldsmar Lodge a few miles outside of town, Coffey met him outside. He wore a golf shirt and khakis.

"C'mon in," he said. "We just got back from a few meetings and freshened up."

Coffey introduced him to Hubred. "Dom, it's Happy Hour right now. You want something to eat or drink? It's free."

"I take the fifth," Coosimano said nervously.

"Dom, this really isn't a formal investigation," Coffey said. "Can I get you a beer?"

"Scotch and water, on the rocks. But I'm still taking the fifth."

While Coffey went to get his drink, Hubred said, "Yeah, this is more like getting background information. Do you understand?"

"I take the fifth. Can I get some snacks?"

Hubred motioned to Coffey and he came back with his drink and nuts.

"Want to find a spot and watch the Bulls game?"

"Yeah, but I want the fifth."

They moved to seats that had a TV right in front of them.

"Isn't Jordan looking great in his comeback?" Hubred said.

"He is," Coosimano said, moving his right fingers as if counting them. "But I'm still taking the fifth."

Picking up on the clue and remembering what I told them, Coffey asked, "Dom, how long have you been a police officer?"

Going quiet for a few seconds, Coosimano looked down, then looked up at the men, and answered in the form of a question like a drunken contestant on Jeopardy, "That's five isn't it?"

Coffey put his right hand on Hubred's leg as if to say, "Don't say a word. Follow my lead."

"Yeah, Dom, that's five. How long you been a cop?"

Dom proceeded to tell the men he had been a cop for 15 years and got a score of 91 on his academy test because he had paid his cousin 91 bucks to fix his score.

"Can't be too smart, you know," he said as he ordered another free scotch.

"No, no, can't do that," Coffey said.

After having two more scotches, Hubred told the waiter to put in more scotch and less water while giving him a $20 tip. By this point, Coosimano really started loosening his lips. He said that Williams realized he needed a big bust to save his job and that he needed to look like the hero.

Then he told of his favorite bust – handcuffing a hooker, then letting her go after getting a blow job.

Coffey and Hubred laughed with him. Then Coffey asked, "Dom, do you know what DNA means?"

"Do not answer?"

Again Coffey and Hubred started laughing with Coosimano, then they raised glasses.

After the laughter subsided, Coffey said, "Good one. DNA is using someone's spit or snot or pee or semen to identify them."

Hubred added, "Sort of like a finger print."

A confused Coosimano replied, "You mean they get fingerprints out of a person's pee?"

Hubred was ready to respond but Coffey grabbed him again, and added, "Yeah, Dom, it's technology from England. They've solved crimes with it. It's been used by the FBI for a few years."

Still perplexed, Dom said, "Doesn't the pee have to be black?"

Biting his tongue, Coffey said, "They've worked the bugs

out. Anyway, the stains on the underwear and bra?"

Coosimano motioned the men toward him, then provided them background information like they were old pals, before he blabbered on, "That's because Jordan Kelly went to the evidence vault and stole an old specimen that hadn't been destroyed. Then they drew blood from an unknowing prisoner in the county jail and transferred the blood, urine, semen and hair samples on the underwear and bra."

Hubred and Coffey nodded. "Anything else you want to add?"

"Well, I can tell you about the time my partner and I around Christmas ..."

"No, no, Dom, you've shared more than enough. We're going up to our rooms."

"All righty, then. Guys, one more thing. I take the fifth."

They all laughed. As they went their separate ways, Hubred turned to his partner and said, "A few more minutes and he might have confessed to the Kennedy Assassination."

Meanwhile, Stu Levin's assistant Jim Brewer, disguised in a beard and Hawaiian shirt, had placed a cassette recorder under their table. He knew what table Coffey and Hubred would use because they had rehearsed it before Coosimano arrived.

————————

Before bringing in other members of Williams' crew, Coffey and Hubred asked me if I knew anything about Volpiano.

"Yeah," I said. "Good kid. Married young, then found out his wife cheated on him. When he entered their home one night to retrieve some of his stuff, she called the cops, made up a story and they arrested him. His dad died at the same time and it sent him reeling. He drove a truck because he had a hard time concentrating."

"Yeah," Hubred said. "Apparently, Williams and his guys ran him through our network 10 days before arresting him."

I told them they needed to know two things about him.

"About 20 years ago, he got in a fight at a bar. Other guys were taunting his black teammate. He beat up a couple of guys and got put in county lockup for six months. Out early for good behavior. Second, the solicitation charge is bogus. Call this number, ask for Yvette Mendez."

When Coffey called, Mendez said, "He's a good guy. We didn't have sex. I came into his truck to get warm and we just talked. He gave me a few bucks because I didn't have many customers that night. When he gave me the money as I left the truck, a cop was right there and saw the exchange."

They brought in Williams' crew three at a time. They also brought Coosimano in for a second time just to show he wasn't the snitch. Coosimano started pleading the fifth again before one of the agents told him to relax and sit in the room with him for 45 minutes. "But if you tell me one story, I'm arresting your ass," he said.

The agents told the cops Volpiano couldn't be the killer because of his location when the victim died, essentially giving him an alibi. And secondly, because of the DNA on the underwear, which they bluffed on Coosimano, they also effectively used that tactic to leverage Williams' men. Williams' crew really screwed the pooch with their "sting operation" by planting evidence. And when challenged, they folded like a cheap suit.

When told they faced 15 years in the clink for taking part in a conspiracy, the men confirmed Williams designed the plan.

———

When Conrad Williams joined three FBI agents in a room, he wore his Sunday best but inside he must have been a wreck. The tables were flipped.

The head cop was now the perp.

When the FBI questioned him, his rants and paranoia resembled those of Humphrey Bogart in Caine Mutiny. He even started twirling golf balls in his hands.

Williams blamed county police, regional police, MAGLOCLEN and JT Hamilton, then the attorney general. He blamed the media, then citizens. He blamed the FBI, then saved his biggest beef for Raven.

"He wanted my job, but he's too reckless, he can't be controlled," he said. "He goes in guns blazing like Wyatt Earp. The man is going to get people killed. He catches bad guys but he's too ..."

"Brave?" Coffey asked, sharply interrupting.

"Yeah, brave and wild," Williams quickly agreed, thinking the FBI was buying his nonsense. "You gotta stay back, see how things play out. Don't take risks, assess the situation. Reassess the situation. Call for backup. Wait for backup. Don't be in too much of a hurry. Can't be too safe. And don't waste so much time on those whores. Whores and truckers. Truckers and whores. Put them in their corner and focus on more important shit. Don't get your hands dirty. Be smart. Play the odds."

After listening to Williams' riff, Coffey said, "Chief, I've been made aware that your department and officer Cindy Esposito agreed to a $250,000 settlement after disparaging things said about her by you and your staff. How safe was that? How smart was that? How dirty was that?"

Williams, fuming and turning red like a ripe tomato, said, "That's classified. How did you find out?"

Hubred said, "Because we're the fucking FBI and your department has a lot of moles."

With Volpiano's attorney Stu Levin threatening to go to the media with another lawsuit, the Oldsmar Police Department released Volpiano.

Williams had no comment but Levin met with Volpiano where he discussed the "negligent investigation" and considered settlement costs. Volpiano didn't want to sue but Levin reminded him he could've gone to jail for years on a bogus charge and that his mother may need round-the-clock care.

The township trustees moved up their monthly meeting to the next day.

Citizens started picketing by the town hall and police department as the community threw its support behind the football coach.

Friend and business partner Travis Simoneau visited Williams in a room at the police station where he said, "CW, I can't help you anymore. You can't fight this."

As he left, trustees Wayne Keller, Dennis Dahl and Jim Hole entered.

"Effective immediately, we are terminating your employment," Dahl said.

"I'm going to get an attorney," Williams said.

Hole, an attorney, replied, "You can but we will work with the FBI to arrest you and charge you with conspiracy to falsely imprison a man. This time, the media will see you in handcuffs as you leave the police station and get taken to the county jail."

Hole had quietly tried to stay neutral in his term as trustee, but finally spoke up as he couldn't in good conscience stand by and watch the law be contorted like origami, and by a police chief to boot. "You have embarrassed this community and this police department," said Hole in his authoritative courtroom voice. "I have personally seen you working side jobs when you're on the clock. That's fraud, theft and double dipping. I consider that to be your severance. By God, if you fight this, I'll work pro bono to build a case against you. I'll find out every job you worked while on the police's clock. Then I'll share the information with the IRS. You'll be audited for years. I'll put your guys on the stand. Have I made myself clear?"

"Yes," Williams said quietly.

"You are dismissed," he said. "Turn in your car keys, office keys and police credentials. Oh, and most importantly, turn in your badge and your gun."

After finding a fourth wife – Muriel Jacobs – who liked him, Bart Gein started to feel normal again. Richard's voice had been temporarily replaced by Muriel's. They had a cottage near the Tennessee mountains.

He took a break from trucking for three months after learning he had Type 2 diabetes. Muriel cared for him.

When Gein said he wanted to work in the shed, she said, "OK, dear."

When he said he wanted pork for dinner, she made the tastiest pork chops with okra, mixed vegetables and homemade apple sauce. No sugar added.

When he wanted to make love, she did so willingly.

And when he said he had to get back on the road again,

she said, "OK, dear," with a tear in her eyes.

But he barely put on 250 miles when Richard returned like a bad habit.

"I'm ready for action," he said.

Gein took off his wedding band but he wasn't in the mood for a teenager or a prostitute. After picking up a load in Georgia, he saw an older woman hitchhiking. He pulled over and put his wedding band in his pocket.

Immediately, the two started talking. She introduced herself as Beverly from Florida.

They chatted about sports for miles and miles but even when they stopped talking, the silence felt comfortable.

He wasn't even interested in having sex so he booked a room with two beds for a night in Pennsylvania before heading west to Illinois.

Richard's voice asserted itself.

"I think you can get lucky," he said.

Gein ignored the comment and took Beverly out for dinner, which he paid for. She thanked him. When they returned to the room, she said, "I want to show my personal appreciation."

Once on the bed, she took off her clothes and put on his T-shirt and underwear. They laughed and drank some wine and had sex. As Beverly rose, she glanced to her right and saw what appeared to be a ring on a table that Gein took out of his pocket. She walked to the table and picked it up.

"What's this?" she asked, agitated.

"That's my good-luck band," he said quickly.

"Bullshit!" she responded. "I can see words inside. It says, 'Love, always, Muriel.' Who's Muriel?"

Before Gein could respond, Beverly gave him a full-force slap against his face and left the room and the hotel. She started walking about 500 feet toward a couple of trucks parked in a lot. There were no lights in the area so she couldn't see if there were men in the trucks.

Suddenly an arm came across her face. Beverly was then hit in the back of the head with a tire buddy.

She fell to the ground, unconscious.

He then sat on her. Her right arm was grabbed and then bit but she didn't flinch.

When she woke up semi awake, Beverly couldn't tell if it was five seconds, five minutes or five hours later.

On her knees, she felt a sharp pain from behind.

"What, who?" she asked wearily.

Before she said another word, Beverly took another hit to the head, going to sleep forever.

For good measure, she was hit a half dozen more times, wrapped up in a sheet and put in a reefer unit.

Victim No. 12.

CHAPTER 16

New Leadership

**"The day is coming when you won't
have to speak softly anymore."**

– Frank Jamison to Cal Raven

While Sue Robinson walked her dog on an early, fall morning at Universal Fuel Station, she saw what she thought was a mannequin. When she brought her husband Fred over, he said, "Sue, that's a dead body."

They called the police, who came and completed their investigation. They found no identification. The woman, who seemed to be wearing men's clothes, became another victim of blunt force trauma.

The couple had stumbled upon another victim.

Charlie Valera, who I knew from my days pumping ethyl at Universal, called me.

"I'll be damned," I said.

While Oldsmar dispatchers didn't tell me, I easily could've gone over there because the police department was in chaos.

After Williams announced his resignation, the department became a classroom study on CYA – cover your ass.

Lieutenants, sergeants and captains jockeyed to show

they deserved to be chief. Many were in Williams' inner circle. They buddied up to search committee members and township trustees and tried to bribe them.

Meanwhile, other people who thought they were top candidates formed cliques, which backstabbed and dished out dirt on competitors. As a result, some Oldsmar officers' candidacies ended up being torpedoed by innuendo, loosely based facts and outright lies.

The inner-office strife basically told the search committee members three things:

1. Any individual hired within the department would find it impossible to unite everyone.

2. The backstabbing and infighting meant that some staff members also needed to go.

3. A national search needed to be done to find a chief who could offer a fresh perspective and overcome the cronyism and factions that had formed.

In addition, because of the nearly half million dollars in settlements, Oldsmar couldn't pay top dollar for a new chief.

Some of my co-workers and community leaders asked if I'd be interested in being chief. While flattered and enticed by a $30,000 pay increase, I also realized how hard it would be for a 31-year-old man who hadn't even been promoted to be captain.

Jan's response? "Absolutely not," she said. "Qualified? Yes. Mentally ready? No. There are a lot of vicious people in that department. They'd set you up to fail."

Dr. Farnsworth shared a similar sentiment when I came to see him.

"Cal, you've made excellent progress but you've also had some setbacks. Williams is gone now but that department is toxic. They need someone to come in and clean house. That is a thankless job, even though many need to go. And firing people who likely will never work in a police department again. That's all some of them know. You have a conscience. You're a former altar boy, right?"

I motioned the sign of the cross.

"God wants you to protect people who can't protect themselves. It's like the man you met, Fred Fry. You represent the dead. Do that work. While everyone else in that department is making a power play, do your job. Put your head down and do it as best as you can."

———

The next day, I arrived a few minutes early for roll call. Sgt. Jamison looked at me with a dry smile.

"Well?" he said.

I smiled back at him and said, "The timing's not right, Frank."

"Good choice. I always tell you, speak softly and carry a big stick."

As I walked away, I could hear him say, "The day is coming when you won't have to speak softly anymore."

———

With the office games still going on three months after Williams' exit, the timing felt right to go to Arkansas for a conference – paid by the department, for a change – on obtaining phone, pager and fax records through the proper filing of subpoenas and court orders.

I connected with a group of law enforcement people from Arkansas – police officers, investigators, sheriffs, deputies and a few attorneys.

While having ribs and beers, I sat next to county prosecutor

Dub Marshall and public defender John Dixon. We talked about gruesome cases we worked on.

"I've got two unusual cases and they may involve the same guy," Marshall said.

"They're beauties," Dixon said.

"Actually redheads, or red-haired women," Marshall said. "Prostitutes found in Tennessee, Kentucky, Mississippi, Ohio, Pennsylvania and West Virginia. All with red hair."

That immediately caught my attention, so I shared details from my case, "You know, we've had a lot of prostitutes killed who spent time at the 105 Truck Stop in Illinois. One of them was called 'Pancho Girl.' She had red hair. It may be the same guy."

"Maybe," Marshall said. "The guy we're talking about also sexually assaulted two young girls. I'm talking like 5 and 7. We'd love to catch that bastard. There's one problem."

"What's that?"

"The man has gone off the grid," Dixon said. "I was supposed to represent him, like nine years ago, and he never showed. We checked around. Gone. Poof. Into the wind."

What's the guy's name?"

"Driller. Fred Driller."

After being home for a couple of days, I was invited by township trustees, search committee members, 105 Truck Stop owners and MAGLOCLEN'S JT Hamilton to attend a meeting in regards to a new chief.

"Cal, we invited you because you seem to be the only person not politicking for a job with the department," Hamilton said. "We wanted you to know we considered you for chief and ..."

"The timing's not good," I said.

"Yes," Jim Dail said. "Personally, we love the work you're doing for us; and with Williams out of the way, maybe the new chief will be more receptive to collaboration. By the way, anything interesting that came out of Arkansas?"

I told them Arkansas police had targeted a person of interest in a few murders, and that the suspect could be tied to the 105 killings. More work needed to be done to connect the dots, but I circulated the photo of Fred Driller as a starting point.

"Let's make copies and put it on our board," Greg Shriver said.

Trustee Dennis Dahl then asked, "Cal, you meet a lot of interesting law enforcement people at those conferences, right?"

"Yes," I said.

"Anyone who you think would be a good fit in Oldsmar?"

"There's a couple I could reach out to. What's the pay?"

Keller cringed and paused, "Tell them it's negotiable, but as much as we can manage for the right candidate."

"I'll make a few calls."

Trustee Jim Hole said, "It's mid November. Holidays are coming. We're likely not going to have our guy in place until the calendar flips."

———

I reached out to a few chiefs I met and who gave me their business cards.

They showed interest in the job but were leery about the vague pay range.

I was resigned to telling everyone I didn't have any luck. I said a prayer to St. Anthony, the patron saint of lost people and lost things.

"Help us find a good chief," I said silently in my thoughts.

———————

I opened up my wallet to see how much money I had when I noticed a couple of cards sticking together. When I pulled them apart, I had a business card for John Powers, police chief in Las Cruces, N.M. My track rival. I called him up.

"Hello?"

"John, Cal Raven, how are you doing?"

"Cal, so good to hear from you. How are things in the Greater Chicagoland area?"

"Excellent John. It was great seeing you and reminiscing at the St. Louis conference; and I remember you said if I needed anything I should call."

"Cal, I did and I meant it. You've made a great impression at these conferences. I wouldn't be surprised if you're asked to be a speaker soon."

"Yeah?"

"Absolutely. I'm not bullshitting you. If you need a reference, let me know. In the meantime, how can I help?"

"Well, it's more like how can you help us. John, you may have heard, we're looking for a new chief. Would you have any interest?"

For a good five seconds, that felt like five hours, I waited for a response. Then I heard, "Hun, can you pick up the other phone?"

As he waited, Powers said, "Sorry Cal, you're not going to believe this. Yes, I knew Williams got the boot, but I thought they filled the position because I hadn't heard anything."

Just then, Powers' wife Donna picked up the phone, "Babe I'm here."

"Donna, this is Cal Raven with the Oldsmar Police Department. They're looking for a new police chief."

"Oh my gosh. God has answered our prayers. Babe, have you told him about my mother?"

"Cal, Donna's mom Bebe, her memory is getting worse. She's nearly 80. Her husband Ned died a couple of years ago. We think she has early onset Alzheimer's. We've talked about moving closer but if Donna took care of her, I would be the sole breadwinner."

Another pause. "Cal, what are they paying?"

"I'm not quite sure, that's above my pay grade. Pun intended!"

Powers paused. "Well, we're very interested in finding out more. We'll be in Shullsburg during the Christmas break. Can we talk then?"

"Let me check."

"Cal, one last thing. If this works out, I'll take care of you buddy. I mean that."

———————

When I told hiring committee members about John Powers, they showed cautious optimism. When they found out he had motivation to return to the Midwest, they smiled; and when they did a background check, they started to get excited after reading an article in the *Las Cruces Star* which read:

In his three years as Las Cruces police chief, chief John Powers has led a charge where crime has gone down 27%. Community leaders, officers and detectives are working closer together. He also forged a student task force at New Mexico State with campus police and local cops. Citizens feel safe.

With Powers looking to start after the holidays and with no chief to pay for more than six months, the department's portion of the $475,000 in settlements was partially paid off. Insurance covered about $100,000.

When he and Donna met with the hiring committee on December 20, they had a three-hour meeting. Township trustees told him he'd be walking into a fractious situation. Powers, who outlined a 100-day plan, said he'd have to clean house. He also said he'd focus on finding the serial killer still at large. "Our citizens can't feel entirely safe if that individual is out there," he said. "We are going to take a more proactive approach to catching this person."

The hiring committee made him a strong offer, plus moving expenses. They also would help him get a good deal with low-cost financing on a new home; and if they wanted to sell Donna's mom's home, they would help them with that as well.

Donna and John Powers agreed to the terms two days later. He'd start work January 15. "We'll have great news to share with Mom," Donna said, tears in her eyes.

The hiring committee offered to take Powers out to dinner.

"We will, under one condition," Powers said. "Cal Raven and his wife Jan have to be invited."

Trustee Dennis Dahl said, "Yes, let's invite all the wives. Great idea."

The group had dinner at Sullivan's Steakhouse. They told stories and laughed. The wives offered to make Bebe and Donna part of their family.

Jim Hole raised a glass for a toast. John Powers rose and thanked everyone for their support while promising to serve the community and get everyone working together.

As the night drew to a close, Powers put his hand on my shoulder and asked me to join him outside.

"Thanks for including Jan and I in your acceptance dinner," I said.

"Well, Cal, I said I would take care of you. I told the hiring committee you deserved a $5,000 raise for connecting us. If they had hired a head-hunting firm, that's what it would cost."

"John, I really ..."

"That's not all, Cal. In my first week, I'm going to give you a new assignment. Don't know what it is yet. But we're going to work side-by-side. This department needs new blood with new perspectives and new techniques."

"John, I'm ..."

"Cal, this is no favor. I'm gonna be on your tail. We need to catch this bastard. You, me, the 105 guys, MAGLOCLEN, your crew, we're gonna work together to catch this cretin and clean up this shit hole town. God, has it gone to pot since I've been gone. I got gas at the 105, walked around, saw that 44 Magnum Lounge and it made me feel dirty. That place needs an enema."

With that, Powers walked back into the restaurant.

It may have been 20 degrees with a stiff breeze but I started to feel warm inside.

This was going to be a Merry Christmas.

Figuring he had God and luck working for him, Bart Gein – aka Bert Driller – had a new resolution for the new year. He thought he'd try to get some money from the government. He ignored Richard's pleas for "a little action."

He saw a TV advertisement about how college students needing financial aid could apply for Pell Grants. Richard told Gein he should get a degree in criminal justice and spend time on college campuses. Gein agreed and loved the irony.

He filled out the paperwork as Bart Gein, did a long-haul job, coast-to-coast, and returned home almost three weeks later. When he picked up his mail from the post office, postmaster Floyd Winchel asked casually, "So you home for a few days, Bart?"

"Yeah, got a few days off, Floyd," he replied while leafing through the mail. Included was a letter from a Washington, D.C. address. When he opened the letter, it said:

> *Thanks for your interest in applying for a Pell Grant, Mr. Gein. We have a few minor questions before we can process your request. Can you call us at 1-800-747-PELL at your convenience. Timothy Baker, student services.*

"Good news?" Floyd asked.

"I think so," Gein answered while rereading the letter. "I applied for a Pell Grant to go back to school. They have a few questions."

"Good luck, Bart."

As soon as Gein left, Winchel called an 800 number given to him by the FBI. The bureau flagged Gein's request for a Pell Grant because the social security number he gave them belonged to a man who had been dead for seven years.

Gein returned home bursting with excitement. Richard also was happy.

"Congratulations Bart College," he said. "Sorority girls. Let's get some action."

"Only when we're in the truck, Richard."

As soon as he walked in the house, Gein went right to the phone and called the 800 number.

"Pell Grant Services, this is Tim, how can I help you?"

"Tim, this is Bart Gein. I received your letter."

"Mr. Gein, oh yes. Let me get your file."

Bart's wait seemed like hours. That's because Baker also made a call to the FBI.

"Okay, Mr. Gein, I have your paperwork here."

Baker went line by line. Boy they're thorough, Gein thought.

"And you've never applied for a Pell Grant before, Mr. Gein?"

"No, I thought we covered that."

"Oh yes, my apologies. Now, Mr. Gein, just so you know, these grants are significant financially so we do background checks. Your address, we have three in our database. Are you still at …"

Now, Richard and Gein got upset. "Give 'em hell," Richard said. "Then, let's find a hooker."

"Listen, Tim," Gein said sternly, cutting off the voice on the phone. "I have written my address on the form and on the envelope I sent you."

"Well."

"Well what?"

"Mr. Gein, your social security number…"

At that moment, Gein knew he had been discovered.

The door bell rang.

"Tim, gotta go, there's somebody at the door. I'll call later."

Gein raced to the door, opened it and saw two FBI agents at the door.

"Oh shit," Richard said.

The agents arrested Gein immediately. U.S. Marshals then took him into custody and drove Gein to the county jail on federal charges.

His wife Muriel, listening and watching the whole sequence

in stunned silence, teared up as she watched her husband being handcuffed.

"What should I do?" she asked.

"Hun, this is just a big misunderstanding," Gein said. "I'll be home soon."

On a Sunday afternoon in January, Ann Matheson, promoted from receptionist to chief Powers' personal assistant, was ready to watch an afternoon film when her phone rang.

"Ann, John Powers, I hope I'm not disturbing you?"

Startled that her new boss would call her on a Sunday afternoon, Matheson cautiously answered, "Good? How can I help you?"

"Ann, with this being my first day on the job, I want to get off to an early start. Are you able to come in at 7 a.m.?"

"Uh, yes. Anything you need?"

"Glad you asked. Do you have a pen? I need assorted fruit, granola, oatmeal, nuts, milk, orange juice and two dozen hard-boiled eggs for an 8 a.m. breakfast meeting with the sergeants, lieutenants, detectives and captains."

"Coffee?"

"Yes, Ann, good catch. No decaf. Low-fat milk. No fake sugar. The real thing."

"Notepads?"

"Yes, excellent. Black ink pens and yellow highlighters at each desk. An overhead projector."

"Anything else?"

"Yes. I'll have the day's schedule on your desk when you arrive. The individuals who have phone numbers next to them are to be called and given their meeting times. That's all for now. See you at 7 tomorrow."

Ann shook her head at the speed and confidence in Powers' voice. Then she realized, "I have to go shopping."

———

When Ann arrived at 6:55 a.m., her hands were full of groceries. Powers already was on the phone. She glanced at the schedule:

8:00-10:30 a.m.: Meet Sgts, Lts, Caps, Dets
10:30-10:40 a.m.: Frank Jamison
10:40-11 a.m.: Dominick Coosimano 773-4200,
Jacob Jefferson 410-2317, Lt. Matthew France 608-
5569, Lt. Jordan Kelly 826-0136
11 a.m.-12 p.m.: Go over budget with trustees
12:30-1:30 p.m.: Meet with MAGLOCLEN, 105 TS
owners
1:30-2:30 p.m.: Talk with officers before and after
their shifts as well as staff in squad room
2:30-4 p.m.: Receive tour of facilities, learn processes
4:00-5:30 p.m.: Do first-day paperwork, get to know
township clerk, treasurer

———

Powers did more listening than talking for most of the day. He wanted to hear what his team and officers thought. He wanted to hear what the support staff had to say. He asked questions of those giving him his tour. He asked every employee their name and repeated it so he'd remember.

He also pulled Jamison aside and told him he promoted him to lieutenant. The old man was shocked.

The only time Powers did more talking than listening was when he spoke to Williams' men.

"In the past seven months, each of you have been on probation for being involved in a cover-up that embarrassed this department and cost it $225,000."

"We were set up," France and Kelly said in unison.

Powers, a solid 6-foot-2, 220 pounds from working out, turned and stared at the two men. He then went over to a table, picked up a paper and gave it to them. "You two have been placed on administrative leave, pending further action. If left to me, you'll never wear a badge again. Lt. Jamison, can you escort these two men out of this room?"

Jamison pointed to the door. They got up and walked out. Jamison slammed the door.

Powers walked around the room, partly to give Jamison time to return, partly to let Coosimano and Jefferson sweat. Having already suspended half a dozen of Williams' cronies, Powers was just getting warmed up.

"Either of you want to lie to my face and waste my time?"

Coosimano and Jefferson didn't say a word.

"As I said, you had seven months to redeem yourself. Get some collars, connect with the community, give us some real tips on the serial killer and stop acting like dick wads. No, you pulled more of the same shit, poisoning the waters on hiring a new chief, putting out lies, spreading rumors.

"So, you also have been placed on administrative leave, pending further action. Get out of my office. Go to HR for further instructions. Lieutenant Jamison?"

"Fucking asshole," Coosimano said.

Powers calmly said, "Mr. Coosimano, stay here. Mr. Jefferson, leave now. Mr. Jamison will escort you."

Following the men as they left, Powers shut the door, locked it, then turned down the blinds.

The color drained from Coosimano's face.

"First of all, I've been a cop for more than 25 years and you may be the most incompetent moron I've ever known. First of all, DNA is not proven in the U.S. yet. If you had read one of a dozen articles, you'd know that. You can read, right?"

Coosimano stared at him.

"Second, you and your buddies gift wrapped this case for the FBI with your botched set up of Volpiano and planted evidence. In some ways, I ought to thank you. On the other hand, the level of stupidity you have is unlimited."

Coosimano asked, "What the hell do you want?"

"I'm fining you $5,000 to pay for your stupidity. Now, you can avoid the penalty by taking a swing at me. I know you want to."

Not knowing that fining him for stupidity wasn't legal, Coosimano smiled devilishly, stood up and faced Powers. He wound up and threw a haymaker.

Powers blocked the shot with his left arm, then gave Coosimano a shot to the throat with his right fist, then quickly countered and went low with his left hand delivering a blow to his testes.

Coosimano fell to the ground gasping and clutching his privates.

"Deep breaths," Powers said. "Deep breaths."

Powers then called Lt. Jamison.

"Frank, assist this nimrod to his car," he said.

Powers didn't even look at me when he gave his opening comments to the officers. I kept waiting for my meeting with him but days passed with no contact.

My agita built up. I took my prescribed medications. Depression started to creep in. I also took an anti-depressant. I felt like I was being shunned.

I needed to make a call.

CHAPTER 17

On The Hunt

"We're going to Disney World."

– Laura Raven

On a windy, bone-chilling January day, I met with Dr. Farnsworth.

My anxiety and stress levels spiked to a 9. I sensed a different Chief John Powers the past few days than the day we talked outside Sullivan's Steakhouse.

Would he renege on his promises? Would he change my schedule? Would he give me my raise as he promised?

Dr. Farnsworth listened attentively before asking questions.

"Cal, do you trust authority? I see you competed in individual sports in high school. You had teenage jobs where you showed you could be self sufficient and often spent a lot of time alone. Now, you are employed by people who question how you do your work and why you work the way you do."

I let those thoughts sink it. He made a great point.

"Well, I tried out for football as a freshman and I thought I was the best wide receiver but the coach started two other guys. After the season ended and I found out the school elevated the coach to varsity, I decided to stop playing football. I wrestled and ran track because I earned a spot based on my merits, not the opinion of another coach who may have been influenced by parents or boosters."

I took a deep breath as my job history flashed through my head.

"The ambulance-and-funeral job would've been nicer to get more guidance and have equipment to help those who were dying but I taught myself to be a good EMT. And yes, I feel stifled by my boss and co-workers. It feels like high school all over again. Cliques, small-minded thinking and being controlled by someone, who, yeah, I admit, I don't trust or respect."

Talking through these thoughts with Dr. Farnsworth definitely helped.

"You know doc, I was given three cold cases by Lt. Vascheck, who was jealous of my work," I shared. "I left the cold cases out in the open and when I returned, he left sticky notes on them with snide comments like, *'Solve this one, asshole;' 'Trying to butt kiss the brass again. Won't work;' and 'You're still a nobody.' "*

I continued to vent. "And now, I help the FBI but they make me feel like I'm not as good as them. The new chief thanked me for helping him get his job but since he's been here, he has acted like I don't exist."

"Cal, this sounds more like the PTSD we talked about earlier," advised the doc. "You have battle scars from people who don't want you to succeed. It's made you slightly paranoid. Why don't you quit? Find a job less political, less stressful. Find something where you get patted on the back every other week for a good deed. Find someone to work with you trust. Hell, start your own business and be your own boss."

Those comments irked me.

"What the hell are you talking about? I'm not a quitter," I shot back as my blood boiled.

"I don't need to be treated like a child and praised by his first-grade teacher for going outside and banging the chalk out of the erasers," I continued. "I want to have the freedom to do my job, be respected for what I do and allow me to be me. I've gone to these seminars, I've read the books, I've had face-to-face discussions with some of the best minds in criminal justice, I have files at home …"

Farnsworth put his hands up to his ears and repeated, "La, la, la, la, la, la," as he didn't want to hear that I had files at home.

It's a violation of police policy.

"Okay, I know I'm not supposed to have those at home. And I see you don't want to hear it, but don't we have a doctor-patient confidentiality agreement here? Doesn't what I say stay between us? Aren't you obligated to plead the fifth? You know, I do feel shackled. I want to break free."

Farnsworth paused.

He took a deep breath and then responded, "Cal, you know I've told you some things that could put my license at risk; but I've done it because I trust you, I respect you and we need people like you doing the things you do. I can tell you have a good heart and a good soul."

I put my head down feeling that maybe I overstepped a bit, then replied, "I trust you, too, doc, otherwise I wouldn't tell you all I know."

"Cal, can I give you some advice?"

"Yes."

"First of all, focus your energies on the task at hand. Draw your satisfaction from the work, not the adulation, but the knowing that you're doing the right thing. Don't look for credit, don't expect it. If it comes, that's a bonus from something you felt you were destined to do."

Dr. Farnsworth then paused and measured his thoughts before he added, "Also, trust Powers. Again, not supposed to tell you this, but I've been told that he's a loyal man, a good man, a fair man. He's got to deal with a lot of bullshit, old-school thinking and a lot of changes here before he gets to you. But when he talks to you, I believe it'll be worth the wait."

I stared back at him like, "How do you know this?" but didn't vocalize my thoughts.

Sensing that, Farnsworth stared back and said, "No questions. Remember?"

I nodded.

"One more thing Cal. Heard this through the grapevine but do you know why Powers not only respects and likes you but admires you?"

"No, why?"

"The story you told me about competing against him in the 800. You didn't tell me that after you finished the race, you wobbled to the grass where you fell to your knees, threw up and gasped for air."

"So, why is that relevant?"

"Well, let's just say I overheard Powers telling that same story. He said, 'Raven spilled his guts, gave everything he had in that race. That's the kind of man I want to work with. He looks like Ken but battles like G.I. Joe.' "

As I started my Friday morning work shift, I received a call from dispatch.

"150, chief wants to talk to you after your day is done. That's 2 p.m., right?"

"Yes, dispatch."

I found it funny as they knew when my shift ended, but I put that thought on the backburner as I focused on the tasks of the day. However, I eagerly awaited our meeting. Farnsworth's words stuck in my head, too, like that catchy tune you can't escape. The words, "Trust Powers. He's a loyal man, a good man, a fair man," kept repeating in my head.

When I walked into the police department after my shift, I saw something from fellow staffers I hadn't seen in a long time – a lot of smiles.

"Hey Cal," Ann Matheson said. "Chief Powers is ready to see you."

As I opened the door, John Powers put his arms out and gave me a big hug.

"Hey Cal, come in buddy," he said. "Have a seat.

———————

"Sure," I said, cautiously.

"Hold on, hold on. A few pieces of business first. And apologies. First, I'm sorry we haven't had this conversation earlier but the more I talked to people, the more I've learned about you."

"That's perfectly fine, I understand John."

"And then I get these, Cal."

Powers handed me letters of accommodation from the 105 Truck Stop, the FBI, MAGLOCLEN and the Illinois Governor, who happened to be close friends with Dorothy Douglas and her deceased husband.

"Cal, there's a lot of people in your corner," acknowledged the new police chief. "The work you did as a youth, the work you've done at the truck stops, and to be treated the way you were ..."

Powers showed a palpable anger that got my attention.

"Well, if you haven't been told, Williams' men are on administrative leave, all of them. If anyone else gives you shit, tell me, and their ass will be gone. I have no time for neanderthals. That's not all. I told our trustees your raise needs to be increased to $10,000 because as of today, Cal, you have been promoted to detective."

I put my head down and gathered my emotions.

"Thank you, John, thank you," were the only words I could muster as I felt a little overwhelmed by the overdue praise while appreciating all of it.

"Cal, when I was chief in Las Cruces, I inherited a man who went through the same shit you did. Four-year degree, knew the police manual front and back, did his job well, immaculate paper work. Fellow cops, jealous of him, almost broke him. When I arrived, he stuttered, he couldn't look me in the eye. We straightened that goddamn situation out real quick. But first, we gave him some time off. And that's what we're going to give you."

"Chief, I don't think ..."

"Cal, that's not a request, that's an order. You got six weeks off. Come back March 3. There's a Las Vegas event I've heard about that you need to attend. Other than that, take some time to decompress, refresh and recharge. Because when you return, you're going to hit the ground running."

Powers also put a wrapped box in front of me. When I opened it, there were a pair of running shoes.

"Almost every morning, before you start your day, you and I are going to walk and run a mile. You will brief me."

"Brief you on what, chief?"

"In due time, Cal, in due time. Now, let's get you out of here. Let me conference in Ann. 'Ann, do you have the envelope for Cal, his tickets and expense check for the conference?' "

"Yes, chief."

Powers gave me another hug. As I opened the door, about 30 cheering faces looked at me. Once again they smiled. Among them were Jan and the kids – Janet, Laura and Clayton.

Powers raised his arms. "I have a plaque here that says: Callaghan Lee Raven, the Oldsmar Police Department proudly has promoted you to detective, effective Jan. 20. Congratulations. You are a credit to God, your family, your coworkers and the Richland County area."

The staff started whistling and yelling as he gave me the plaque. My family quickly came and hugged me.

"Dad, rumor has it you're taking us to Disney World," Clayton said. Everyone laughed.

I looked at Jan. She had tears of joy as she shook her head.

Before we went to Disney World, Jan and I spent a few days in Chicago. We toured Chicago's mob history, attended a concert, and had some of the best Italian food I've ever had. Mob-owned, of course.

Jan and I were shopping in the Galleria Mall when she saw a man grab an entire rack of Lady & Duke's clothing and flee the store.

I chased after the suspect, who ran into St. John's Church, ran past the food kitchen line, then entered the basement where I apprehended him at gun point. A Chicago Police Department mounted unit in the area responded to assist me in the arrest.

I later learned CPD had felony fugitive warrants on the suspect for assault and resisting arrest.

I received another accommodation from the store's loss prevention manager that stated:

Dear Detective Raven:

I am writing to thank you on behalf of our company for your help during a shoplifting incident at our Lady & Duke's store in January. Because of your awareness and quick response, an individual was arrested and our merchandise was recovered. It is always comforting to know that the police are there when needed.
Once again I offer our sincere thanks for your efforts.

Sincerely,

Vincent DiMaglio
Loss Prevention Manager
Amy Stiles

———

We used 10 days to drive from Illinois to Orlando and back – we returned on President's Day, Feb. 19 – and the kids were thrilled to take off school for five days.

Jan and I then flew to Las Vegas for the Convention for the American Truck Stop Foundation (ATSF) and the National Association of Truck Stop Operators (NATSO). The groups formally announced Operation Roadblock, a wide-reaching national program designed to encourage action and call attention to the problem of drug abuse in the transportation industry.

Again, to my surprise, Jim Dail and Greg Shriver worked with NATSO to honor me for the work I did in reducing crime and prostitution at their truck stop.

Dail, Shriver and their wives treated us to a High Wire

Circus Show at Blackbeard's Resort. Beforehand, we had a meal at The Pyramids where we stayed. The 105 owners treated us so well, we hardly could spend the stipend John Powers gave us.

"Cal, what do you think the chief has in store for you when you return?" Dail asked.

"Jim, I'm not exactly sure," I said. "He said he wanted me to enjoy my time off; but he did say when he took the job that he wanted to clean up the 44 Magnum Lounge.

Shriver added, "That would be great. That area has been a stain on our truck stop; and we're still feeling the effects of Williams' stunt with the media."

————

Jan and I returned home a good week before I returned to work. I used the time to review notes I took from conferences in Cleveland, Rochester, St. Louis and Arkansas as well as my visit to The Forensic Body Institute.

I reviewed the different types of serial killers. Victimology reports. Creating an investigative plan. Reviewing solvability factors. Case processing. Crime scene checklist. Obtaining phone, pager and fax records through proper filing of subpoenas and court orders. Entomology training. Using the National Crime Investigation Center as a tool.

As I studied, the phone rang.

"Cal, John Powers. Got a minute?"

I barely got a "sure" out of my mouth when he jumped in.

"Cal, meet me at the YMCA, 6 a.m. It has a track inside. I'll be up there. Bring your running shoes and a recorder. Hit the ground running. Enjoy the rest of your day."

————

The next morning, the sun looked ready to pop out but cold winds reminded me spring hadn't quite arrived as I got out of my car and walked into the YMCA in a grey warm-up suit and my new running shoes. I wiped my feet heavily before walking upstairs and meeting John Powers at the track. I pulled a cassette recorder out of my warm ups. We started with a walk.

"Cal, you're going to be the lead investigator on these serial killings. You have the respect of the FBI, the regional and state police and your fellow cops. Rely on them to do the background work, the database stuff and overall grunt work. I want you thinking about the big picture. First instincts, how should we proceed?"

I had waited six years for someone to ask me this question.

"This is a cold case. Review the victims' deaths one by one. We need to obtain the evidence from the other states, other counties in Illinois and have everything mailed to us. That includes the private coroner's reports. Then, we need the victimologies, case comparisons while cross checking the deaths to see if they match.

"Look at the evidence we have. See if there's anything that's been missed there or in the case files. Check the police reports. Interview the coroners and cops from other states. See if there's any imprisoned serial killers who could give us a lead."

As we continued walking, Powers took in the information, and said, "Good, good," then stopped. I also stopped.

Powers looked at me with that stone-cold gaze.

"Are you mentally and physically prepared to see this thing through?" he asked. "I need to know that you can handle all of this."

I looked him squarely in the eye and said, "I'm refreshed, mentally and physically prepared. This is why I wanted to join the force, to do this kind of work. I mean, what do you want me to do, kick your ass in an 800-meter run, to show you I'm ready?"

Powers laughed out loud, then replied, "All right. That's what I wanted to hear. And when you catch this guy, you and I will have that race and raise a lot of money for charity."

Before I called anyone, I wanted to get a composite analysis based on the police reports. Were they all prostitutes? How many had been beaten? How many had been strangled, gagged? Were they killed in any other way? Any other noticeable traits?

I started to notice a few patterns after the first six victims; and relayed them to Powers during our morning walks.

"One died by strangulation, one by blunt-force trauma and four by both," I said. "However, I still need to make calls to coroners."

"Did you call the prisons?"

"Yes. I am waiting back on those calls."

"Think you should talk to the ladies again?"

"I'm working at the truck stop tonight. I will."

"Cal? One more thing. I know you're working more than 40 hours a week on this. I know you're working about 12 hours a week at the truck stop. I don't want you working on any other side jobs, OK? I want this to be your focus."

"OK, chief."

It took about six months to go through all this information. Making calls. Remaking calls. Driving to interviews. Connecting with sources. Updating myself on the most current technology. Reviewing periodicals.

———

After finishing all but one of the victims, I visited three

prisons and conducted five interviews with men charged with murders. I came away with the following notes:

If I brought a food they liked – fried chicken, apple pie, candy bars, a burger, fresh fruit – they talked more.

Some serial killers were killed themselves. "If you live in that world, karma and some nasty-ass motherfuckers can often get you," one prisoner said.

I learned that I have to think like a criminal. As one said, "That'll take you to dark places, white boy."

Some killers can change their routine, but most don't change unless they almost get caught.

Rarely do killers stick out. They often fade into the background.

Four of the five interviewed thought there may be two or even three different killers based on the information I gave them. All four asked for time taken off their sentence. I told them I'd have to check and see if the information they gave me was accurate. I also would have to use what they told me in court and they needed to know they may have to give testimony.

I also got sidetracked for a few days by my old friend Yvette Mendez tipping me off that I should take a look at Bobby Whitfield – who pimped five women – as a possible suspect. He had a reputation for roughing up girls and having gambling debts.

Mendez said a couple of other prostitutes disappeared while three women in the town of Oldsmar were found dead. The ways they were found – wrapped in a jacket – resembled one of the victims, Mary Beth Peters.

Their tips led us – four cops and detectives in two undercover cars – to three different places where we were told Whitfield lived.

In two of the locations, Whitfield had lived there but not recently.

When we arrived at the third location, a good mile off a back road, Whitfield was home, all right, but dead. Had been for days. Shot three times, once in the head. He smelled bad enough but it could've been a lot worse had it been warm.

While we closed off the scene, we called coroner Jeff Bingham.

The prison guys were right. If you live around death, it finds its way to your doorstep.

———

Just before looking over evidence of the 11th victim, I got a call.

Effingham County Jail, a three-hour drive away.

"Callaghan Raven?" Warden Dale Downie quickly and confidently introduced himself. "I've got a prisoner on death row but he's not gonna make it. Edmond Travers. Former truck driver. Had a stroke. Wakes up in and out of consciousness. Blathering a lot of stuff. We can't understand him. I think he's got a couple of days, tops. You left a message with our receptionist that you were working on a truck-stop serial killer? Wanted to know if you wanted to come up."

I said yes and jumped in a squad car. Because most of the drive was interstate, I could go about 85 mph and make it in three-and-half hours.

Illinois didn't make a habit of executing prisoners, but they made exceptions. And this one killer was a doozy.

John Wayne Gacy. Jaycees member. Posed for a photo with former First Lady Rosalyn Carter. Dressed up as a clown for children's parties. The state of Illinois killed Gacy by lethal injection after he was found to have sexually assaulted, tortured and murdered at least 33 teenage boys and young men between 1972 and 1978.

The similarities between Gacy's case and ours were eerie.

Gacy should have been locked up for at least 10 years after molesting a child. The psychological report said the sexual deviant couldn't be rehabilitated.

Gacy hunted a lot of gay men, many of whom were hitchhikers. About a third of his victims were never identified.

Police, who seemed to have a bias, didn't take their investigations seriously.

Lazy police work led to leads not being followed.

Edmond Travers wasn't as deviant. However, he had killed his wife and her lover. Also had priors for other arrests. Assault. Armed robbery. He would've killed himself after he killed his wife, but he passed out with a gun in his hand before he did so. Too much liquor.

The state psychologist said Travers was fit to stand trial. Travers said he needed to be punished for his sins. Said if he received a life sentence, he would kill prisoners. The agreeable jury gave him the death penalty.

While in prison, Travers suffered a number of health issues because his sister-in-law asked for and was granted a stay of execution. Knowing he had health issues, she wanted to make him suffer.

Then Travers had his stroke.

When I arrived, he spoke incoherently, then mumbled, then had seconds of clarity.

When I showed him a photo of Bert Driller, he looked at me and said, Drill, Gein, Drill, Gein, Two, two, two, per... per... per... eh, eh, eh, s, s, s, evil.

With that, he went incoherent again.

"What did he mean?" Downie asked.

"I'm not exactly sure," I said. "When I figure it out, I'll call you."

As I drove home, Travers' comments kept rolling around in my head.

Could Bert Driller and Bart Gein be working together?

CHAPTER 18

Key Tip

**"We'd like nothing better
than to put an apple in his
mouth, baste him and roast him
over some white-hot coals."**

– County Prosecutor
Dub Marshall, Arkansas

I had a chance to supplement my $10,000 raise but turned it down.

While working the early morning shift at the truck stop, we arrested a Korean prostitution ring working out of a building in the 44 Magnum Lounge. The prostitution ring employed a madam and about four or five women who gave massages and just about everything truckers and wayward souls wanted.

A got a tip from some little birdies who saw their paydays being diminished. Hell hath no fury like birdies losing their worms.

Depending on what the truckers wanted sexually, it could cost them about $200; and they could be out in 30 minutes, max. However, the truckers didn't like the idea that some

Koreans charged more for less-than customary service and happy endings.

So, we planted one of our cops, Ron Buffet, who looked like a seedy truck driver when he didn't shave. The work was kind of dangerous because we didn't know who the Koreans had for protection – or should I say muscle.

Ron also was literally naked. In police lingo, that meant he had no badge, no weapon, no wire, and ultimately, in this case, no clothes.

The women usually offered a routine massage, rubdown, then ran their thumbs up the crack of Buffet's ass. That will get even the most modest of men to stand at attention.

All Buffet had to do was turn down their sexual advances and price offering, put on his clothes, come outside and give us the all clear to do our raid.

When we pulled out approximately $20,000 from their money purses and mattresses, a woman said to us, "You keep evidence, you keep evidence."

Now with some crooked officers, if there were four guys, they would take half and put the other half in evidence. Each man pocketed $2,500.

If a guy felt uncomfortable about taking the money, he was encouraged to "put it in the collection basket at church." If he didn't take the money, the other three would think he was too clean and maybe working with internal affairs. If he did take the money, his personal ethics started to blur. It's an incredibly difficult situation to be in.

Fortunately, the four guys I worked with were honest and followed my lead. I also had the perfect excuse.

"Look guys, I don't want any of this," I said. "I just got promoted, I got a raise and I'm working a big case."

They quietly shook their heads up and down, then said, "Cal, next round is on you."

————

A few weeks after I was back on the job, John Powers and I met for our routine exercise and did our first outdoor walk, circling around the track at Oldsmar Central High School.

We had a lot to talk about. The bust, the discovery of a dead man and another dead man's confession all happened within a week. Edmond Travers died six hours after I met with him.

"You've had quite a month in a week," Powers said. "Outstanding work. Your connections with the ladies have led to a good bust. And it'll put some money in the police till when we get guilty verdicts."

"Unfortunately, we didn't exactly bring that man to justice," I said.

"At least he's off the streets, Cal. I have to tell you some people are glad he's dead so we don't have to spend money on a court case. Find out what you can on this guy. If there's enough to link the man to some murders, we can say we believe he's played a role in deaths within the Oldsmar city limits."

I nodded.

"Anything more on the trucker deaths?"

"Yes," I said. "The dead man, Bobby Whitfield, could be linked to one of the girls."

Pulling out my recorder, I said, "I also went to Effingham County Prison where I taped a serial killer on his death bed saying this:

Drill, Gein, Gein, Drill… Two, two, two, per… per… per… eh, eh, eh, s, s, s, evil.

Powers walked faster, said nothing. After about 150 yards, he said, "Thoughts?"

"Maybe Driller and Gein are working together."

Powers walked some more, then added, "Maybe. Didn't you say in your reports that some witnesses said a clean-cut guy while some mentioned a bearded, fat guy?"

We walked some more, then almost simultaneously we said, "Could it be the same person?"

"Play the tape again," Powers said.

After listening to it again, Powers said, "Could the eh, eh, eh be a – as in alias?"

"Could the s, s, s mean the same as in same person?"

Powers and I looked at each other and smiled. "Cal, how many of the victims have you reviewed?"

"All but the last one."

"Great. I believe we're about to break this baby. I can feel it. How about you, Cal?"

"I do, chief. What we talked about is the first step. I'm going to call coroners, review the 11th victim and let you know what I find. Do you know we still don't have a name for our latest Jane Doe."

"Or two of the others, right? Cal, you are going to find something."

With Jane Doe, I figured I'd lay out all the evidence on a table, then call the coroners. It has been my experience that I'm often put on hold when I make my calls. Apparently, dissecting bodies and finding causes of death delayed phone calls. While waiting, I looked over the evidence. This visual exercise helped me process the medical findings and usually provided clues.

I needed to call six coroners. I left messages with the first four. As I guessed, I got placed on hold. I laid the phone down and pushed the speakerphone button.

As I listened to the instrumental "Chariots of Fire," I went over to what was on the table – a crushed pack of cigarettes, probably in a pants pocket, three sticks of spearmint gum, a few quarters, tube socks, $33, cubic zirconia earrings, a man's pair of underwear and a man's shirt with a pamphlet in the pocket.

As I took the pamphlet out of the pocket, a voice answered back.

"Yes, how can I help you?"

"Is this Jeff Bingham?"

"Yes, Cal, I recognize your voice. Thanks for your help a few months back. A lot has changed since then, hasn't it?"

"Yes, it has Jeff. Have you noticed any similarities between the deaths?"

"Yes sir. Several. Besides not being identified, the women had red hair. They both had an object stuffed down their throat, then they were strangled and beaten. Based on the indentations of the victims, I believe it was what they call a truck tire buddy."

"I'm familiar with that."

"Also, a leather nylon cord was used. The victims seemed to be wearing the killer's underwear and T-shirt. In return, the killer took the victims' bra and underwear. Why? Your guess is as good as mine?"

"Yeah, a lot of possibilities there. Anything else?"

"Yes. The bite marks on this last victim. Didn't see that on the other one."

"And, uh, something I didn't have in my reports," Bingham added. "Something I didn't want a reporter knowing in a do-not-release medical examiner's report. Something I found disturbing."

"Jeff, besides being a detective, I also worked for a man

who had an ambulance and funeral service. I've seen a lot."

"Okay, okay. Are you familiar with the term necrophilia?"

"Sex with corpses?"

"Yes. Both victims."

As Bingham started to describe how he knew this to be, my mind – and ears – didn't want to go there. I looked at the pamphlet and opened it fully. As I glanced at it, something immediately caught my attention.

Chicken scratch. Hand written notes. A pager belonging to Bart Gein: 1-877-TRUCKIN along with Secure Trucking. Also the name of a school: ABC Truckin'.

After he finished talking, I said, "Jeff, thank you so much. You've been such a big help. Something has come up. Can I follow up with you if I need to?"

"Yes Cal, keep me informed. Hope you catch this bastard!"

I immediately called Ann Matheson: "Ann, tell Chief Powers to come to the evidence room immediately. It's urgent."

Powers arrived in two minutes.

"John, take a look at this."

Powers got a big smile on his face as he saw the writing on the pamphlet. Then he got pissed.

"How the hell wasn't this caught a year ago?" he asked.

"The men who went over this evidence a year ago aren't working here any longer," I said.

Powers shook his head and angrily asked, "Anything else?"

"I also spoke with Jeff Bingham. There's a lot of similarities between the two victims. Red hair. Object stuffed down their throats. Strangled. Beaten. Leather nylon cord and tire thumper used. The victims wore the killer's underwear and T-shirt. No bra and underwear found. Also, our killer is into necrophilia."

Powers calmly but authoritatively replied, "That sick fuck. Bulldog, start making calls."

Just then my phone rang. The coroner from Ohio said besides the police report, there was necrophilia. In the other two out-of-state murders, there was not.

While I'm on the phone, two messages were left at the front desk that confirmed two more victims of necrophilia.

After getting a breakdown on the killer or killers, Powers scratched his head, walked around, gathered his thoughts.

"Okay, Cal, let's focus on Gein. Start sending out subpoenas."

———

When I looked closer, the pager also needed a four-digit pin number. Rather than call it and alert Gein, I wanted to see what I could find out about him.

I went to a clerk of courts in Richland County that I knew, Karla Bakke, and made a request for a subpoena for Gein's phone records as part of a murder investigation. I included probable cause as the justification for my wanting the phone records.

Morschauser then quickly went to the assistant county prosecutor who reviewed and authorized the subpoena within three days.

Back then, we had to do things by fax and registered mail so it took days for me to get the subpoena and mail it to Secure Trucking and then receive mail from the trucking company. We included in our letter the urgency of receiving the phone records.

But it was worth the wait.

We learned a few things. ABC Truckin' sent Gein's records for a five-year period, but there was a gap since he hadn't been working there the past few months.

No names but a lot of phone numbers. His wife or girlfriend, dispatchers, customers at the district center and who knows who else.

I started calling phone numbers. I did so from an Oldsmar Police Department landline in case people wanted to call back and verify I was a cop.

Some people didn't answer at first so I had to call at different times. I had to be aware that some numbers were in places where there was a one- or two-hour time difference. If I kept getting no response, I had to subpoena phone records from that phone while getting an address.

When I identified myself and told callers this was part of an active homicide investigation, I received a number of responses.

Some wary people wanted more identification so I had to fax them our letterhead. I told others to look up the Richland County Sheriff's Office and ask for the Oldsmar Police Department and detective Cal Raven.

Some wanted to help – especially the single females – but could offer little assistance.

Some gave me a big "fuck you." I subpoenaed their records.

And some were flat out scared.

One couple – Terry and Patricia Ehrke – said Gein "invited" them to his truck in the Tennessee hills to smoke some pot and just hang out.

"He hugged me and just creeped me out," Martha said while Jonah said Gein made a sexual comment that didn't sit well.

"Thank God we told him we'd think about his invitation," Jonah said.

Another person, Hailey Dickinson, said she traveled with Gein to her native Canada. When authorities wouldn't let him cross the border, Dickinson said her instincts told her to get out of the truck.

"You're fortunate, ma'am," I said.

I also called a Muriel Jacobs. She had no idea who Bart Gein was.

———

At the 105 Truck Stop, we put up an identikit drawing – an artist's rendering and likeness of a person's face based on the description from a victim or witness – that drew a lot of nutcases.

Psychics, tarot-card readers, paranormals and crystal-ball gypsies. They annoyed the hell out of me.

After sending out the second batch of subpoenas and waiting for callbacks, I started contacting people who worked with Gein – his bosses, dispatchers and customers. After exploring every avenue I finally hit paydirt.

During one conversation with a dispatcher, Kevin Smith, he offered a huge tip.

"Yeah, I know that Bart Gein," Smith said. "A real turd. But I overheard him tell another trucker that his real name is Bert Driller. He dresses like a slob, too."

"Whoa, whoa, whoa," I said. "What did you just say?"

"Yeah, his real name's Driller, Bert Driller. Dresses like a slob. Mussed-up beard, stinks, real attitude."

Thank you Kevin Smith.

I called John Powers and reported the huge tip. "John, your instincts were great. Bart Gein is Bert Driller."

"Knew it, I goddamn knew it. Just like a case in New Mexico we tracked down. Meet you at the dispatch center."

I race-walked to the dispatch center where we met up with Sue Wentland. After three straight days of checking parking fines and traffic tickets, she got just as excited as we did when we gave her the name – Bert Nelson Driller – along with a birthdate.

Wentland typed Driller's name in the National Crime Information Center and the Illinois Law Enforcement Center. It's the same place where a dispatcher put in the license plate information on that $50,000 Mercedes-Benz that I noticed at the 105 Truck Stop.

"We've got a hit!" Wentland yelled. We could hear the "tat, tat, tat" of the printer spitting out information on silver thermal printing paper.

Wentland was so excited, she partially ripped the report. She had to tape it.

Powers and I didn't care.

We quickly scanned the report.

- *Larceny and sexual abuse of a child, Arkansas*
- *Skipped hearing with judge, Arkansas.*
- *Fraudulent breach of trust, Kentucky*
- *Grand larceny, Kentucky*
- *Worthless checks warrant, Kentucky*
- *Sex with a minor, Nevada. Report processed, not enough evidence to hold.*
- *Person of interest, red-hair killings*
- *Hit-and-run of victim with truck. Also spit on him.*
- *On parole in the state of Tennessee.*

While we let the information on the report sink in, I asked Wentland if she could run a report on Bart William Gein. She had a quick response.

"Only a fraudulent claim of a Pell Grant," she said. "That's why he's on parole in the state of Tennessee."

Powers and I looked at each other.

"So he had this alias, this double identity and whenever he got in trouble, it was Bert Driller," Powers said.

"Except for the Pell Grant, which now has led us directly to him," I said.

"Outstanding work Cal. Outstanding. Keep making calls on these charges but it won't be too long before you're flying to Tennessee."

I called Jan, I called my partner Tony Blackstone, I called Dr. Farnsworth and I called my parents to tell them the news.

Almost in unison, they said, "We're so proud of you. This is what you were meant to do."

Jan added, "Come home. I have something special for you."

I replied, "I have one quick stop to make."

I made a trip to St. Michael's Church. Just three years earlier, I thought of ending my life. Now, my life couldn't be better.

After I kneeled in a pew and said a prayer of thanks, a familiar friend patted my shoulder. Father Hallahan.

"Callaghan, me boy, how are you?" he said with a teary-eyed smile. "I've been praying for you."

"Many prayers answered," I said, tears rolling down my cheeks. "Three years ago ..."

"I know, Cally, I know. I could see the despair in your eyes. You trusted God to guide you and He did. How are you doing now?"

"Terrific, I just got a big tip on a murder case."

"Let's talk about it over breakfast sometime. My treat. We can make it your confession."

I laughed. It felt good to laugh.

———

I now had a true fugitive on my hands with the history, means and personality to commit heinous crimes. Anytime you have a crime, you're looking for means, motive and opportunity to commit such an act.

I also had what could be the proverbial smoking gun: bite marks on Jane Doe's skin.

My first call: Tennessee State Police.

I talked to two people: Detective Terry Shannon and Parole Officer Ed Sunday.

As he read my fax and I told him some of the key details, Shannon said, "Congratulations, we got a bad guy on our hands. Whatever paperwork you need, let me know. When you fly in, I'll pick you up and we can talk strategy over breakfast. Thanks for calling us."

Sunday then started by saying, "That sloppy pig, greasy truck driver" before giving me everything he knew on Driller. After telling me nice job, he said he'd also take care of the subpoena and mail it to me. He closed by saying, "Raven, when you want this guy in here, he'll be in here."

I next called Arkansas County Prosecutor Dub Marshall, who I met at a conference in his home state. We also exchanged information.

"Great job, man," he said. "We have very detailed interviews with the victims, who still are minors."

"How are they?" I asked.

"Okay, but jittery," Marshall explained. "They stutter. They're delayed developmentally. They're 14 and 16 but they act like pre-teens. It's sad but they have loving parents who are extremely protective. And embarrassed."

He paused to reflect on the lives negatively affected, then added, "Let us know if you need anything. And if you want to hand 'em off, we'll gladly take that sum bitch. Frankly, we've got a couple of rangers with this huge pit; and we'd like nothing better than to put an apple in his mouth, baste him and roast him over some white-hot coals."

I had heard they grill just about anything in Arkansas.

After I talked to Kari Wolfgram, part of me agreed with Marshall on how to punish Driller.

Now 23, Wolfgram was hard to find. She no longer lived at previous addresses on file in the state of Washington.

When a forwarding address in Montana found Wolfgram, I found she didn't have a phone. Thank goodness for the police in Bear Creek. They didn't get any benefit out of finding her but they did and she willingly went to a pay phone.

She also willingly told me her story. Getting drugged, chained up, forced to put her hand on the bible to marry him, having sex with him, being hit by him, strangled, not being believed, disappearing, then hearing Driller/Gein got nothing more than a slap on the wrist for what he did to her.

"You know, he said he belonged to the mafia," she said. "He bragged about killing one of his wives. And he bragged about what he did to those girls."

Wolfgram was remarkedly strong and coherent; but she also was extremely angry and bitter. After we talked a few times, she shared more of her story and I sensed it helped her recover.

"You know, I kept a knife under my pillow for three and a half years," she said. "That piece of scum. I've needed therapy for the assaults."

I told her I felt honored that she trusted me enough to share such awful, demented things.

She told me she trusted me because I sounded like her uncle Paddy, and then challenged me, "I also trust you'll put away this beast so he can't hurt anybody else."

"That's the plan," I said. "He's on parole, a long way from here. Would you be willing to testify against him?"

"Absolutely," she said. "That bastard deserves the death penalty.

"Then I can sleep comfortably."

As Jan drove me to the airport, I looked at her and gave her a big smile. She sure knows how to take my anxiety and stress away.

"Be careful," she said while giving me a warm kiss goodbye.

As I waited for my 6:30 a.m. flight to depart, John Powers got clearance from the Transportation Security Administration to come over and visit.

"This is when I would be working out anyway," he said. Then he turned serious.

"You know, Cal, we and everybody who's been involved have talked about how we want this guy to either fry, hang, face a firing squad or to be drawn and quartered."

"Or roasted on a spit," I jumped in, referencing the preferences of the Arkansas police – and probably our counterparts in Tennessee, too.

"Yeah, yeah, exactly," he said, looking at me warily. "Here's the thing. I know you're a pro; but you'll have to control every urge where you want to slap, punch or beat this guy, whether you're interrogating him or whether you're handcuffing him. You've been at these conferences. Focus on getting this guy to confess, even if it means you have to be his friend or agree with him or condone what he did. We want to send this guy to a place where he sees darkness for all but 30 minutes a day. Let the inmates do the dirty work. Understand?"

"Yes sir," I said. "I'll be on my best behavior. Scout's honor."

CHAPTER 19

Caged Killer

**"We want to send this guy to a
place where he sees daylight
for about 30 minutes a day."**

– Chief John Powers,
Oldsmar Police Department

As I made the short flight to Knoxville, Tennessee, Powers' words resonated with me regarding Bert Driller/Bart Gein.

Focus on getting this guy to confess, even if it means you have to be his friend or agree with him or condone what he did. We want to send this guy to a place where he sees daylight for about 30 minutes a day.

The training he talked to me about is called the Reid System or Reid Technique.

Developed in the 1950s by John E. Reid, a polygraph expert and Chicago police officer, the technique is known for creating a high-pressure environment for the interviewee.

Before our interview with Driller, Terry Shannon and I talked about taking a more passive approach because we felt we had enough evidence against him. However, we also used empathy and offers of understanding and help because we thought a confession would be forthcoming.

Pardon the awful pun, especially in this case, but you have to feel the suspect out, mirror the person until they deflect.

Reid's interviewing approach included 15 suggested questions as the foundation for establishing a rapport with a suspect.

Another part of the technique is to let the suspect sit closer to the door so they don't feel like they're trapped. Giving the suspect space at first is good, but as the interrogation goes on, the goal is to move closer and closer. Think of it like this: If a person in the Men's Room is in the farthest urinal of six and the others are empty; and you go to the urinal next to him, he's likely to squirm, feel uncomfortable and look away. Proximity is a good thing to exert control.

Having been sent Shannon's photo – short haircut, comb over, clean shaven, square jaw, pug nose – I recognized him immediately as he honored his promise to pick me up at the airport.

We drove for just a few miles before stopping at Cindy's Café.

"What are you thinking about Cal?" Shannon asked me while I ate my eggs, bacon and pancakes. I never tasted them.

"Anxiety, excitement, relief," I said. "If we can end some people's suffering …"

I never finished my sentence as I wanted to control my emotions and follow Chief Powers' advice, even toward the good guys.

Before we brought in Driller/Gein, I wanted to do a bit of a role reversal. Surveil Gein and be the hunter. We staked out where he lived: 1724 Volunteer Circle.

He and his wife Muriel lived on the bottom floor. I wanted to see if he somehow escaped, what his options were.

The first two days Shannon and I did our surveillance, he wasn't home so we went to visit his wife.

Muriel Jacobs, who I had called months before, knew nothing about Bart Gein's life. Either she put on an Academy Award-winning performance or she had me completely fooled.

I don't think it completely sunk in when Shannon and I told her we were part of an active homicide investigation. She welcomed us in for coffee and allowed us to search the home. We saw nothing that could tie him to any murders.

"Bert and I have lived here about five years," she said. "He's gone a lot but it allows me to do things with my friends, plant flowers in the backyard and sing in the church choir."

She revealed more insight into her world. Most people will offer up plenty of details with simple small talk, especially if they think they are helping the police and don't know they are under investigation.

So she continued, "He's always been respectful to me. I do what he asks and he asks nicely. I think he knows I wouldn't respond well if he wasn't nice."

Muriel Jacobs then asked us if we had any other questions about "a murder."

I then asked, "Muriel, do you understand that the homicide investigation involves your husband?"

Taken aback, she replied, "Oh, I thought it was a murder in the community."

"Muriel, I'm a detective in Illinois. Mr. Shannon is a detective here in Tennessee. It's a multi-state investigation."

Just then, it hit her how serious this was.

"Oh my," she said. "My husband does travel a lot. He drives

through Illinois. Is there anything else I should know?"

"Ma'am you may want to get checked for a STD."

"What does that mean?"

With a sad look in my eyes, I handed her a pamphlet that said, "Sexually Transmitted Disease (STD)."

Trembling, she took the pamphlet, held her stomach and said, "Thank you officers, I think I need to lie down."

As she closed the door, Shannon looked at me and said, "That sucked."

———

On Day 3, an old, beat-up pickup pulled into the driveway and our suspect arrived. He looked as described. Fat, slovenly, hair disheveled, he walked with a limp, back hunched over.

Amazingly, because he hadn't violated his parole, Driller couldn't be arrested.

We took our time driving back to the parole office. Didn't want to alarm Driller by calling him in minutes before he arrived home.

Ed Sunday looked like he could be Shannon's brother. Same hairstyle. Similar jawline and nose.

Sunday had been a parole officer for 22 years. If he felt you were worth saving, he'd act like a brother or father and offer advice. If he didn't, he'd help authorities any way possible to bring a criminal in and send him back to prison.

We chatted for about two-and-a-half hours and I added gory details about Driller/Gein.

"Which one do you think will show up?" Sunday asked. "I hope it's Gein. Driller is one big, fat, barnacle-riddled whale we're reeling in."

When Sunday called our suspect, he told him to "come in

for a quarterly drug screen."

In most cases, parole and probation officers helped reintegrate offenders back into society while safeguarding public welfare; and that was Gein/Driller's path until I shared with Sunday and Shannon his transgressions, heinous acts that would make most people's skin crawl. And that's before you add in murder and the whole serial killer thing.

As Sunday promised, Gein/Driller arrived at the station 45 minutes after being called.

He weighed every bit of 275 pounds. He did have a chance to shower but didn't shave. The clothes looked tight on him.

Gein/Driller looked confused when Sunday said, "We're taking you to a room instead of my office today."

When they went into the interrogation room, I was waiting for them. Sunday said, "Bert, there's a man here who wants to meet you."

His look of confusion turned into this oh-fuck glance in a millisecond. I could see it in his eyes briefly. However, he kept his composure.

But Richard spoke to him: "Buddy, you're on your own. See ya."

Our objectives were to not only get a confession on Jane Doe's death but any other major crimes of interest or murders he may have committed. We didn't want to get tunnel vision on just one case or focus on the details we knew. We didn't want to miss something that we may not have known from his long list of crimes.

———

Sunday left the room. Shannon entered and began with the formalities of introductions and giving Gein/Driller his rights, which he said he understood. He also understood this was a "non-accusatory interview" and that he didn't have to stay and could leave any time he wanted. He waived his right to an attorney because he said, "I ain't got nothing to hide. I don't know what this is all about."

Surprising move but maybe he thought bringing an attorney in would be a sign of guilt.

I then started my question-and-answer session.

Q: "There's some things I need to know Bert. First thing, I think you know why I'm here. Do you know why I'm here?"

A: "No."

Q: First of all, do you want me to address you as Bert Driller or Bart Gein?

That immediately put him on the defensive.

A: Ah, um, Bert Driller.

Q: And who's Bart Gein?

Silence.

Q: I'll repeat that Bert. Who is Bart Gein?

A: A name I picked up along the way.

Q: How did that happen?

A: I got in a little trouble in another state so I got this name.

Q: Okay Bert. The real reason I wanted to meet is that an acquaintance of yours was found dead about a year ago. On one of your routes. There's a truck stop, small grocery store, K-Mart, Secure Trucking and ABC Truckin'. Are you familiar with that?

A: Not really. I don't know where the terminal office is.

Over the next 20 minutes, Driller became like Sgt. Schultz – "I know nothing, I see nothing."

To refresh his memory, I showed him photos of the victim, told him people saw him and her together and showed him a map of the area.

Still, his answers early on were "No" and "I don't know."

Because he didn't have control, Driller started tapping his fingers on the table while his eye contact was horrible. He never showed out-and-out concern for the dead woman in the photos. We also couldn't use DNA because it was in its infancy at the time.

In these moments, you want to slap them or pop them in the nose to refresh their memory but this also is when you have to have the most restraint. Like Chief Powers said.

It didn't take long for Driller to give conflicting answers.

He said he gave one woman a ride; a few minutes later, it was three.

Driller claimed he gave a woman a ride to Knoxville, then gave her $80 "to take a bus." While he remembered the names of some women, he didn't remember others.

When I asked about his female escort to Canada, he finally admitted he took her, probably because he remembered he didn't do anything to her. It's always easier to remember the truth than a lie.

Driller said, "If anybody beats up on anybody or tears them up, they ought to be punished."

But when asked if he raped anyone, he said that was different than assault. He added he was accused of rape, but not convicted. He explained, "It was thrown out of court and come to find out it was my ex-wife's husband that put the girl up to it."

When Driller said he would do anything to prove his innocence, we took him up on it.

Q: Would you be willing to take a polygraph test?

A: Yes.

Q: Would you be willing to give me blood or hair samples?

A: Yes.

Q: Could I get your dental impressions?

Driller gave me a wary look but repeated, "Yes, I've got nothing to hide."

But when Shannon asked if he could take a look at the watch Driller wore, he said, "It's mine and you can't have it." Sometimes, dried blood seeps in between the bands and makes for excellent evidence.

I told Driller if he could help me solve this case, that he could be a great help. He responded, "I ain't guilty of what you're asking me."

For a second, I thought I had him when I asked who could've done what I said.

He replied, "I have no idea. It could've been another trucker, anybody the woman got involved with. She could've done something and he threw her out of the truck or something. I have no idea where she was."

Q: Threw her out of the truck. Why did you say that? Threw her out of the truck.

A: Because I've known of people doing that.

Q: Like who?

A: I can't remember their name.

Q: Have you ever killed anybody, Bert?

A: Nope.

His answers returned to being short again. He responded to my questions with questions. When I said I had his log book, he played dumb.

Q: Did you have anybody with you on that trip?

A: Yeah.

Q: Who did you have with you?

A: I can't even remember who she was.

Q: Bert, why don't you ever pick up male hitchhikers?

A: They could beat me up.

Q: But females are less of a threat?

A: Um, uh, what do you mean by that?

Q: They're less of a threat. But they can test your patience. Bert, I don't think you did it intentionally. Things got out of hand. You know women. One minute, they're fine, the next they start acting up. Something accidently may have happened?

A: Not sure I'm following you. I never hurt anyone.

Then I pulled out the pamphlet with his alias, pager number and ABC Truckin' written on it in his handwriting.

Driller admitted that was his pamphlet and that he changed his name to Gein and that he stopped at the 105 Truck Stop from time to time but when I asked him about picking up a woman, he turned into Sgt. Schultz again and changed the subject.

And then I asked if the T-shirt on the victim was his. Two photos showed he wore similar shirts. He again changed the subject.

When I asked if the relationship with one of his passengers started as one thing, then turned to another, he claimed to be confused and put his hands against his head.

"I'm trying to remember what it was," he said. "Shut this (recorder) off so I can think."

When we turned the recorder off, Driller had stalled enough to buy time and talked more gibberish.

While I didn't get a confession, I did get a suspect who wobbled while trying to bob and weave with his answers. He made some missteps and recovered but he didn't sound convincing, to say the least.

"If I think of something, I'll let you know," he said.

"He's got nothing on you," Richard said, finally speaking up, the cynical voice controlling his alter ego was taking charge. "Be cool, we're getting out of here and then let's find some action."

Amazingly, because he hadn't violated his parole, Driller had to be released.

———

While the interrogation ended, our evidence discovery was fast-tracked. We had a few more stops to make.

Besides having a renowned Forensic Body Institute in the area, Tennessee had a top-notch forensic odontology or dental department. One of their forensic odontologists completed the dental impressions.

We also took the blood swabs and hair samples from his head, body and privates and mailed them to the Illinois State Police Division of Criminal Investigation (DCI).

Our last stop: Driller's home.

A day after the interrogation ended, he called the district attorney. First, he said he didn't want to do a polygraph, "because of the severe stress the cops put me through." He'd decide on the polygraph after he talked to his doctor.

When I returned home to Oldsmar, a lot of questions went through my mind.

Could I have asked the questions a different way? Should I have pressed him when he became evasive and didn't answer the questions? Should I have kept the photos of a beaten Jane Doe for him to look at? Did the grand jury take into account how much Driller showed a memory lapse and avoided questions in charging him? Was our mounting evidence enough to overcome the fact Driller didn't confess?

The next two months were a series of highs and lows.

First came good news from Tennessee dental specialist Neil Jones, who lifted the bite marks from the victim's arm.

"Are you sitting down?" Jones said. "It's a perfect friggin' match."

That night, Jan and I had a wee bit of our favorite Irish whiskey. However, a week later, we drowned our sorrows. First, Shannon sent me a message that photos of the bite impressions came back poor.

In addition, tests on Driller's blood and hairs did not match hairs on the ball cap or the T-shirt or the underwear.

However, the grand jury looked at the evidence I gathered, circumstantial and otherwise, and combined with Driller's responses in the interrogation, they felt there was enough to indict him.

The grand jury charged him with three counts – murder, rape and abuse of a corpse.

———————

Two days after receiving all this news, I met with Chief John Powers and trustees Dennis Dahl, Wayne Keller and Jim Hole.

They shared the always-present concern of what a trial would cost. Using their clout, prosecutors voiced their concerns and recommended we should pass the case on to Arkansas. Oldsmar's police budget had been stretched thin already by trials and hearings related to organized crime figures.

However, they showed a lot of respect and even some deference to me when they said, "Cal, what do you think? We're willing to back you if you believe you can get a conviction."

I looked each one of them in the eye. I kept my ego on the shelf. While I had solid evidence against Driller, it wasn't perfect.

"Men, to be honest, I think we ought to extradite Driller to

Richland County and then to Arkansas," I said. "They have a testimony on paper of young girls who were molested at ages 5 and 7. They also will fly in Kari Wolfgram, who Driller forced to marry and then raped her and held her as a hostage. Even though it's a small county, the police have the resources because they haven't had a case like this in five years. They also want this guy – badly. In the words of their prosecutor, 'We'll take the som bitch in a heart beat.' "

Powers and the trustees chuckled, partly because of my quote and partly because I just made their decision a lot easier.

"Cal, we really appreciate your humility," Dahl said. "You've done a helluva job on this case; and your ambition could've put this conviction at risk. But you made a good choice."

Hole added, "This just about guarantees you take Driller off the streets – forever."

Powers said, "Gentlemen, I think you owe us some beverages."

As we left for O'Quinn's Restaurant, Powers said, "The Tennessee folks believe you've earned the right to pick Driller up in Knoxville and bring him back to Richland County. Is that good with you?"

"Yeah," I said. "I'll drink to that."

CHAPTER 20

Opposite Destinations

**"I guess the game is afoot. ...
Sherlock Holmes, sillies."**

– Wendy Thomas to stupefied
fellow passengers

After having never visited Tennessee in my life, I made three visits to the Volunteer State within a three-year period.

Most plane flights are happy occasions. They're usually for visiting family or friends, starting a vacation or traveling for an important business trip.

But this plane trip felt different, weird; and in a way, unsuccessful, unfulfilling.

It didn't have the classic, Hollywood ending.

In my hands, I held an indictment from the Illinois grand jury with its three-count charge.

Bail set at $225,000.

I wanted in the worst way to charge Bert Driller with all the murders he committed. I wanted him to stand trial in Illinois. I wanted him to face the victims' families.

But we had the cost of a court case going against us. It costs money to fly in witnesses and put them in hotels. It costs money to go to trial. It costs money to pay the prosecutor and judges when they are pulled off other cases.

Meanwhile, Arkansas wanted Bert Driller – badly. No murder charge but Arkansas officers may be able to "persuade" him to a confession. Three females testifying as to what he did to them. I wouldn't be surprised if they constructed hanging gallows outside the courthouse.

The best evidence we had was from these females who said Bert Driller sexually assaulted them. As I told the trustees, sometimes you have to put your ego aside and get him convicted of the sure thing.

Because of these factors I had a short conversation with Driller.

"You're going to be extradited to Illinois and then Arkansas where you will stand trial for sexual assault with minors."

Driller seemed distracted.

Richard told him, "This isn't good pal. Do something."

"You can't do that," Driller said.

"Yes we can. We have the testimony of three girls you raped. Three underage girls."

Driller paused. I let him stew in that sauce.

He said nothing but muttered something like, "Richard, help me."

"Is there something you have to say, Bert?"

He shook his head.

———

I wish Bert Driller had the courage to not only admit killing Jane Doe but admit that he killed others. Whether it be some or all of the red-haired girls or other women who worked at the 105 Truck Stop, I had hoped he would've had the balls to say, "I did it."

But besides being controlling, cruel, brutal and evil, serial killers' narcissism has no limits. They actually want to make people feel like they're the victims.

At least Bert Driller did.

To avoid him needing to go to the bathroom or just pooping on the plane, authorities gave him an enema before he boarded the plane. You'd think he was being tortured.

"That's really affecting my blood sugar," the diabetic whined. "I feel faint."

As authorities put handcuffs and shackles on his wrists and ankles, he also cried at how uncomfortable he was.

"This sounds more like you're transporting a spoiled 8-year-old than it is a fugitive," Sunday said quietly in my right ear.

"Baby wants his lollipop," Shannon added in my left ear.

I so much wanted to have Shannon and Sunday join me and take Driller into a side room and tell him we'll take the restraints off for five minutes alone with him. I would've loved to have seen his response. Would've loved to give him a beating like they did in The Shawshank Redemption.

But I shook off the image and gave Driller a big smile.

Police bound Driller in handcuffs and leg shackles. The handcuffs are connected to a belly chain and the leg shackles are about six inches apart.

With his 275 pounds jammed into an economy-class seat, he squirmed, twisted and agonized. After the thought of ejecting Driller out of the airplane through the exit row passed, I just couldn't help myself.

"What were you expecting, a big comfy recliner?" I asked.

That shut him up for a few minutes, anyway.

———

Richard, in panic mode, pleaded with Driller.

"Make him an offer," he said.

"Okay, I will," Driller said aloud.

That got my attention off a book I was reading: *Execution Techniques in the 1800s.*

"What did you say?"

"Nothing. Raven, I've got $100,000 stashed up in my cabin in Tennessee," Driller said. "And I have another $50,000 in the house. You can have that, anything else you want, just let me escape, please. I can't go to jail. Word gets around about me, and you know."

"And I know what? You should've thought about this 10 years ago. Driller, you have lied to me on just about every question I asked you. I'm not going to start believing you now."

Richard said, "Shit. He's hardcore. He's also right. You weren't convincing in the interrogation."

An unmarked car drove us from Chicago to Oldsmar where TV and print media greeted us as I took him into the Richland County Jail.

After getting peppered with questions, TV reporter Jamie Conom asked, "Why did you bite her, Bert?"

Driller looked at the reporter and said, "I didn't bite her. I have false teeth."

I chuckled inside.

My prisoner continued the processing ritual for the charges against him. A lot of paperwork.

I then handed him over to the jailers.

"This is where we go our separate ways," I told Driller, who started to tremble.

"I'm low on insulin," he said. A jailer gave him his shot after sticking him a few times.

In a bit of irony, Driller had to undress and bend over while he was given a cavity search.

As I stopped to chat with one of the deputies, I heard this high-pitched squeal.

"He must have had something suspicious up there," another deputy said with a straight face.

"Yeah, like his personal manifest," I said.

For the next six months, Driller remained in the county jail until Arkansas authorities extradited him to Little Rock, where his trail for raping those three poor girls began.

Yes, Bert Driller and I headed opposite ways – in the courthouse and in our lives.

While he would face an angry jury who wanted to give him the maximum penalty it could, I returned to the Oldsmar Police Department and was greeted with more smiles.

Chief John Powers had another announcement.

"Callaghan Raven, on behalf of every police officer, detective and staff member of the Oldsmar Police Department, I am honored to announce you as the unanimous winner of our Detective of the Year."

Once again, Jan and the kids got to celebrate this moment with me. Everyone clapped and whistled. They all came up and hugged me. I mustered a few words.

"This is quite the journey I've been on, chasing Bert Driller, Bart Gein or whoever or whatever he thinks he is. And you've been on this journey with me. I can't thank you enough."

Powers put his arm around me and said, "Let's take a walk outside."

Most of the leaves had already fallen from trees. Pumpkins were prominently displayed on nearly every porch in town. Halloween was just around the corner.

He handed me a letter.

"Open it," Powers instructed excitedly, breaking from his usual imposing demeanor as chief. "Next month, the Texas district attorneys and investigators will have their annual conference in Austin; and you've been invited to be a speaker. I thought your work with Driller made the timing perfect for me to suggest your availability."

"Thanks for believing in me, chief."

"Cal, since I've been back here, I didn't realize how fucked up this area is. The truck stop culture. 44 Magnum Lounge. The mafia. Illegal gambling. Drugs. Scams. There's lots of shit out there."

Then he paused, looked at me, and said, "Glad you're one of the good guys."

We went out and celebrated with dinner at Sullivan's Steakhouse. I think this is going to be our hang-out joint. Sorry Costello's.

Even though I should have been feeling on top of the world for bringing Bert Driller to justice, I didn't have overwhelming satisfaction. In fact, I felt a bit hollow, which I shared with Dr. Farnsworth. First, I had to ask him about Driller.

"Doc, you know I swear a couple of times I thought he was communicating with someone, even though nobody was around. Could he have been hearing voices?

"Possibly, Cal. Maybe schizophrenia. It can cause hearing hallucinations that may influence behavior. If incredibly serious, it can lead them to cause harm. But that's in rare cases. It's like one in 10 people who have schizophrenia are violent."

"Well, maybe he was a 10 percenter, Doc. You know he actually tried to bribe me to let him free. Said he had a lot of money stored away."

"Desperate times, desperate measures. If what he said is true, you should tell his wife. After what he's going to put her through, she may sell everything and disappear for a while.

Dr. Farnsworth then shifted the conversation back to me and asked, "Cal, now that your professional career is great with catching a child rapist and helping to put him away for life, being honored, how are you doing?"

"Well, that's why I'm here. I should be euphoric. But I'm not. I wanted to see that scumbag be put on trial. I wanted to see him answer for his sins. I wanted him to confess. I wanted him to look at the mothers and fathers of those he affected. The award is great. But the joy, the pride, the accomplishment, I just don't feel that."

"A lot to unpack here, Cal. Can I offer a few thoughts?"

"Please do."

"Well, I know your ego is safely in check because of you handing over Driller to Arkansas. I can't tell you how big of a step that is for your growth. But you know, you told me how you took pride in your appearance – pressed shirt and pants, combed hair, buffed shoes. And then you'd get sweaty or hailed on or snowed on. You'd step in shit or slip on black ice or have to tackle a suspect to the ground. That's what the Driller case was like. That's what being an officer is like. You can only control so much. The job doesn't allow for a neat and tidy way for it to be done. It's often dirty. It's hard to put a ribbon and bow on this case. The bad guy will lie, cheat and steal to stay out of jail. If there's hell on earth, Mr. Driller will experience it in prison."

We both reflected on that statement in silence, then the

doctor asked, "Can I offer more?"

"Sure."

"You may have saved a lot of people pain, grief and suffering by him not going on trial. Like you, they may have suffered PTSD. If you want to have closure, fly to Arkansas. If you're 80 to 90 percent sure he killed other people, you can meet with their families and explain to them why you think their sister, daughter or mom's killer is behind bars. Maybe that will give them closure without the pain of a trial. Those who want to share their anger or sadness can do so in their living rooms."

The doctor continued and prefaced each thought with a question, "And you know what else, Cal?"

"What?"

"You sharing moments like these with me helps me help other people. Through your stories, I now have a different perspective of what it's like to be a cop with its politics, stresses, highs and lows."

"You know, I do take tips, doc."

———

After listening to various speakers at conferences over my 11-plus years on the police force, I now had a chance to share my thoughts with district attorneys and investigators as a speaker. And I talked about everything. I shared as much of what I learned on the job as possible.

I talked about following the chain of evidence. I talked about being persistent. I talked about graphic information that led to people making funny faces. I joked. And I showed Fred Fry's bumper sticker, "I represent God."

I used up all the battery power in a laser pointer. I wore out a whiteboard. I wrote information with a black magic marker. After filling the board, I wiped it off with my sleeve, then wrote some more. All the while, I'm sweating, pitting out. My shirt is soaked.

When I finished, I received a nice ovation. When I put my right hand over my chest, I felt the soaked shirt and tie and my heart going "bah-dump, bah-dump, bah-dump" really fast.

After grabbing lunch and a beverage with some of the other cops who attended my presentation, I received a variety of responses.

"Great job, great passion."

"You looked like G.I. Joe by the end."

"I filled up the notepad they gave us."

"Slow down, partner, slow down."

"Can I get a copy of your slide show?"

A couple of cops just out of the academy looked at me a bit stunned. "Some of what you said is downright scary," Matthew said.

Terrence added, "Makes me wonder if I'm ready for this."

"I know the feeling, guys," I said. "I know the feeling."

I then grabbed county prosecutor Dub Marshall of Arkansas and asked him for an update on Driller.

"The judge put the trial on fast track and the defense is asking for continuances," he said. "Denied, denied, denied. Honest to God, Cal, I think they're trying to delay it so he dies in his sleep. He's in really bad shape. Complains all the time. Says he's stressed, wants a change of venue, change of bedding, change of food, change of everything."

"Sounds familiar, Dub. Is John Dixon still his public defender."

"Yes. Dixon told Driller, 'Take your medicine. And take your diabetic medicine.' Being a pussy doesn't sit well in these parts. And if you have a diabetic episode and the judge thinks you're faking it, he told me 'I'll keep Driller on that goddamn stand until he's answered every question. Then he can die.' "

I chuckled a bit at that one.

After lunch, I went over to another conference, sat in the back and took notes. A veteran officer I had seen at past conferences sat next to me.

"You know, there's a lounge for speakers who want to sit next to other speakers and talk about how good their presentations were, right?" he said.

"Yeah," I said. "This morning, I was the teacher. This afternoon I'm the student."

"Well said, Cal. Keep learning. I think more big stuff is coming your way. Stay humble and carry a big stick."

That was good advice I'd heard before.

———————

Cold December winds and a light snow greeted us as Jan and I walked a few steps before going inside the Edgar Tews Hall for The Oldsmar Optimists Club Detective of the Year ceremony.

Partner Tony Blackstone and his wife Phyliss picked us up. Dressed to the nines, the flakes seemed to bounce off me as I strode confidently in my new dinner jacket. Maybe they could feel the intense heat I felt with an honor I was about to be given.

Jan wore this beautiful leather coat that made her look like a movie star. I took the coat off her and dropped it at the coat check so she could show off her beautiful flowing, red, off-the-shoulder dress.

"Eat your hearts out Gloria and Gina," she said a bit sarcastically. "Oh, they're not here."

The governor arrived with his wife and Dorothy Douglas, who winked at me, then said, "My son will be here, Cal. I want him to meet you."

I gave her a big hug and said, "Your support has meant so much. You know, you're pretty crafty."

"If I was so crafty, Cal, you should've had me join you interrogating Driller. I would've liked that."

I smiled.

City and county officials attended as well as judges, attorneys and prosecutors. District attorney Thomas Elkington, who poo-pooed Jan's and my idea of suing the police department, stuck out his chest and said, "I'm glad we made the choice we did."

Cop Cindy Esposito, who successfully sued the city, overheard the conversation, then said, "Counselor, you didn't have the balls." Then she gave me a hug.

Dr. Robert Farnsworth caught my eye and he gave me a quick salute, then walked away.

My guys all hugged me and we posed for photos.

This was going to be quite a night.

I prepared talking points for my acceptance speech, but I chose to go off the cuff. The most memorable thing I said was, "the support I received from many of my fellow officers and my family has meant so much to me. Starting with nothing in my investigation and turning it into everything made me feel like a somebody instead of a nobody."

———————

It took us almost an hour to get back into our cars. It seemed like everyone who attended wanted to shake my hand. I warned Jan not to put on her coat.

Thomas Maxwell, the Illinois Fraternal Order of Police

president, said his organization would pay for any travel costs on my family victim visits. Overhearing that, 105 Truck Stop owners Jim Dail and Greg Shriver said they'd offer scholarships to any of the victim's families who had children.

Powers and I took photos with different dignitaries, including the township trustees. He told them about an idea he had of us competing in a run at Oldsmar Central to raise money for police training. They loved the idea of community outreach in a fun way.

In a final, cool touch, Thomas Funeral Home officials brought their new limo to pick us up. Owner Mack Thomas and his wife Wendy opened the doors.

Jan and I laughed as we got in the limo and she blushed when I told Mack we made out in a previous model.

Mack Thomas then chauffeured us to Sullivan's for a few beverages.

We all were having a great time when Jan reached into her coat pocket and pulled out an envelope. My name was on the front.

"Cal, what is this about?" she said nervously.

"I don't have a clue," I said.

When I opened the letter, it said: *I confess, you confess. Only bring your partner or I disappear. St. Michael's Church, 6 a.m.*

"Anything wrong, Cal?"

"I'm not sure, Mack. I have a note here that someone wants to meet me at St. Michael's tomorrow morning.

"What does it say?" Wendy asked.

"Wendy," Mack said. "That's privileged."

"Sorry Wendy, he's right."

Oblivious and curious, Wendy responded, "That's okay. I guess the game is afoot."

When we all looked at each other in confusion, Wendy noticed and said, "Sherlock Holmes, sillies."

————

As soon as I got home, I called Chief Powers and told him of the note in Jan's pocket, which had been in the coat check room all night.

Powers paused and said, "Call Tony Blackstone and alert him. Exchange thoughts and ideas. Call me back in 15 minutes."

I called Father Hallahan but he didn't answer. Then I called Tony, and he, Jan and I considered possible suspects on the note and where Tony should be positioned as backup at the church.

After calling Powers back, the chief asked for my thoughts.

"I don't have a clue who wrote that note," I said. "I attend that church. Everyone in town knows that. I know Father Hallahan well."

"I'm tempted to take my binoculars, get up on the roof of the church and watch for anyone who comes out."

"Isn't that dangerous, chief? It's still dark."

"Yeah, it could be slippery and I don't want him to see me. Any ideas?"

"How about the Kratzke home across the street from the church?," Jan asked.

"That's as good as any elevated place I know,"I said.

"Tell me Cal, could this be a clue to another serial killer?" Powers asked.

"Maybe. I don't think Driller was the only one."

————

The alarm went off at 4:30 a.m. but I didn't need one.

Even with a nip of Irish whiskey I couldn't sleep. So many scenarios went through my head.

Who is this person? What did he want? What did she want? What did he want to share? What did she want to share? Could there be another killer? Did I miss something in the investigation?

Dr. Farnsworth said I should take deep breaths when I'm stressed. That helped.

When I got up, I quickly dressed while focusing on the unknown variables behind this meeting.

"How do I look?" I asked.

Normally impeccable in my dress, I don't know why but I had Jan look at me.

"You look fine other than your hair is messed up, your tie is off, your zipper is down and your shoes are untied."

"Oh."

"Mind at work, Mr. Holmes? The game's afoot, you know."

"Uh, yeah. You're funny."

"And you need to get going. If nothing else, don't forget the zipper."

———

The drive from my home to St. Michael's is a short one I've made hundreds of times; but on this morning, I made a wrong turn. That's how distracted I was.

But I made it on time. Waiting for me, Tony Blackstone said, "I haven't seen anybody go into the church in the last 20 minutes."

"The suspect could've been in church all night. The doors are kept open."

We walked to the church entrance where Blackstone

stopped. He cautiously opened the door and I walked in while he stood guard out front.

I took about 15 steps toward the altar when a voice I didn't recognize called out in a loud whisper from the left side of the church and said, "Confess."

It came from the confessional. I turned and walked toward it. A confessional has two darkened rooms, which are separated by a screened lattice. The idea is that the priest, who is in one room, can't see who is in the other room. Anonymity is respected. As a child, I told of my transgressions in the confessional. The priest listened, made suggestions on better behavior and then told me to say five Hail Marys and five Our Fathers for penance.

As I cautiously entered the darkened room and gave my newfound source his privacy, my heart skipped a beat. What if he wanted me to confess to something I didn't do?

But none of that happened. The voice whispered, "Mr. Raven?"

"Yes."

"Mr. Raven, turn off your recorder."

He could hear me clicking my device as I entered.

"Now. Bert Driller should go to prison for the rest of his life; but he did not kill Jane Doe."

"How do you know?"

"I'll explain later. First, review the police report. You overlooked something," the voice instructed. "Now, I'm going to give you three questions. The answers to those questions will give you a name you need to look into. Don't answer now, figure it out later. First, who did Sam I Am give green eggs and ham to? Second, what's the first name of the Major League Baseball player with the most hits? 3. A phalange is in what part of the body? Got it?"

"Got it. So why ...?"

"That will be answered soon enough," the voice quickly cut me off. "Please tell me, is there any information you haven't told the media? What evidence links to Driller, and what info links to other killers?"

"Well, that will take time."

"I'm all ears."

I tried to answer briefly but it took me a few minutes. While I spoke in a loud whisper, the voice quietly left his confessional room.

Suddenly, a familiar voice called out, "Callaghan, is that you?"

Startled, I rose up, immediately recognizing Father Hallahan's voice. It sounded as though he had just stepped out of a room next to the altar at the front of the church.

I jumped up and shouted, "Yes!" as I left my confessional room. I then quickly pulled the velvet drape back on the other room, it was empty.

"Father, I'll explain later," I said. "Isn't there a basement here?"

"Yes, follow me."

Father Hallahan led me down a short walkway behind the confessional. The walkway led to stairs and then the basement, used for church socials. As we reached the bottom of the stairs, we walked through the basement to a second exit that led to a small alley, then a parking lot.

As I walked through, I could smell a faint scent of aftershave. Then I saw a business card on the ground. I made a mental note and kept walking quickly.

When I opened the unlocked door to the alley, I saw no one. When I quickly went to the parking lot, I saw no one.

I looked across the street where Powers stood on the roof and waved him over. I called out to Blackstone and he came around from his position at the front of the church.

"Did you see anyone?" I asked. They all shook their heads.

"What did the voice say?" Blackstone asked.

"You got to speak with him?" Powers asked.

"Yes," I said. "He told me to re-review the case file on the last victim. Then he asked me three questions: Who did Sam I Am give green eggs and ham to? What's the first name of the hitter who has the most number of hits all time? A phalange is in what part of the body? Got it?"

Father Hallahan, "I read to children and Dr. Seuss is one of their favorite books. Guy is who Sam I Am gave the green eggs and ham."

Blackstone, who knew his fair share about sports, said emphatically, "Pete Rose is the all-time hits leader. More than 4,000."

Powers added his input. "I remember when I ran, I had an issue with my toe," he said. "I remember the doctor referring to a phalange. So it's either toe or foot."

"It's Foote," I said. "One of the police reports I read vaguely mentioned a man. Spelling was F-o-o-t-e. Guy Peter Foote."

I went back to the basement where I picked up the card. A business card, it gave the address and phone number of a George Rollins in Chicago.

"Oh, Father Hallahan, I almost forgot," I said. "I called you last night but there was no answer."

"Oh yes, Cally. After I attended your wonderful event, I was called to give last rites to a member of the church, Finbar Corr. I didn't get home until after midnight."

———————

When Powers, Blackstone and I went to Sue Wentland's desk, her eyes lit up.

"Another hot one, guys?" she said.

"Yes," I said excitedly. "Guy Peter Foote. That's it. No birthdate."

"Let me see," she said as she quickly typed the name into the National Crime Information Center and the Illinois Law Enforcement Center. We heard that melodic "tat, tat, tat" sound again. Music to our ears.

Third-degree sexual abuse of a youth under the age of 18.

Assault of a fellow trucker.

Cocaine possession.

———————

However, when I looked at Powers, his reaction varied from what I saw before.

"Cal, let's talk in my office," he said.

When we arrived, he said, "Cal, of all the cops, is Blackstone who you trust most?"

"Yes," I said. "Why?"

"I want him to lead the Foote investigation. You can help but the trustees want you to focus on something else. Remember last Sunday when one of the county's richest men and his son were killed?"

"Yeah, Charles Forsight, really sad, right before Christmas, chief."

"Well, that's how the trustees and community leaders and county officials feel. They want to put our 'Detective of the Year' on the job. There's rumors that Chucky, as the mob called him, got in too deep. There's a saying, 'When children are killed, it's gone too far.' Cal, I want you to see what you can find."

"Okay chief."

I left Powers' office with my head spinning.

Mob action escalating.

New lead on a truck stop serial killer.

Did I catch the right guy?

More emphasis being put on who killed a prominent citizen than a number of prostitutes.

A prevailing thought went through my head.

The more things change in our department, the more they stay the same.

Epilogue

The horrific crime statistics below are true, but as stated before, the names, dates and locations throughout this book and below have been changed to protect the innocent.

There have been at least 850 murders across the United States that are believed to be connected to long-haul truck drivers, according to the FBI's Highway Serial Killings initiative.

Frank Figliuzzi, author and former FBI assistant director for counterintelligence, said 25 long-haul truckers are in prison for multiple homicides. However, he said there are 200 killings still unsolved and 450 suspects being looked at in those cases.

Many police officers and detectives around the country must settle for lesser charges on some long-haul truckers because of insufficient evidence as well as the cost to put them on trial. As a result, many of those 200 victims murdered will likely remain unsolved cold cases.

Some long-haul truckers/serial killers die before they are apprehended.

According to the National Missing and Unidentified Persons System (NamUs), at any given time, up to 100,000 persons may be reported missing in the United States with as many as 600,000 reported annually. While many of these individuals are found alive and well, some become long-term missing persons.

After 28 years Jane Doe No. 1 was identified thanks to DNA matches. Jane Doe No. 2 and Jane Doe No. 3 were identified after 17 years and 21 years, respectively thanks to improved forensics. That has led to certain serial killers being charged with their murders.

The daughter of Jane Doe No. 1 (Mary Masters) continues to search for her mother's killer.

Yvette Mendez has found a better path in life and now operates a couple of Mexican restaurants.

Harry Blacksmith has apologized numerous times for threatening my family. I remind him I still have dents in my shin from when he kicked me. However, I consider him a friend.

As for me, Callaghan 'Cal' Raven, I still have nightmares, and still work to overcome post-traumatic stress disorder, yet I remain vigilant in helping families find justice.

If You Need Help

Nearly 200 police officers take their lives each year, according to First HELP, an organization that tracks law enforcement and first responder suicides.

In addition, approximately 18% to 24% of dispatchers and approximately 35% of police officers have post-traumatic stress disorder (PTSD), according to the National Alliance on Mental Illness. The exact number is not known because these first providers want to maintain privacy and avoid the stigma.

Also, there is a term that differs from PTSD called moral injury. Moral injury is the harm to one's values, conscience and world view from witnessing or perpetrating acts that violate one's moral code, according to *Psychology Today*.

In addition, harming others, whether in military or civilian life; failing to protect others, through error or inaction; and failure to be protected by leaders, especially in combat — can all morally injure or wound a person's conscience, leading to lasting anger, guilt and shame and can fundamentally alter one's world view and impair the ability to trust others.

Police officers dedicate themselves to protecting us from harm yet unknowingly cause harm to themselves.

———

If you work in law enforcement or know a police officer who may be struggling, there are many organizations that can help, which include:

The National Fraternal Order of Police (FOP) is the world's largest organization of law enforcement officers, with more than 373,000 members in the United States. In times of crisis, the FOP wants to ensure that each officer has a competent place to turn for help. The Officer Wellness Committee engages in a thorough vetting process of available resources and has deemed these hotlines approved for its members. To reach its national headquarters in Nashville, Tenn., call 615-399-0900.

COPLINE is a hotline exclusively for current and former law enforcement personnel and their families. To use COPLINE, call 1-800-267-5463.

If you need to talk, **the 988 Lifeline** is available. Whether you're facing mental health struggles, emotional distress, alcohol or drug use concerns, or just need someone to talk to, caring counselors can assist you. Just dial 988.

For law enforcement officers in crisis, text: **BLUE to: 741741.** The crisis text line is free 24/7 and is confidential.

Blue H.E.L.P. honors the service of law enforcement officers who died by suicide. Offering comfort and honor to the families who have lost an officer to suicide is necessary to maintain the credibility of the thin blue line. All officers, regardless of method of death, deserve thanks. And all families deserve support. For more information, e-mail contact@1sthelp.org.

The Wounded Blue is a police officer peer support advocate program, which can be reached online at https://thewoundedblue.org or by calling the Help Line: 833-892-8255 or text "Blue" to 877-810-0911 for 24/7 confidential support.

The **main treatment for PTSD** is psychotherapy, according to current treatment guidelines and as written in the National Library of Medicine. However, PTSD continues to be a chronic condition even after psychotherapy, with high psychiatric and medical illness rates. There is a dire need to search for new compounds and approaches for managing PTSD. The usage of psychedelic substances is a potential new method. For more information on this, go to: https://pmc.ncbi.nlm.nih.gov/articles/PMC9710723 or https://www.theilluminating.co/justinlapree.

———

Recommended Reading:

Three books should be required reading for all police officers: *Rocks in the Roadway* by Dan Hollingsworth; *Officer Down Code 3* by Pierce R. Brooks; and *Street Survival Tactics for Armed Encounters* by Ronald J. Adams, Thomas M. McTernan and Charles Remsburg.

Dr. John Violante has written many books about the profession but three of his best are *Police Trauma, Police Suicide and Dying For The Job: Police Work Exposure and Health.*

———

Missing Person Organizations:
If you need help locating a loved one, these organizations may
be able to help:

**The National Missing and Unidentified Persons System
(NamUs)** is a national centralized repository and resource
center for missing, unidentified and unclaimed person cases
across the United States. NamUs helps investigators match
long-term missing persons with unidentified remains to
resolve cases and bring resolution to families. At any given
time, up to 100,000 persons may be reported missing in the
United States with as many as 600,000 reported annually.

The Doe Network is a nonprofit 100% volunteer
organization devoted to assisting investigating agencies in
bringing closure to national and international cold cases
concerning missing and unidentified persons. Its mission is
to give the nameless back their names and return the
missing to their families. For more information, call 931-
397-9610.

––––––––––

Human Trafficking Organizations:
If you see human trafficking being done, here are numbers
to contact:

Polaris is a 501 nonprofit that works to combat and
prevent sex and labor trafficking in North America. The
organization's 10-year strategy is built around the
understanding that human trafficking does not happen in
a vacuum but rather is the predictable end result of a range
of other persistent injustices and inequities in our society

and our economy. Contact the National Human Trafficking Resource Center to report sex trafficking, forced labor or to get help at 1-888-373-7888 or text "BeFree" 233733.

The Blue Campaign is a national public awareness campaign designed to educate the public, law enforcement and other industry partners to recognize the indicators of human trafficking, and how to appropriately respond to possible cases. To report suspected human trafficking to federal law enforcement, call 1-866-347-2423.

Truckers Against Trafficking (TAT) is a nonprofit organization that trains truck drivers to recognize and report instances of human trafficking. This national organization formed in Oklahoma in 2009. For more information, call 1-888-3737-888.

Acknowledgments

Craig Handel

I want to thank my wife Isabel for her understanding in me writing my first fiction book. She may have rolled her eyes at some of things Don and I talked about but she gave me the creative license to take this story where it needed to go.

I'd also like to thank my parents, Joan and John, for their continuous support. They have been married for a year longer than I've been alive. Mom showed great spirit in recovering from hip and femur surgery while Dad visited every day as she went through her rehabilitation. They continue to inspire me.

Thanks to my friends, teachers and coaches – past and present – from my hometown of Deerfield, Wis. I couldn't ask for a better place to grow up; and they're a big reason why. That's also why many of their names are included as fictional characters in this book.

I also want to thank our dog Ollie, whose desire to be taken for long walks pulled me away from my computer, provided me some fresh air and gave me a chance to collect my thoughts.

And my appreciation to detective Don Corbett and publisher David Kratzke for collaborating on this book. Their attention to detail and constructive criticism gave perspective, a peak behind the curtain and depth to a book that goes far beyond fiction.

We brought up topics like post traumatic stress disorder, moral injury, sexual harassment and police corruption.

Meanwhile, we revealed the humanity and danger prostitutes deal with on a regular basis.

Don Corbett

To all of the people that have played a significant and major role in my life, thank you. Each one of you has made me a better person and has helped lead me to complete this book.

While there are too many individuals to list, I'll do my best to recall the vast majority of those who were special to me and who I owe a deep debt of gratitude and love.

First and most importantly, without my wife, mother of our children, partner, best friend and confidant Marsha, I would have ceased to exist decades ago. Her unconditional love, endless support, energy and forgiveness have kept me alive even in my darkest hours. I have never met a more caring, loving and compassionate human being than my wife. She is the reason I am able to cope with my demons, nightmares, anhedonia, anxiety and PTSD. Without Marsha I am nothing. Thank you Marsha! I don't know what I would do without you. My love for you is forevermore. I love you.

Thank you to my mother Margaret, father Donald and mother-in-law Margy Porter. Without them, I would not have been able to get through many of my darkest struggles, difficult times and issues that nearly destroyed me. I remember from a very early age that the love from them was unconditional and I knew that whatever harm, crisis or misfortune may come my way they would be there with open arms, they were my safety net. They were my biggest cheerleaders anytime I chose to take a risk or try something new. I was always proud of my parents who were very respected and liked in the community. I was a very lucky man to have been raised by my mom and dad who paved the way for me, always leading by example.

I always relied on my only older brother Tom, who now suffers from Parkinson's disease and makes his home with us. I always bragged about him being such a phenomenal cross country and track star. He always supported me and was a great friend, companion and mentor to my son Mark.

I also was fortunate enough to have some of the best teachers throughout the Austintown (Ohio) School District who made me look at all sides of a situation and listen to friends and family who I trusted the most before making difficult or sensitive decisions.

Mr. Richard Peduzzi and Mr. Al Cervello were the greatest but on occasion they also deemed it necessary to present my backside with a number of rounds from the infamous red-wood fly swatter paddle which always had a calming effect when I had a difficult time learning to keep my mouth shut in class. It always did the trick and made me respect them even more.

Father John Lyons, my Catholic church priest at St. Joseph's, where I was an altar boy, was always there if I needed someone to talk to that would ensure my words would not be repeated or used against me. I confided in him for years. He also understood what a difficult job being a police officer was and offered me continual guidance that I could count on in even the most difficult times.

I'll always be forever grateful to Joseph Lane, owner of the Lane Funeral Home and Ambulance, who had enough respect and trust in me to give me a job at the young age of 17 that would prepare me for being a clean-cut, responsible adult and police officer. I also will always have fond memories of an old neighbor of mine as I grew up – Mr. John Sabo. He was more than happy to listen to my whining and tell me to grow up and give me a good kick in the behind when I failed to listen.

Then there was Don Bloom, "ah yes," one of my first partners on the ambulance who taught me more about what it would take to succeed in life more than anyone else. However, he also taught me a great number of things that I promised I would never share with anyone else because it could result in both of us burning in hell. Thank God there's a statute of limitations. Don Bloom ended up being an extremely successful business owner after his career as a paramedic, embalmer and funeral director.

I learned a lot about being a successful and trusted cop from Sergeant Harry MacDonald, Lieutenant Richard Bullen, Lieutenant Ron DeAmicis, Lieutenant Mark Skowron, Detective Lieutenant David Allen, Sergeant Norm Gallagher, Detective Sergeant Dan Kosco, Officers Larry Asdell, Jim Cerimele, Richard Brincko, Michael McCreary, Bill Saltsman, David Thoreson, Tom Heinz, David Bernat, Dan Mikus, Dan Hageman and retired former Austintown Chiefs of Police James Hazlett and Jack Scott, Director of Security Fred Prassack and FBI Special Agent John Stoll.

One officer in particular that I trusted with my life and who always had my back was Detective Sergeant Frank Tomasino. They don't make them like Frank anymore.

Another individual that I learned much from and always trusted was Art Powers who never steered me wrong, offered good sound advice and gave me hell when I was out of line. We have remained close friends through the years.

Also, officers Jim Pastore, Andrew Maddox, Marc Mattmiller and Richard Hamaker made a difference and supported and stood by me because they knew what I was about. They also gave me knowledge and trusted me.

A couple of my old bosses, Blair Staud and Rodney Armstrong, were always there when I needed them and turned into good friends.

One of my longest friendships has been with John Cornelius, who never gave up on me and was the first to call me in one of the most difficult times in my life when I thought everyone had forgotten me. My parents always loved John like a son.

Two great businessmen who I had extreme respect for and learned much about business operations in the private sector and living a good life were Ron Glove and Steve Johnson. I had the pleasure of working for them over the years.

Another person who I have the utmost respect for is a former partner and Retired FBI Assistant Special Agent in Charge Robert Clark who is now the Los Angeles Deputy Mayor for public safety.

Trustees Bo Pritchard, David Ditzler and Ken Carano never forgot how much of a dedicated caring officer I was even when things went south and they could have forgotten about me or thrown me under the bus. For that I will always respect them.

Several couples who have been long-time personal friends of ours that Marsha and I love and think the world of are Bob and Sharon Agler, Peggy and Bill Cochran and Linda and Scott Edge. And how could we forget Lori Andrews and Dan Mancuso, LouAnn and Ron Tindle.

I also want to share my appreciation to doctors Dr. Adam Levin, Evelia Iglesias and John J. Passias. And a special thank you to lifelong friends Fritz Weidner, Lloyd Vandervoort and Mike Carr.

Lastly I'd like to thank Craig Handel, author, and David Kratzke, editor, publisher and owner of Big Kat Kreative, who made this book a reality. Without their knowledge, experience, professionalism and friendship it would never have gotten off the ground. Most importantly they believed in me, for that I'll be forever indebted to them. You guys are the greatest.

About The Authors

Craig Handel

Craig Handel has written for newspapers in Wisconsin, Arizona, California, Massachusetts and Florida since he started writing in junior high.

As an author, Craig has collaborated on a wide range of books, including *The Sodfather*, which chronicled groundskeeper George Toma's career working the first 57 Super Bowls; *5 Days to Grow*, on optimizing mental performance in sports and life; *Resilient Spirit*, an entrepreneurial journey; and *Interview with a Spy*, which revealed an untold aspect of the Kennedy assassination.

He considers working on a documentary *Curveballs* with John Biffar and David Van Sleet to be one of the most inspiring projects in his life. This film chronicles a team of amputee baseball players that compete against able-bodied teams. Craig feels these men offer an amazing perspective on overcoming adversity and living a life of purpose and meaning.

An avid gardener and swimmer, Craig and his wife Isabel live with their puppy Ollie in Florida.

Don Corbett

Don Corbett is a retired police detective who has been honored with many awards and commendations over the years, including the State of Ohio Fraternal Order of Police candidate for Member of the Year as well as the Austintown Optimist Club Detective of the Year. Acknowledgements from people whose lives he's positively affected also have been gratifying.

Don has been a guest speaker in Montreal for the National Association of Truck Stop Operators; the Annual Investigators' School in Austin, Texas; the Arkansas State Police Major Crimes & Narcotics Conference on Traveling Criminals; and the International Homicide Investigation Seminar in Ohio. He has been a guest expert on CNN and HLN, and he's the Past President of the Ohio FOP Lodge 126.

After leaving law enforcement, Don became the Senior Board Certified Investigator with NetJets, and took on the role of Assistant Airport Security Coordinator.

Among the officers Don has mentored is retired FBI ASAC Robert Clark, who serves as the City of Los Angeles deputy mayor for public safety overseeing police and fire issues.

After retiring, Don has used his expertise to review cold cases pro bono for victims' families concerned that law enforcement officials didn't do all that they could to solve their cases. He has rigorously fought the system by going above and beyond his responsibilities to obtain justice for those victims who could no longer do so for themselves.

Don's law enforcement career came with costs. He has suffered from the effects of post-traumatic stress disorder, moral injury and workplace bullying, which ultimately resulted in his disability retirement from a profession that he loved.

Don and his wife Marsha live in Ohio with Marlee, their Cavalier King Charles Spaniel. They have three grown children and six grandchildren.

Thank You

Thank you for reading *Trucker's Deadly Haul.* It has been our pleasure to share this story with you. If you enjoyed this book, please consider leaving a review on the website where you bought the book.